Solo Variations

CASSANDRA GARBUS

A DUTTON BOOK

DUTTON
Published by the Penguin Group
Penguin Putnam Inc., 375 Hudson Street, New York, New York 10014, U.S.A.
Penguin Books Ltd, 27 Wrights Lane, London W8 5TZ, England
Penguin Books Australia Ltd, Ringwood, Victoria, Australia
Penguin Books Canada Ltd, 10 Alcorn Avenue, Toronto, Ontario, Canada M4V 3B2
Penguin Books (N.Z.) Ltd, 182–190 Wairau Road, Auckland 10, New Zealand

Penguin Books Ltd, Registered Offices: Harmondsworth, Middlesex, England

First published by Dutton, an imprint of Dutton Signet, a member of Penguin Putnam Inc.

First Printing, February, 1998
10 9 8 7 6 5 4 3 2 1

 REGISTERED TRADEMARK—MARCA REGISTRADA

LIBRARY OF CONGRESS CATALOGING-IN-PUBLICATION DATA:
Garbus, Cassandra.
    Solo variations / Cassandra Garbus.
      p.   cm.
    ISBN 0-525-94380-3
    I. Title.
    PS3557.A653S65   1998
    813'.54—dc21   97-34053
                                                 CIP

Printed in the United States of America
Set in Garamond No. 3
Designed by Eve L. Kirch

PUBLISHER'S NOTE
This is a work of fiction. Names, characters, places, and incidents either are the products of the author's imagination or are used fictitiously, and any resemblance to actual persons, living or dead, events, or locales is entirely coincidental.

This book is printed on acid-free paper.

To my husband, David Moreno

Like us, music must inhale and exhale to be alive!

—Marcel Tabuteau,
former principal oboe
of the Philadelphia Orchestra

Part One

1

I was losing heart. I didn't know when it started, this feeling that maybe I couldn't continue. Maybe a few months ago, maybe even years ago. Maybe I just noticed it then, sitting on the train to Philadelphia. The dug-up fields, the yellowed factories, passed faster and faster beyond the frame of my window, and I pressed my head against the glass, trying to lose myself to the steady, uneventful churning of the train. The faint clattering of the window was a D, I thought, and I imagined myself playing a D, a rich, dark, beautiful D.

Imagine a perfect sound, my mother would say, closing her eyes, touching her chest. For years, I had ignored her advice. It seemed silly and I thought there was no reason to listen to my mother, who had never been confident enough herself and had quit the piano by the time she was my age, twenty-six.

Concentrate. Listen. The sound is inside of you, my mother would tell me, and now for the first time I listened. I closed my eyes to feel each pulse, each jolt of the train, and I imagined myself breathing once, deeply, and drawing from my oboe a sweet, pure sound, the perfect sound that had always eluded me.

The train lurched and my oboe slipped from my knees. I grabbed the case and caught my breath. One small screw turned, one key slightly bent, one pad slightly uncovered, and my sound could be ruined in a hundred different ways. And I imagined what I would say to my teacher, Mr. de Laney.

"My high register isn't full because this screw is loose. Maybe that's the reason. Maybe the C pad isn't covering."

Impatient with my reasons, Mr. de Laney would shake his head as he looked over my oboe.

Maybe I would be right, maybe I wouldn't be. Maybe the C pad wouldn't be covering or maybe my high notes weren't full just because they weren't.

We were passing Trenton, New Jersey: the factory towers, the trudging brown river, the crooked white letters on the bridge, TRENTON MAKES THE WORLD TAKES. The *W* was dangling. Timed from here, the trip was forty-five minutes. Forty-five minutes and I would be playing, and maybe Mr. de Laney would tell me I had a chance of winning my audition for the New York City Ballet Orchestra, the tenth audition I had taken since Juilliard.

I opened the case of my new oboe and ran my fingers over the keys. The new silver shined. I oiled the keys and tiny screws every day. The intricate branching of joints and keys moved effortlessly and soundlessly, except for the small thud of cork on wood. The wood was a deep reddish brown like rich, stirred clay.

I'd bought my new oboe four months ago when I first started with Mr. de Laney. He'd been principal of the Philadelphia Orchestra for thirty years, made dozens of solo recordings, and taught countless great students. More than anything, I wanted his praise, his blessings. At first, my new oboe seemed too perfect. I missed the familiar efforts of my old oboe and felt guilty sticking it in my bottom drawer. I'd gotten so used to it—its stuffiness in the low register, the same out-of-tune notes—that I no longer noticed its weaknesses. My new oboe was easy; my breath just melted into the wood. It felt like Tom, like our first weeks together, so right and creamy and smooth I had to keep steadying myself. It was two summers ago, and in darkness we would lie for hours on the covers on my bed, two stacked mattresses, while the distant horns of merengue churned in the bottom floor of my building and Bach violin sonatas played softly in the living room. Occasionally the aboveground subway swooshed through the night, adding another line to the fugue, and Tom would stroke my arms and shoulders and knead the extra lip of flesh on my stomach, the part of myself I disliked most.

"But I like it," he'd say softly, squeezing my stomach, his curly hair falling over his eyes, his forehead sticky from the heat. Even then

I knew that he would be there every evening and every morning, at least for a while, and I tried to relax into his hands, to let him touch me without flinching or moving away.

Tom was a violinist and he never got that anxious when he performed.

"Just pretend you're not nervous. Fake it," he'd tell me as if it would be that easy to change myself. "Convince yourself you're the greatest player in the world."

He had risen to the top of Juilliard violinists by his senior year. He'd been concertmaster of the top orchestra and won some of the toughest competitions. He had never fallen apart. Not like I had, eight months ago at Merkin Hall. My old teacher, Mr. Barret, the principal of the New York Philharmonic, had recommended me to be the soloist with the Philharmonia Virtuosi. It was an honor and my chance to make my mark. Critics, New York oboists, my parents, and everyone I'd known from Juilliard were among the audience of twelve hundred people. But under the hot spotlights on the dark stage, my lips felt as if they had lost all muscle, all control; my uneven tone blared bright and my own sound shamed me. My fingers shook so badly I couldn't even get through the fast passages. The violas plucked their strings: small, shallow sounds where my solos were supposed to be.

In the front row of the audience, my mother covered her eyes. Tom, who was playing assistant concertmaster, averted his face and stared down at the stage floor. The conductor frantically mouthed measure numbers to me as if that might help. Every averted gaze and every gaze that stayed fixed on me, horrified and amazed by my mistakes, felt like blows I would never forget.

The crumbling roofs, the burnt-out windows, the deserted blocks of North Philadelphia piled up outside the train window, and I tried to blot out the memory of that awful silence in the hall after I played. The frayed edges of *Le Tombeau de Couperin* by Ravel, the most difficult excerpt for the oboe, stuck out from the rest of the music in my bag, but I resisted pulling it out for one last anxious study.

To win my audition in two weeks, *Tombeau* would have to be flawless.

"You're going to do well this time, Gala," my mother had told me last weekend, her voice bright and strained as we sat together on her bed, a twisted pile of covers between us. The bald afternoon sun

streamed in through her closed windows. Her purple silk bathrobe
hung too loosely over her narrow shoulders, and her face, once delicate
and pale, had turned bitter and creased. She had barely been eating
since my father left three months before.

She clasped her hands as if in prayer. "They're going to love you.
I can just feel it," she said, and then suddenly she shivered, pressing
her fingertips to her forehead.

We had just spent the afternoon watching the video of Passover,
the last holiday my parents were together. Our seders were mostly
makeshift, unreligious. My father, who was leading the service, kept
breaking into lectures about the collapse of Russia, the subject of his
new book, or making everyone laugh at his jokes about the suffering
of Jews. He skipped over the parts of the Haggadah my mother had
carefully selected or else he made a joke of them, faking the Hebrew
and making up nonsense words.

"Baruch maruch faluch Adonai. Oy," he'd chant, davening right
down into his matzo ball soup. His imitation of old Russian rabbis was
perfect, and our relatives laughed and cried for all their dead fathers.

My mother, though, had spent hours preparing the Haggadah.

"Gordon, this is where you skipped." She pulled on his sleeve. "I
wanted this."

"Roberta"—he flicked his wrist dismissively—"we're having fun."

"Please, please." She was laughing, but her face was red, near
tears. She had also chosen poems, some Yeats and Pound and then
some women's spiritual songs, New Age stuff, which my father always
made fun of.

" 'We are Mother Earth, we are Mother Earth,' " he chanted,
interrupting her as soon as she began.

"Gordon never takes anything I do seriously." She tugged on his
arm, but he closed his eyes, droned on. If she had laughed it off or paid
no attention to him, he would have stopped. But instead she pleaded,
"I can't take this anymore. Stop. Please."

My mother switched off the video. "I can't stand my voice. So
needy! You can tell he was planning to leave, can't you? You can just
see by the way he treated me."

"We shouldn't watch this," I told her. My absent father, so
present on the screen, dizzied me as the sun drenched my mother's
bedroom.

"I can't help it." My mother clutched the neck of her robe as she flicked the VCR back on. The next shot was of my profile as I played an easy Chopin nocturne on the piano for the guests. My long hair was tucked behind my ears, and my mouth moved along with the music. I was in my own private world, unaware of who was listening, until I messed up a right-hand run.

"Let's turn it off." I reached for the remote, but my mother held it above my head.

"I'll change it." She fast-forwarded through me playing, through my youngest cousin looking for the afikoman, and then all of a sudden, blurring across the screen in fast-forward motion, was my father kissing my mother.

My mother stopped the video, replayed the scene. It wasn't my father's usual public kiss, affectionate and paternal after twenty-eight years of marriage. My mother had started toward the front door to open it for Elijah, but my father grabbed her hand, pulled her to him, as if he were suddenly afraid that she would leave him, leave through that door to God, and he kissed her on the mouth, wholly, fully.

Leaning against the marble walls of Thirtieth Street Station in Philadelphia, I inhaled deeply off a cigarette, but this did not calm my rushing heart or the heat rising to my face. My beta-blockers were still in my purse. Keisuke, an oboist from Juilliard, had given them to me. If I took one, he said, the nerves would still be in my head, but my fingers wouldn't shake. But I would lose something, too, he said. I would lose that rush, that joy. The Inderal would flatten my playing. Keisuke took them for the first two rounds of the Boston Symphony auditions. For the final, he didn't. In finals, the intangibles that the Inderal flattened and ruined were what made the difference.

Slumped on a bench, still trying to calm my racing heart, I couldn't decide whether to take a beta-blocker or not. It seemed like cheating. But that wasn't why, in the end, I chose not to take one. If my playing lost its rush, its joy, I didn't think I would have anything good left.

The full trees, lush and humid after the August drizzle, swayed above me in the breeze, and I filled my lungs with the soft air. I had always lived in New York City and I got easily lost outside of it.

Twice I had taken wrong turns down these suburban streets and arrived late for my lesson. The de Laneys' ivy-covered stone home was on a thickly wooded road, and I was relieved when I finally saw their giant, silver Chrysler gleaming alone in the driveway. There were never any guests, and Mr. de Laney was always home when I phoned. I didn't know what he did with his time, except teach, since he'd retired.

Mrs. de Laney rushed to the door, her hands in dishwashing gloves. The scent of a lemony fish wafted in from the kitchen. Every Saturday, she seemed to be cooking another gourmet dish just for them.

"Mr. de Laney is on the telephone. He will be just a few minutes," she told me in her thick French accent, her pumps with the bows pressed tight together.

I waited until she had disappeared into the kitchen, then I lingered in the living room, taking only baby steps toward the studio. I wanted to discover something—the secret to his greatness—but the living room didn't reveal much to me. Between the matching yellow sofa and chair was a glass table with nothing mysterious on it, just an unused, glittering glass ashtray and a statue of Cupid.

The history of the Philadelphia Orchestra woodwind sound lined the shelves of Mr. de Laney's studio. There were pictures of Mr. de Laney; Richard Woodhams, the new principal; Tabuteau, the founder of the Philadelphia oboe style; and recordings of all the great players. Unlike mine, Mr. de Laney's reed-making desk was perfectly ordered: knives lined up, plaques in a thread box, string neatly fastened around the spool, and no cane shavings on the floor. His old oboe, the one he'd used for most of his time with the Philadelphia Orchestra, was on its stand on his desk. It didn't play well anymore. The wood had blown out, but I loved looking at it, the acid-roughed silver, the worn wood.

I ran my fingers over the shiny keys of my oboe. If I could just play well today, I thought, in this one moment, one hour of life.

In the living room, Mr. de Laney was speaking to his wife in French. I strained my grade-school French to hear if he was saying something about me, expressing some hope, some special promise he'd observed, but their conversation had nothing to do with me; it was about dinner and which wine to get. They had been married for forty-five years, longer than anyone else I knew, and I thought his greatness and that he could have loved someone for so long must have been somehow connected.

I picked out my best *Tombeau* reed, a light reed, easy in the low register, and I went through *Tombeau* once with no preparation, no worries or thoughts of the music beforehand. My fingers were fast and fluid over the keys. They moved automatically as if unattached to any other part of me. I'd done it. *Tombeau* was perfect.

"Ready for that audition?" Mr. de Laney asked in his gruff Midwestern accent as he tapped open the studio door with his rosewood cane. At the top of the steps, he towered over six feet tall. He was around seventy years old, and he did not look at all as I had imagined when I'd studied his recordings, memorizing his Mozart, every phrase somehow ethereal and triumphant at the same time. He had the look of an old-school musician, conservative and well-kept in his starched chinos and red and green cardigan sweater, but also jaunty in his black fisherman's cap. His face was large and long.

"I don't know," I answered, then corrected myself. "Yes. I practiced very well this week."

"That's the way," he said, like an athletic coach. He tipped forward his fisherman's hat, adjusting it. His hair underneath was thinned to wisps. Every time I saw the whiteness of it, I was surprised.

"Got any reeds?" he said, sticking on his black reading glasses, which hung around his neck on a chain.

"No." I laughed, then covered my mouth.

"Just let me see what you've got. I'll tell you if it's good or not. None of this." He waved his hand chaotically in the air, the gesture he used to describe me.

At his desk, he squeaked on my reed, testing the crow, which was too low, he said, and then he scraped the tip of the reed so fast I was sure he would cut off a corner.

"See here." He pointed to the tip, now paper-thin. Up close, he smelled musty, as if his wool sweater had been locked away damp for years. I didn't like to think of him as someone with smells.

"But the crow is still closer to a B." He shook his head. "You're going to have to start breaking that habit." The crow of a reed was supposed to be a C, otherwise the reed would be flat and unstable. Last year, when all I could think about was getting a deeper, thicker sound, I had gotten into the bad habit of making flat reeds. Now, to compensate, I bit with my embouchure to keep the pitch up, and my high register was pinched. That was what was so difficult about reeds. You kept adjusting yourself to your bad habits until only the bad felt good.

I played a quick scale down to low C. My low register was my best. I knew how to sink into the notes, to play right into the rich core.

"Let's hear some long tones. Two, three, four . . ." Mr. de Laney conducted, and ready or not, I had to come in on one.

I closed my eyes and listened for the sound before I began. The sound must come from nowhere, he'd said. It must start as if it were already there, resonating in the farthest reaches of the room, where we couldn't hear it.

"Don't overblow," he told me. My forte sound had become harsh.

"Now decrescendo." He swayed on his feet, his arm almost touching mine on its graceful loop to three. "Down to nothing. Magic," he whispered. "Let me show you."

My oboe was small and skinny in his hands. He looked as if he were going to attack the instrument; he took a huge breath, raised his eyebrows and shoulders, but then he started so softly, I could barely hear his sound. Quietly, it shimmered, intense and dark and alive. There was no edge, no falseness. He had the most beautiful, pure sound, the sound I would have done anything to have.

"You know, Gala, none of this is any mystery." He knotted his eyebrows, studying me through his black glasses. "There's no reason why you can't do it. It's ninety percent practice. If I can do it, you can do it."

He always said that.

"It's all hard work. Perseverance. From point A to point B. You can do it." He searched my face, waiting for an answer.

"I don't know," I said nervously, and he frowned.

"It's been four months, hasn't it?"

It was the first time he'd mentioned anything about the six months. Giving it six months and then he'd see. That was what he had said when he first accepted me as a student. I braced myself for him to tell me I had not improved. Every lesson, I pinned up my long black hair and wore my prim navy skirt and white blouse, hoping for his approval. I wanted to appear as I imagined his Curtis students had looked: serious, contained, unsexual, and undamaged by humiliating experiences.

Mr. de Laney sighed, lowering himself back down to his chair. "Let's hear some *Tombeau*. You can be sure that's the first thing they'll ask for."

Tombeau was still at the front of the stand. Just one moment of life, I thought. Just one moment to play well.

"Focus," he told me. "Feel the tempo, the dancing before you begin. Imagine the dance has already started and you're just joining in." He sang the opening phrase, his voice so high and girlish I nearly giggled.

"I know you're nervous. This is one problem. But if your technique were more solid, it wouldn't matter how nervous you got. Everything would be automatic. Let's hear it." Mr. de Laney closed his eyes, and his curved fingers patted the air lightly as if the music had already begun. I could feel how much he wanted me to play well. I was one of his last students, he must have thought. There wouldn't be too many after me. All he wanted was for me to play well. I felt my hands shaking. The music was hectic and black with thirty-second notes. I took a deep breath. Mr. de Laney was conducting. "Two, three, four."

My fingers slipped out of control. I told myself to just keep going. To just get through it: the fast trills, the triplet thirty-seconds down to the low B's. But then my fingers got scrambled. None of the low B's came out.

"Sorry," I said.

Mr. de Laney leaned back in his chair. He had a funny smile on his face as if he didn't know what to say.

"Let's slow it down a bit." He conducted slower this time.

My fingers were trembling. All my red warning marks glared at me.

"Three, four . . ." Mr. de Laney counted the beats, and I tried again, but couldn't do it, couldn't do it at all as I had before.

"Gala," he said slowly, "it's hard to work on music if you're having a hard time getting the notes. Your audition is in two weeks?"

I nodded, and he told me how to practice it, how to switch the rhythms, how to start playing just two notes and then add on. He had told me the exact same thing for my past three lessons. I didn't listen. I had practiced it this way. I hoped he would put *Tombeau* away and that I could play something else.

"Let's hear it again. We'll use this." He set the metronome to one of the slowest speeds. It was humiliating. A beginner played it this slow. He stood a few feet away from me, his arms folded across his chest.

Immediately, I messed up. My fingers were shaking too much.

"I can't do it."

"Didn't you practice it?"

"I don't know." I shook my head. "I had it before," I said, but I felt as if I were lying.

Mr. de Laney turned to the window overlooking his patio, the ordinary white tables and chairs, wet from the drizzle. He lifted off his fisherman's cap, ran his fingers through his hair. Midway through he stopped and dropped his hand to his side.

"Let's hear some Tchaikovsky," he said.

The solo from Tchaikovsky's Fourth Symphony was slow with awkward intervals; it could easily sound clunky and directionless.

"Let's hear it," he said. I watched his back, the red and green squares of his cardigan sweater. Just play, I told myself.

I did. I let it sing. I played the first phrase, the call. The sound lilted up, yearning, and then the next phrase answered, a sad answer not really meaning enough. I let it fill me.

Mr. de Laney faced me, his finger pointed in the air. He looked almost angry.

"You have something special. You know that, don't you?"

I nodded. I did know it.

He looked back out onto the drizzle. He was thinking, thinking about what to do with me. I held my oboe at my side, letting it swing a little, the bell tapping against my leg. I wanted to keep myself sharpened, awake, and away from sadness. I tapped myself harder with the bell.

"Let's work on *Tombeau* again," Mr. de Laney said finally. "I want you to play well at that audition."

2

onday, two days after my lesson, Tom and I saw my father with another woman. It was at Columbia where my father taught Eastern European Jewish Studies. Arms loosely locked, in a comfortable silence that was new to us, Tom and I were shuffling up Broadway, our Woolworth bag of cleaning supplies dangling off his forearm between us. Our sandals squished on the wet pavement, and every so often, Tom forgot to keep the umbrella over both of us and I had to tug his arm to remind him. We both had dark eyes and the same wild, dark curls, and we both wore good leather sandals and a lot of black—I had a short, black shirt on, Tom jeans. We could have been brother and sister. Anyone who saw us, I decided, would think we were a happy couple.

"You never cleaned before in your life," Tom teased. "I have to train you."

"We'll see about that, my friend."

Tom laughed once loudly and tugged my arm. "The problem is you think it's beneath you to be domestic. You don't think it's important to have a nice home."

"Home shlome." I flicked my wrist, my father's gesture, but I did find it comforting that Tom cared so much about making a home, unlike my last boyfriend, Wendel, a pianist, who was moody and difficult and never kind for long. As soon as Tom moved in two months ago, he had talked of wanting a solid family, a better apartment, and

nice things—clothes, furniture, luxurious food—all that he hadn't
had growing up in the South Bronx.

"I'll be better after the audition," I said, and Tom rolled his eyes.
"I promise. I just have to do well."

"Just convince yourself you're not nervous. Repeat it over and over."

I nodded as if that might work, as if that was not what he always
told me. The rain pattered unevenly on Tom's umbrella, avoiding
rhythm, and I squeezed my eyes shut against the memory of *Tombeau*,
my flubbed notes two days before.

We were making our way uptown through the crowds of students, back for the fall semester, when I glanced through the iron
gates of Columbia and saw a man who looked like my father with his
arm over an unfamiliar woman's shoulder. The woman slipped on the
wet brick walk and the man steadied her, his hand lingering intimately on her lower back, her shiny, expensive raincoat. First I was
sure the man was my father, then I convinced myself it couldn't have
been him. The man had my father's gray overcoat and his frizzy,
unbrushed hair. He lumbered like my father after years of jogging
without stretching, and his free hand was clenched in a fist like my
father's when worrying. But the man was nearly old, his messy hair
white and thinned, and my image of my father was of a much younger
man.

"Stop." I jerked Tom's arm.

"What?" He pulled back, and by the time I looked again, the
man and the woman had turned off the brick walk and were gone.

"I think I might have just seen my father with another woman."

"That's weird." Tom laughed, glancing back. "How'd you know
it was him?"

"I mean I'm not exactly sure but . . ." I shrugged my shoulders high.

"At least he's not living with your mother anymore." Tom's own
father, a numbers runner in the Bronx, had carried on affairs right in
front of his mother and then left for good when Tom was four. Tom
hardly ever saw him.

"He should be seeing other women. He shouldn't be alone," Tom
said, and I winced. "What? You think I'm being insensitive? You
want him to be miserable for the rest of his life?"

"My father with another woman." I tested the feel of it. A short-
skirted woman heading down the 116th Street subway steps took a

second look at Tom. He was especially handsome in his white linen shirt, which set off his tan, almost as deep as the varnished wood of his violin. I checked Tom's gaze, but he hadn't seemed to register her. I wanted to love so much better than my parents had loved.

My parents had threatened to leave each other so often, I never believed it would happen, and I tried to react as little as possible to their fights. They'd jumped out of cars, disappeared for days, left each other standing on highways. My mother would cry to me—in front of my father, to get him back for something—"This is the last time. The last time. It's over." But it never was.

Always they came back to each other and nearly—but never fully—forgave each other. Home again after fights, my father would not leave my mother's side. He'd follow her around the house as she cooked and cleaned, then insist that she play through all the pieces she used to play for him when they first fell in love. He'd lie in his puffy bathrobe on the couch, a book open on his chest, and he'd tell his favorite stories of their romance.

"After our first date," he said, "I made a bet your mother would marry me. I had never met a woman like her. A woman who knew about Bach and Beethoven. Everyone said she was too high-class for me, the son of a candystore owner."

My mother laughed softly, looking down at her fingers as she played Chopin's E-flat Nocturne, the piece that had won her a full scholarship to Juilliard over thirty-five years before.

"Isn't your mother beautiful?" my father said to me, and she was, with her pale skin and long black hair falling onto the keys.

"I'm like a dog," he told her. "A bad dog, and I can't be without you. All I need is a little . . ." He pretended to be screwing in something at the side of his head. "A little tune-up."

"If only I could get this kind of treatment every day." My mother smiled to herself as she produced as seamless a run as she might have years ago when music was still her private devotion, separate from him.

I never thought that after twenty-eight years together one of them would finally decide to leave. Three months ago, they had invited me, without Tom, for dinner to talk about something important. I had my own news, which kept me from thinking of theirs: Tom was giving up his studio, the great deal in Chelsea, and he was moving in with me. Neither of us had lived with anyone before, and I had already anticipated my parents' reaction. My sentimental father would cry big, silly tears over the fastness of time and the vanishing of years, but my mother would be more reserved because she had always secretly believed in the inevitable passing of love, even in the best years of their marriage. She liked Tom, though. He was "nice," and "niceness," she told me, was more important than brilliance or drive or unpredictable bursts of affection.

"There she is! There she is! My big love!" my father had shouted inside the apartment, lumbering on his bad leg on his way to the door. He held my head against his old wool sweater longer than usual, then he piled books into my arms: Elie Wiesel, Dylan Thomas, and Camus.

"So you won't be an illiterate musician," he said, his usual joke, but then wouldn't look me in the eye. "Did I ever tell you the story of *Night?*" He described how the narrator, in Auschwitz, had pummeled his own starving father for a piece of bread.

"Thanks, Dad." I punched him in the arm. "When will you ever tell me a happy story?"

"That's me, Mr. Cheerful." He laughed his silent laugh, his round stomach shaking, but his face became red, too red, and he looked away and exhaled long streams of air.

"Wait for me! Don't do anything important!" my mother called brightly from the hall, and then she appeared, a whirl of perfume, colors, and jangling beads.

"Is he giving you things again?" she said, hands on the hips of her long purple skirt. "You never give me anything."

"I never give you things? What is this? What is this?" My father waved his hands comically in the air. "I gave you an apartment, vacations, summers in Woodstock." His voice became fast and livid. "I gave you books, I gave you a daughter, I gave you—"

"All right. I heard you," my mother interrupted, her lips quivering. "I gave *you* a daughter by the way," she said with a small, twisted smile, knowing how ridiculous she sounded.

My mother had made an elaborate dinner, salmon and salad and steamed vegetables. Purple, red, and yellow candles flickered in the center of the mauve tablecloth, and the track lights were dimmed. In the half-light, my parents' faces appeared flushed and overexcited with their news, and they kept pouring each other glass after glass of wine, like their last offerings to each other.

"Before you tell me your news," I said, "guess what."

"What?" they said. Both had forgotten I had something to tell them.

"Tom and I are moving in together." I smiled stupidly.

"That's great, sweetie. Wonderful," my father said. He clutched me to him, his chest heaving.

"What's wrong with you, Dad?" I pushed him away. "Are you happy or sad?"

"This calls for another glass of wine. A celebration." My mother raised her glass. Her face suddenly looked stained and horrible in the candlelight. "To love!"

My father turned to the bookshelves, unable to stop crying, not just his usual silent tears, but gasping sobs, which embarrassed me to hear. Fifty paperback copies of his last book on the Holocaust framed his head. "Your mother's leaving me," he said.

"I'm leaving you?" She laughed sarcastically, thrilled that she had hurt him, that she had jolted him out of what she thought was his usual disregard for her. "You dismiss me, ignore me, never listen. And now you cry as if you're the one who's hurt."

She cleared a stack of dishes from the table and dropped the clanking silverware into the sink. She expected it to go as it usually did. She would threaten him, maybe kick him out for a few days, to scare him into valuing her, but he would never leave.

That night after dinner at their house, I didn't even tell Tom what happened. Even though a persistent dread gnawed at me, I still waited for the call that usually came within a few days—the call that would let me know everything was all right. My family would continue.

3

I rang my mother's doorbell three long times, but there was no
answer. The sound of her ocean-music tape was faint inside the
apartment. It was exactly two o'clock; I was on time. Though
it had been three months, I still expected to hear my father, shouting
to me as he rushed to the door, his arms open. I called my mother's
name, but only a somber wave answered me. I imagined her lying on
her bed, listening, sleeping, I didn't know what. She might do anything to herself alone in her apartment where no one thought about
her enough. I rang my mother's bell again and again, but still she didn't
come. Panic dizzied me and I shook the door by the knob.

"Mom," I shouted, pounding on the door, not caring who heard
in the nearby apartments. The waves stopped abruptly, and I heard
her footsteps—that quick, stiff walk—to the foyer.

"I couldn't sleep all night," my mother said. She led me into the
living room, then sat up straight on the sofa, her purple bathrobe tied
tight at the waist. Her skin was still damp, scented with lilac soap,
and the wet ends of her hair, shorter now, darkened her robe where her
collarbone jutted through.

"Don't be as brokenhearted as me, promise?" She waved her finger at me. "Women are trained to have broken hearts. I thought there
would be some kind of reward for unhappiness." She gave a short,
bright laugh, then fumbled with the neck of her robe. Between us was
the slate table, Navajo vase, and laughing brass Buddha, his arms

raised with joy, and I didn't move to touch her or hold her as I should have. My father's first book on the Jewish Resistance lay open, facedown, on the table. Thirty years ago, he had dedicated it to my mother: *To Roberta, for her understanding and patience.* Patience, I thought, for all the years she'd endured his absolute devotion to his work and not to her, the years when his work had come before hers until she had no more work, no more music.

"Hard to believe, isn't it?" My mother caught me looking at the book. "It all goes by so fast. My mother used to say that, but I never believed her. Every day had a weight. A certain awfulness."

I nodded, smiled at her, though that wasn't the right thing to do.

Stella, my mother's old gray cat, rubbed up against me and purred immediately when I scratched her ears.

"See," my mother said. "Look how happy she is. All she needs is a little attention. A little love." She watched my fingers and her thinned face nearly relaxed, becoming again what it once was: exquisite with her small, fine features, sharp or delicate, depending on her mood, and her long, arching neck, which my father had always loved.

It kept changing, the memory of the man and woman I had seen at Columbia an hour before. First I was sure the man was my father, then I persuaded myself I had been too far away to tell.

"So how was your lesson, darling?" my mother asked too cheerfully, clasping her hands under her chin.

"It was good." I shrugged, tossing it off.

"I'm so glad." She sighed with both mock and real relief, and though I had promised myself not to, I told her something that wasn't true.

"Mr. de Laney thinks, he's pretty sure, I'll make it to the finals this time."

"Wonderful!" My mother clapped. She knew how many famous players Mr. de Laney had taught.

"He told me my Tchaikovsky was beautiful."

"You always played that so well. Always."

When I was thirteen, I'd played the Tchaikovsky with the All-State Youth Symphony. I felt so full of myself because I'd been chosen to play first oboe so young. I didn't think to be nervous, though great players have studied and honed the Tchaikovsky solo all their lives. It didn't occur to me that I could fall apart.

"Mr. de Laney said if I played the Tchaikovsky that well next week, the judges would be sure to like me."

"Oh! I'm so happy." My mother laughed, her first hearty laugh in a while. I wanted to close my eyes and shut everything else away so that I would remember the sound of it, full and strong, and always have it with me. I felt almost as relieved as if Mr. de Laney had told me I'd won.

"You're too much like me," my mother told me. "Not enough confidence. You hang on to the bad. You have to forget what happened."

I looked away to ward off any more discussion of Merkin Hall.

"Have you been doing what I told you? Just close your eyes and visualize." She closed her own eyes, curled her fingers into om signs on either knee. "Concentrate. Feel the sound inside of you. The most beautiful sound in the world."

"Mom . . . ," I interrupted.

She blinked her eyes open. "Have you spoken to your father recently?" she asked, trying to sound offhanded. "What's he up to? Business as usual?"

"You know, working hard. Frantic." I always spoke badly about my father around my mother.

"Well, that's your father!" She laughed, short, ringing. Her eyes were glassy. "What else is he doing?"

I shrugged and pulled Stella onto my lap. It wasn't just what I'd seen today that made me suspicious; I never knew where my father was. There were always different backgrounds to his calls and reasons why I couldn't call him back. Last night on the phone, clinking glasses and laughter rose and fell behind him, but when I asked, he told me in a purposely distracted voice that he was at a friend's house and then changed the subject.

"He's not seeing anybody, is he?" my mother asked breezily. The dim light in the mauve room made her cheeks look hollowed.

"No." I petted Stella, but she struggled away.

"Your father doesn't tell me anything anymore." My mother narrowed her eyes at me from across the room, trying to elicit a response.

When I was silent, she gave a short laugh. "Whoever knew what he was doing anyway. You saw the way he would flirt."

I fought not to take her words in and to pretend she'd never said them. Even now I kept expecting my father to suddenly appear in the living room door, as if he'd only been in the bedroom sleeping. "My big love. When did you get here?" he'd say, and then sentimental as always, he'd admire us from the doorway. "Look how lucky I am. This is all I've ever wanted. My daughter and my wife, together."

These months of visits and endless worries about my mother would be over. I wouldn't have to call her twice a day, once at night, to make sure the darkness fell more easily, and once again in the early morning, her most relentless hours. It was then that if her phone rang too long, I clutched the receiver, afraid she had given way to sadness.

"Play a little piano for me. Please?" My mother showed only a little space between her thumb and index finger. "Just a bit?"

I knew it would make me sad to play now.

"Just a little?" she said. "It would cheer me up."

I couldn't say no.

My mother opened the piano bench where all our old music was stored, then flipped through the leatherbound books of Chopin nocturnes, Bach preludes and fugues, and Beethoven sonatas her first teacher had given to her.

"What will you play?" She smiled to herself as she skimmed the table of contents. I waited, my fingers poised on the keys. We sat so close to each other on the piano bench that I could feel the dampness of her skin and smell her lilac soap. I didn't remember the last time I had been so close to her, and I had to force myself not to pull away.

"My teacher gave these books to me just as I was getting on the bus to come to New York. And I was so afraid of crying I didn't open them, I just clutched them, wrapped, on my lap. I was so frightened."

Her father had never wanted her to leave Bearsville, in upstate New York, to come to Juilliard. He told my mother she would never succeed at music or anything else, and he dismissed her scholarship to study with Horowitz, the only full scholarship awarded in piano that year.

"That trip was my one big moment of courage." My mother laughed at herself. "You know how good everyone else at Juilliard seemed?" She widened her eyes as if she were still amazed. "Of course, then I met your father. And I was so in love, I did everything, centered my whole day around trying to make him happy. So weak." She shook her head, staring down at the leatherbound books.

"Oh, well," she sighed all of a sudden, then smiled at me, holding up one of the books so I could not refuse. "Play a little Beethoven."

"I can't play Beethoven anymore," I said, but my mother had already opened to the *Pathétique* Sonata. It was not something I could really perform well, now or ever. But my mother loved the startled, passionate way I played those opening chords. She'd never wanted me to choose the oboe over the piano, even though a wind instrument felt much more natural to me, just like singing through the reed.

"All right." My mother pointed her finger, imitating her old teacher. "Let's hear it. Two, three, four."

I had my fingers on the keys, ready to play, but my mother started to laugh.

"Oh, boy." She wiped her eyes. "When I think how terrified that teacher used to make me."

She tried the opening on the high register. "How did that sound?"

I nodded.

"I've been practicing every day," she told me. "If you can believe it."

Her fingers were no longer pianist's fingers, strong and agile over the keys; they were clunky, bunching at the knuckles. She couldn't get the right-hand run smooth. She tried again. Missed notes.

"Jesus." She shook her head. And her voice got brighter. "You wouldn't think I had been practicing."

I slumped beside her. I wanted her to stop playing. She tried hands separately, just her right hand, but still couldn't get it.

"I had it this morning." She dropped her hands flat on the keys. The sound clanged loud, and she covered her mouth.

"I don't know what's wrong with me." She blinked at her tears and I had to look away, around the living room at all her things—the Buddha, the Moroccan tapestry, the lush plants by the windows, their vines draped across the radiator. I thought my father had held her down in a good way, too. Without him, everything about her seemed invented, scattered, ungraspable.

"Won't you play a bit for me?" my mother asked.

The opening chords of the *Pathétique* were so weighted and grave I didn't want to play them.

"Just a little bit." My mother's lips were taut, her chin trembling. My fingers felt muscleless, as if they could not possibly hold firm to the keys.

"Please," she said, and her sadness swallowed me up. I played, and the somber chords felt like her formless grief overtaking me.

"You just play so beautifully." My mother touched her chest. "It's just so beautiful."

I knew it was beautiful, but when I looked at my mother, her face lit up bright, I told her, "No, it wasn't. I am the worst pianist in the world."

My mother knocked my fingers on the keys. "Gala!"

"I'm terrible." I had to hold back my desire to laugh, to make a joke of it. "It's true."

My mother nudged my arm. "You play beautifully. Don't say that." Her words seemed distant and quite separate from me. I wanted to leave.

"I have to go. I have a student at five o'clock." I was lying and immediately felt guilty.

"You told me you could stay until dinner," she insisted, and I felt my will slip away.

"I'm sorry, Mom." I made my voice small and childlike. "My student called at the last minute."

My mother took a deep breath and ran her hands down her face. "I understand," she said, but I couldn't tell if she believed me.

Glad to feel the cool rain on my forehead, I walked slowly with no umbrella away from my mother's house. Cars splashed down Broadway, umbrellas bobbed by, and I tried to lose myself to the sounds of wetness all around me: the horns, the splashed gutter water that seeped through my sandals, sticking to my ankles. I went past the row of Chinese restaurants, the rain beating on the swirl of fluorescent letters, and the two-dollar clothes that hung under plastic on the sidewalk in front of Vims. Next to the T-shirts, a tiny boy in a yellow parka was riding the single carousel horse ride. People passed on the sidewalk and he stared out into the rain.

As I wandered toward my apartment on 124th Street, I passed Columbia, hoping to see my father through the black iron gates. Even if he was with a woman, any woman, I would pull him away and tell him about my mother and her sadness. First, he would be stunned by my anger—so few were the times I'd truly been mad at him—and then he would cry again as he finally realized how much he loved my mother. He could never leave those twenty-eight years of his life, the woman he'd given his youth to.

I stopped at a pay phone. Raindrops rolled down my forehead, tasted salty when I wiped my mouth. I huddled into the booth and dialed my father's office number.

"It's the big G! It's my big daughter!" my father shouted into the phone, high and full of himself from teaching well, I could immediately tell. I imagined him in his office, the stacks of books on the Holocaust and the nature of good and evil on the cluttered, ugly metal desk, and the pictures of me taped haphazardly to the wall.

"Your father was brilliant today," he told me. "My students were on the edge of their seats. You should have heard me."

I smiled, cradling the phone closer to my ear though I had wanted to be angry. The rain beat on my back, but my father's voice filled me, made me forget about getting wet. It was as if the whole world had suddenly become focused, clear, intense, and it contained only my father and me. I did not ask him about the other woman as I had intended; I listened for the full five minutes about how brilliantly he'd lectured.

I stuck in another nickel.

"You didn't call me after your lesson," he said. "I was so worried."

I groaned impatiently at him, though the more he worried, the more I craved his attention. I lied to him as I'd lied to my mother.

"Mr. de Laney said he was sure I'd make it at least to the semifinals."

"Sweetie," my father sighed with relief, "you should have called me before. I was up all night. How's the practicing going?"

I told him all about how I was waking up at 5:00 A.M. to practice and doing six hours a day. It was all true and it pleased him immensely. Those were his habits when he'd been writing his books.

"You're like me," he told me. "You know how to work."

I smiled, glad for his compliment, though I felt like a traitor to my mother, who he said never knew how to push herself. The difference between my mother and me, he said, was that I had discipline.

"Did you hear what happened with the Menendez case today?" my father said, then he gave me his daily report from Court TV, which we were both secretly addicted to. He spoke in his teaching, lecturing voice. "Lyle claims that not only did his father have sex with him but that his mother fondled him, too."

"It's true!" I slipped up and laughed, though I hadn't meant to with him today.

"You just like them because they're cute. Especially Eric. Just don't ever try to kill me in my sleep. I want to be awake."

"Sleep with a gun near your pillow."

He laughed at my rudeness. "Guess what I was looking at before you called—those pictures of you dancing. You were always such a great dancer."

"I was not." I giggled because I knew it was true. My father had taken a whole series when I was twelve, and now they lined his office walls.

"No one has your rhythm. I love to watch you dance."

"Dad . . ." I giggled again and held the phone away for a moment to calm my anxiety, flushed and chaotic but not altogether unpleasing. We liked to have secret, outrageous conversations together. It was like a game.

It had started raining harder. My old leather sandals felt muddy and wet and warm, sort of oozing around my toes.

"Who do I love most in the world?" my father said.

"Me."

"And who will always be your father?"

"You."

"And what will you read at my funeral?" he joked. We'd already planned the whole sermon—Dylan Thomas, "Do Not Go Gentle into That Good Night," and Robert Hayden, "Those Winter Sundays," about a father who dies unappreciated.

I knew my three minutes would soon be over and that we would hang up. Through the wet iron gates of Columbia was Low Library, where my mother used to wait for my father after his classes every day. She'd pack his lunch and dress up in her red swing coat and suede thigh highs, his favorite, just so he would feel that same rush when he spotted her on the steps every afternoon.

"No two people have ever been so happy," my father used to tell me, and I felt almost in love with them, their younger selves. I imagined my parents' first years as perfect and blessed, unlike any love of mine.

I turned away from the library steps, empty in the rain, and I huddled into the phone booth.

"Dad? Do you miss Mom?"

"Of course, I miss your mother. I will always miss your mother," he said, but his voice was too large, sweeping over everything.

"Why did you separate?"

"Why?" My father repeated as if he could never answer. His breath got heavy on the other end of the wire. "We were mean to each other. We didn't know how not to be."

*M*usic made Betty Blue sing. While Tom and I practiced, she chirped a constant accompaniment. It reassured me to play in the bedroom while Betty Blue sang in her cage by the fire escape and Tom practiced for his Prokofiev Quartet audition in the living room. Their music kept me going, kept me focused, and I didn't drift off into useless anxiety.

My audition was in one week. Five times since Juilliard, I'd made it past the first round, four times I'd gotten nowhere, and only once I'd made it to the semifinals.

My mistakes were never the same. It wasn't one problem, easily located, then solved. I made different mistakes each time. Maybe my reed would be flat, droopy in the high register, or maybe it would be too resistant and I would miss my low attacks. Or maybe one minute before an audition, I would realize that I had not practiced the easiest piece enough; I had left it for last and suddenly it seemed insurmountable.

But more often than not, it was my finger technique that I didn't trust, that made me unable to sleep the night before, worrying. My fingers would tremble before a technically hard piece like *Le Tombeau de Couperin,* and then I would make that one crucial mistake.

Every morning at 5:00 A.M., I woke up to practice in the kitchen, my bell facing into an open cabinet to dull the sound while Tom half-slept. My lungs felt tired at first. I couldn't get enough air and it seemed as if my sound would never come. I would never feel that fullness, that completeness, when my sound, my very own voice, filled the room. Sometimes I thought I could feel my sound getting richer and more controlled, my technique more thoughtless and fluent. This new hopefulness felt uneasy and not quite real though. At any moment, it seemed someone might take it away from me and tell me I had no chance of ever playing beautifully.

From point A to point B. Hard work, Mr. de Laney had said. As simple as that.

Sometimes I did not care about this audition or winning anything at all. I thought I could simply live on these early mornings. The white sky spread over the aboveground subway tracks a half a block away and it seemed perfect; I would crescendo just as the subway lurched closer and closer over the tracks, gathering sound.

As it grew closer to nine, the subway would come and go much more frequently, and I timed how long I practiced each scale by its arrival. I was lucky, I knew, to be playing, to have music, while so many people got on the rush-hour subway every day. I liked to have my scales and exercises done by noon before I left to teach my few beginning students or to play my few scattered gigs.

Nearly every day I jogged a slow four and a half miles down to the bottom of the Seventy-second Street boat basin and back. I had never been athletic, and I didn't try to prove anything to myself now. I kept jogging for pleasure only and focused on the details: the exact feeling and texture of the weather that day or the relative strength or sluggishness of my legs. I often ran with my friend Daphne, a dancer, whose family had known mine for years. She was ten years older than me, and as a girl, she'd studied with Balanchine and wanted to dance in the New York City Ballet. She'd ended up teaching in a small school on Broadway, but she said it was all so much more pleasurable now that she had stopped pressuring herself. Now she remembered why she danced in the first place.

"It's easy to forget, you know," she cautioned me as we dodged Rollerbladers on the walkway along the Hudson. Her baggy sweatpants flapped against her long dancer's legs, and her leotard clung to the wiry muscles of her shoulders. On a bench, two men with babies watched us go by, our ponytails, hers blond, mine black, bobbing behind us.

"I haven't forgotten why I play," I told her. "I love the work. I love practicing."

"You should remember that, whether you do well or not."

"Of course," I agreed, though failing to make it at least to the semifinals seemed intolerable to me. It wasn't even an option. I had to do well this time.

We stretched side by side on the stone steps of Grant's Tomb. Her leg on the railing, Daphne did a perfect split, head to her knees, and then she massaged her thighs vigorously, lovingly.

She told me that when she studied with Balanchine, she would get sick before classes.

"Once Balanchine was criticizing my arabesque and my knees trembled so much I was sure they would collapse. Right there, in front of everyone. What a waste." She shook her head. "I was always putting off being happy."

As I reached for my toes, she touched that perfect place on my back, and tension, which I didn't even know was there, drained out of me.

"I didn't see how much larger life is than every little success or failure," Daphne told me. "It wasn't worth it anymore. Don't let that happen to you."

Two nights before my audition, I stopped being able to sleep. While Tom clutched his pillow, his lids fluttering with his dreams, I stared up at the live, shadowy ceiling. The light through the shade cut across the bureau, my overflowing jewelry boxes, and the picture of my parents, peaceful and at ease together, reading on a field in Woodstock, their long hair curtaining their faces. At 3:00 A.M., I kicked the covers off my bed. I was sure it would happen again. My fingers would go flimsy and my sound would humiliate me. The conductor had nodded to me, raised his eyebrows in a question. I can't, I tried to tell him with my eyes, but he lifted his baton and the orchestra played its first note.

I swung my legs off our bed, our stacked mattresses, and Tom mumbled in his sleep, grasping the pillow tighter. I lit a cigarette in the living room and the nicotine buzzed through my veins. My mouth and throat were dry and tasted of ash and I knew I would not sleep.

I sat on the edge of our bed and touched Tom's naked shoulders. "What's going on?" He blinked open his eyes once quickly, then squeezed them shut again. "What time is it?"

"It's late. I'm just so nervous."

Tom sighed into his pillow, but then he held my hand limply in my lap. The white vinyl shade moved in the slight breeze, and the light opened and closed across the bureau.

"I'm afraid you'll stop loving me if I lose."

"What? Stop loving you?" he repeated, not lifting his face from the pillow. "Haven't I always been loving?"

"You got impatient."

Tom let go of my hand. "You really think that?"

I knew if I said yes, we would have an argument, right there in the middle of the night. After Merkin, I'd hidden my shame from him, first in the basement where I crouched among the microphones after the concert, and then every day for months when he grew impatient with my worries. He kept telling me to just make myself get over what had happened. We were living apart then and I stopped admitting that I still hadn't recovered, that every rehearsal, every lesson, the memory of my ugly sound echoing in the huge hall still haunted me.

I spoke softly, placing my words in the dark room. "I'm just afraid. That after all this with Mr. de Laney, I still won't do well."

Tom sighed once more. "I can't take this anymore. You worry all the time. You're making me crazy, too."

I watched the vinyl shade, the string at the bottom knocking against the window ledge, until the sting of his words had almost disappeared.

"Can you just hold me? Please," I said like a little girl. His eyes were still closed but I felt him thinking.

"Come here," he said, his voice strained between love and impatience as he opened the covers for me. I lay on my stomach and he stroked my shoulder with his fingertips. Our faces were inches apart, his smushed on the pillow.

"You can't be so nervous all the time. It's insane," he whispered.

I nodded. I knew it was. "I can't help it."

"Don't say that. Of course you can," Tom told me, because he had been able to reinvent himself. I wanted him to stay up with me, to speak tenderly, to comfort me. But a few minutes later, his breathing had grown heavy again. I thought I wanted too much. I needed for him to make up for something too big. I remembered how my mother used to sing me lullabies at night. She would wrap her body around mine, her breath moist in my ear, her hands playing with my hair. I didn't know why I fought so hard to keep her away from me.

I slid Tom's arm off my back, this time trying not to wake him, and I left the bedroom. My cigarette burned beside me on the kitchen counter. My bell facing into the cabinets, I played a quick scale. I had been practicing so much lately that I didn't need to warm up. My fingers felt as if they were always playing.

"*Tombeau,*" I told myself, and it came out of me perfectly, naturally. I did it. I kissed the tip of my reed and hugged myself.

"Brahms," I said. I pretended I was in an orchestra. I heard the soft, sustained chords of the violins and horns, then I began to play that sweet opening. It was supposed to be soft and yearning, but I couldn't stop from playing more, from filling the whole room, letting my sound call out through the quiet apartment.

5

The beta-blockers rattled in my purse as the number 1 train lurched over the rails. I gripped my oboe tight on my lap. Beside me was a woman with a long, chinless face and stringy hair. Her boyfriend stood over her, not looking at her. She kept gazing up at him.

"Charles." She tugged on the bottom of his jacket.

At Seventy-second Street, the local doors shut just as the express arrived, and a man in a blue suit pounded on the glass. The next stop was Lincoln Center. I fingered my reed case in my bag, and suddenly I was sure my reed wouldn't work. I'd chosen the wrong one. It was dark, but it sunk in the high register. My high notes in the Brahms would be flat.

The train screeched into Sixty-sixth Street and I covered my ears, as my mother always told me to do. The huge square in the middle of Lincoln Center looked deserted, as if all the life, the concert crowds, the tourists, had been sucked away. Only two middle-aged women, tourists in boxy khaki shorts and pastel sweaters, were taking pictures, posing for each other in front of the fountain. In exactly forty-five minutes, I would be playing.

In the lobby of the New York State Theater, I was alone. The ticket windows were closed and the marble, spiraling stairs looked immense and empty. The low ceiling with its hundreds of rows of tiny lights dizzied me. There were no signs and no one around. Muffled through thick walls came the sound of fifty oboists warming up. Occasionally, one player rushing up to the high register would become distinct from the rest, and immediately I judged the player, his technique, his tone, his style of playing—whether he had more the Philadelphia sound, dark, resonant, and intense as mine was now, or whether his sound was bigger, brighter, and more spread out like Mr. Barret's. Twenty-five oboists lined the backstage hall, at least two from Juilliard. Noel was leaning up against the water fountain. His windbreaker sagged at the middle pockets with the weight of his hands, and his eyes were half-closed. He probably had just played. By the EXIT sign, Jason was talking too loudly to someone I didn't recognize, but who obviously wanted to get away from him. I didn't see my friend Pam, who was playing at 11:45.

My warm-up room, number three, had yellow walls, a plush yellow chair, and a mirror with ten tiny lightbulbs around it. I set my oboe, music, and reeds on the desk and took a deep breath. This was it. My heart was beating too quickly and I tried to make it stop. I clasped my new oboe with both hands and tried to send it a message through my clenched fingers. Please.

I still had enough time before playing to take a beta-blocker. Yesterday, I'd tried one while I was practicing and it had made my playing tired and listless, but I knew if I took it, my fingers wouldn't shake. It was a trade-off.

I tried to think good thoughts—of how many good, confident performances I'd had in my life and how many times, especially when I was very young, performing felt natural to me, not like something I had to brace myself for. I thought of how it would all be over in two hours, about how I would see Tom tonight and whatever happened he would be there. I never appreciated that enough.

Dimly, I could hear someone warming up in the next room. His technique was seamless, and I felt a wash of loneliness. I wished that someone could be with me now, could hold my hand and make sure I was okay, that I was protected from failure and making a fool of myself. I cupped my forehead in my palm and then remembered that I always had this loneliness before playing. Suddenly I felt lighter and that my despair a moment before was silly.

I imagined Mr. de Laney standing and conducting beside me. I heard his words: "Every note must be perfect and whole. Like it is the last and only note in the world." I took a deep breath from my abdomen and played a D, so soft and clear and resonant that I could just barely hear it, suspended, shimmering in the room.

I stuck my beta-blockers back in my purse without taking one. I was to play at 12:00. There were so many corridors and doors on the way to the stage that I was sure I would get lost and miss my audition. I almost hoped that would happen. As I weaved my way to the backstage door, I fought against the memory of those minutes before playing at Merkin, how I'd huddled into the dark fold of the curtain and wished to disappear. I'd pressed my face into the musty velvet, knowing I would not be able to play.

A woman with a clipboard was in front of the backstage door. She had on thick glasses and her hair was pulled back in a bun.

"What number please?" Her voice was squeaky.

I cleared my throat. "Number sixteen." Then I had to wait. The backstage door was closed. I couldn't hear the person playing before me.

"Are they running on time?" I wanted to talk, to distract myself.

"Yes."

"I heard they were a little late."

"Nope." She looked back down at her clipboard.

My hands were sweaty, slippery on the keys. My reed was still in its cup of water. I worried it had been soaking too long. What if it had been soaking too long and my sound was soggy and flat? I couldn't remember how long it had been in the water. It was 11:57. Three more minutes. In twenty minutes it would be over. I tried not to think. "Visualize, Gala," my mother always told me, and I tried to hear the music in my head but couldn't. I couldn't remember the music. I looked at the clipboard woman again. She was chewing on her pencil.

"Are you sure they're running on time?" I asked just as the oboist before me opened the door. She had long, heavy hair, and she stumbled down the steps.

"I'm done," she breathed at me, though I'd never met her before.

I had to wait for the judges to call my number. The woman with the clipboard went through the stage door and then came back.

"They're ready for you now."

I panicked just as the clipboard woman pulled the curtain aside. Knees shaking, I passed through the curtains onto the stage. In front of the stage was an opaque silver screen that blocked the judges' view of me. Above the screen were the empty, yellowish rows of chairs and the three tiers of balcony. I tried to convince myself of my insignificance and how little this audition mattered, but my hands were still trembling as I organized my music on the stand according to the judges' order: Mozart Concerto, *Tombeau*, Brahms, then *La Scala*. The hardest things were first.

I stood behind the screen and waited for the judges to tell me to begin. In the audience, they whispered and shuffled their papers. Across the empty stage, the porous lights streamed down on the black floor.

"Number sixteen, you can start whenever you're ready."

The voice jolted me. I started the Mozart too quickly without taking a breath. My fingers rushed up the first scale. They felt as if they didn't belong to me. I heard myself reach the high C, and as I sustained the note, I tried to focus again, to concentrate on the music. I imagined the orchestra parts beneath me. I listened for the violins and cellos, and I felt part of the music again as I came off the high C and played the pressing, light phrase into the G's.

"Thank you very much. Ravel, *Tombeau de Couperin*, please." The voice stopped me before I felt I'd even started. My fingers fumbled as I moved *Tombeau* to the front of my stand. I remembered how I'd messed it up in my lesson, and I begged for this one time to be right. Just this one time.

"*Tombeau*, please," a woman's voice called, impatient.

I began before I was ready. My fingers were going way too fast, much faster than I'd ever played it before. I was racing, but somehow not messing up. I thought I was going to make it through a perfectly clean run. Not particularly musical, but still clean and very fast. I thought I would do it, was sure I would make it, but then, for some reason, right at the very end, in the very last bar of triplet sixteenth notes, my fingers moved unevenly. One note was nearly swallowed into the others.

"Brahms, please," the woman's voice called, and then the judges were silent. They seemed so far away all of a sudden. Across the stage, the corridors of lush red curtains were dark and empty.

The mistake in the last measure of *Tombeau* was so slight, I thought, I could easily make up for it.

I played the Brahms as I'd never played it before. I pressed into the first note, that high A, and gave it an extra pang, making it bittersweet, then I milked the next two phrases, teasing into notes and then pulling back, just the right amount. I gave everything on the F—all of my warmth, all of my love. I knew it was beautiful, and for a moment I felt so happy I wanted to laugh, I wanted to scream, this was my music, my voice.

When I was done, I heard a silence, the kind of good silence when an audience is moved.

An older man whispered something. "Yes, yes," the woman agreed.

"La Scala di seta," the woman said.

I began and my tongue was light and quick. The music sounded easy and playful, exactly as it should. I hammed it up, making the last run to the low C raucous and drunken-sounding.

"Thank you very much," a woman's voice called, ending the audition.

I blinked my eyes against the light. The sky had turned bright and silver, the sun beaming through the clouds. I walked a few feet from the audition hall and then stopped. A family near the fountain was feeding the pigeons. The father tossed out pieces of bread and the little girl clapped her hands when the pigeons swarmed around the crumbs. Other oboists slowly filtered out of the huge revolving doors of the New York State Theater building. Most looked dazed, only one looked happy.

At the phone at the bottom of the square, I called my mother first.

"I can't tell if it was good. Maybe it was."

My mother squealed so suddenly, so girlishly, that I laughed, too. "I know you. If you say maybe it was good, then it must have been wonderful."

"I made a slight mistake in the last measure of *Tombeau.*" I told her what had happened and she reassured me. Usually my mother was scattered and couldn't listen to me for long, but now she asked me about every piece, and my need for her attention felt bottomless.

"Next week is Rosh Hashanah." She changed the subject and I tried not to feel disappointed. "What will we do?"

Without my father, his scrambled Hebrew, his made-up words and davening imitations, I worried my mother and I might sink together to a place I wouldn't be able to come up from. "Let's just skip it." I hadn't intended on being mean, but my mother was quiet, her breath squeezed on the other end of the wire. I tried not to absorb her sadness. It took so little, just a moment hearing her loneliness, to make me feel it, too.

"You have to make yourself happier," I said carefully into her silence. "Have you sent out any résumés?"

"A few," she answered too quickly, but I knew she was lying. It had always seemed true to both her and my father that after giving up the piano, there could be nothing else. She'd tried teaching yoga and meditation, leading consciousness-raising groups, and even going into real estate—all professions my father did not respect. Even when she had finally finished social work school, my father criticized her. He'd told her once in the middle of a fight, "I never expected to be married to a social worker." He apologized over and over, but my mother never forgave him. I was like my mother in this way, and I didn't know if it was normal, how much we held on to the cruel things people told us.

Pam pushed out the doors of the New York State Theater building, and I told my mother I had to get off the phone.

"When will you visit me?" she said, and I promised I would soon, not this week, but the next, but she sounded so forlorn that after hanging up, I almost called back to say I'd visit sooner.

"Well, that's over with," Pam said sourly, flicking her black lighter three times before leaning into the phone booth for shelter. She looked prim and unstylish, unlike herself. Her short blond hair was headbanded back, and she wore a drab, navy blue audition skirt and high-necked blouse. I asked her about her audition.

"It was great," she yawned in a voice surprisingly confident. "Everything was in place." She firmed the air with her hand. "Solid. What about yours?"

"I don't know," I said, a knot tightening in my chest.

"I bet your Brahms was good. That's your thing. The soul thing."

"Yeah, right."

"You know it's true." She elbowed me and I laughed one little puff into the wide, gray square. We crossed Broadway to Orloff's, the bright, overpriced diner we used to always go to after rehearsals. We didn't see each other as much anymore. Mostly it was Pam, who was too busy with gigs or her boyfriend, Kurt. She played with half a dozen pickup orchestras, all better than any of the groups I played with. At Juilliard, we'd been best friends in that girlish, loverish way I'd never had before, but always missed. We spoke on the phone every night, confessed everything to each other, and even practiced together. We locked ourselves in practice rooms, stuffed towels under the door, and we smoked and played and made reeds for hours. If we skipped a day, Pam kissed me twice on either cheek and said she had missed me. I had wanted a girlfriend like her all my life.

"Of all the instruments to choose." We'd roll our eyes together at the unfortunate luck of playing the oboe, the only instrument, along with the bassoon, that required that its players remake part of their instrument, their reed, every day. Then I was a better reed maker than Pam, and I taught her everything I knew. Reeds were terrible, I told her, volatile, undependable, and it was impossible to ever copy exactly what you had done to make your last good reed; each piece of cane was different. I loved the craft of it, though. I loved stirring my hand through a box of smooth tubes of cane, fresh from France, and examining each one till I picked out the best. I gouged the chosen pieces, hollowing out the first layer of excess cane, then showed Pam how to tell by the hardness and softness of the grain how the reed would eventually sound. If she had no good cane, I would give her mine.

The hostess, an older woman with dyed red hair, showed us to our usual table in the back corner. Pam ordered a diet Coke immediately. Her long arms didn't have enough room on the table so she moved everything—the Sweet'n Low, the sugar, the oil and vinegar—to the next table. When her diet Coke came, she gulped down half.

"I feel better already." She shook off her headband, then puckered her lips at herself in the wall mirror. I admired her perfectly smooth skin. Once a month she treated herself to Erbe facials, a pleasure I allowed myself only occasionally.

"Beautiful," I told her.

"You always say that." She lit her cigarette and blew the smoke straight up, fluffing up her bangs. "And today I know I look like shit."

We had opposite looks. Different but equal, Pam and I used to say in our giggly vain moods. Pam was very white, blond, and angular; my hair was black and frizzy and my face was round, too round, I thought. "Kurt kept me up all night." She rolled her eyes. "He was in one of his moods, and of course, he expected me to take care of him. 'Take care of yourself,' I told him."

I tried not to look surprised.

"He adores you, Pam." I always stuck up for Kurt, who had wanted to marry her for the past two years.

"He's too depressed half the time. Needy. I like a certain boundary." She made a wall in front of her with both hands, which I couldn't help feeling was like the distance she'd put up between us. Or maybe I just wanted too much. Her mother had died of an aneurysm when Pam was twelve. Sometimes I thought she was still a little in shock. "It's kind of liberating," she'd said once. "You get used to loss." I wasn't sure whether to believe her.

A handsome Italian waiter took our order. I got a frozen yogurt because I always pretended to myself I was on a diet. Pam ordered a cheeseburger.

"And another diet Coke!" she called just as he was turning around. She did not sweeten her voice when she spoke to men.

"So," she said, "are you happy in your new nest?"

"Still adjusting."

"Tom's good for you. Wendel was too moody."

"I need someone who can be kind," I agreed. It was our most common discussion, whether we were happy or not. Pam offered me a cigarette and I couldn't resist; her tobacco was so fresh and potent.

"It's too much of a pleasure," I said, and we sat, smoking together, watching our puffs meet and then dissolve in the center of the table. We were back in our rhythm, smoking buddies, best friends, as I wished we'd always be.

"How's the gig in Brooklyn?" I tried to keep the jealousy from my face as she told me about the conductor, whom she was, of course, flirting with because she wanted to steal the first oboe position from the guy on vacation.

"You bad girl," I said.

"Then I could get you in to sub for me. But then I'd have to watch my back with you."

"Oh, come on." I made a disgusted face, though I felt myself blushing as if I had, in fact, been plotting to steal her gig.

"You don't realize what an honor it is to be studying with Mr. de Laney." She craned her neck to see over my shoulder. "Don't look now, but guess who's at the counter."

"Who?" I turned around quickly. Elaine Douvas, principal of the Met and one of the judges, was buying a frozen yogurt. She was petite and trim in her conservative pants suit.

"I can't believe it." I scrunched up my shoulders.

"She sees us. Turn around. She's waving."

I smiled foolishly at Elaine Douvas and she nodded to both of us, her head pulled slightly back, as if to say she'd been impressed by our playing.

"What do you think that meant?" I asked Pam after she had gone.

"Nothing. Maybe. She probably doesn't know so quickly which number goes with what person. Or maybe she does."

We pondered that, crunching on our ice.

"You have more the playing style she likes." Pam frowned.

"No way," I said, though I hoped it was true.

"She likes very soulful players."

"You're extremely soulful. What are you talking about?" Secretly, however, I did hope Elaine Douvas had been nodding mostly to me. "And your technique is so much better," I added enthusiastically to hide how much I didn't want that to be true. "I hope we both make it to the finals this time."

"That would be a trick." Pam sucked on her cigarette, then looked back at me and smiled. For a moment, though, something else was in her eyes, something that said she did not want me to do well if she failed.

For the first two weeks of September, I didn't have to worry. Even when I checked the mailbox, I knew the notice would not yet have arrived. The humid days of summer were gone, and I jogged with Daphne faster than I ever had before. My legs took off beneath me as I fantasized about winning. I imagined how proud my parents would be, how Tom would no longer see me as sad and needy, but as glamorous and successful, and Mr. de Laney would love me and count me as one of his greatest successes. I might even dedicate a toast to him at my victory dinner. The best teacher in the world, I would say, the one who had saved me.

I practiced lazily with long breaks at Manhattan School of Music, where one of the small orchestras I played with rehearsed. I loved to rest between scales, the silver of my oboe cool on my bare knees, and listen to all the sounds from the other practice rooms drifting in with the warm wind over Broadway: the flutist fluttered through scales, the trombonist droned, and beside me, Stephen, the composer, puzzled through his weighted, abstract forms. His writing rhythm was slow with long silences, just like the way he spoke, his Mississippi accent so gritty and thick our conversations were filled with misunderstandings.

He had come to New York in July on a grant for the doctoral program, and he spent his days composing in the loneliest room, the one farthest down the gloomy hall. At one o'clock exactly, he took his breaks outside his practice room door and read long biographies of famous composers. Sometimes I joined him and we talked of everything musical, my audition and his symphony and our struggles with each. But he never mentioned anything about having heard me play, and this made me more intent on making him listen.

After the audition, I was in a loose, flirty mood, and I stood in front of the open window and played "Niobe," the mourning song, one of Britten's *Six Metamorphoses After Ovid,* which I had not played since Mr. Barret's master class, the performance that had won me Merkin Hall. Nothing told me beforehand I was going to play well. I was as nervous as I ever was, but by the time I reached my music stand alone in the center of the stage, something locked inside me and I felt safe, protected, unlike myself. I had no thoughts of nerves, of places I might mess up. Selfless, I was inside "Niobe." Closing my eyes, under the hot lights, I felt the audience breathing with me, sighing with the music as I sighed. I imagined I was onstage again, and I played "Niobe" now as I'd played it back then, with all of myself.

When I was through, I heard Stephen's footsteps coming down the hall. The outer door of my practice room creaked open, but I swiveled on the piano bench just as it swung shut again. I set my oboe and reed down carefully, but when I looked through the window into Stephen's room, he was gone.

Stephen was tall, easily over six feet, and thick-boned, though his footsteps were light and quick ahead of me on the stairwell a few days later. His shoulders looked strong and sturdy, pulling at the fabric of his blue shirt, neatly tucked into his jeans. Under his arm, he carried an old, thick paperback and a worn leather briefcase, stuffed with his manuscript paper.

He must have heard me close behind him and he turned around. The broken sunlight from the barred window washed over his face, and he squinted at me, surprised. We hardly ever saw each other anywhere but in the dim, gloomy halls, and there seemed an enormous amount of space and light between us now.

"What are you doing here?" His voice, gentle and slow, echoed on the stairwell.

"I have a rehearsal upstairs with that terrible orchestra. Unfortunately." I laughed a little and stayed where I was, a half flight below him. I felt his gaze, slow like his voice, travel over me. I hoped my legs looked long and lean in my cut-off shorts, but I hadn't shaved in nearly a week and the stubble was black in the sun.

"What are you reading?" I asked, and he held up his book, *Doctor Faustus,* about Schoenberg, one of his favorite composers. He said he'd never read another writer, besides Mann, who could describe music so well.

"Why is that?"

"You try it," he challenged, his thumb looped over his brass belt. His thighs were thick in his jeans. "Describe the bassoon solo in *The Rite of Spring.*"

"It's like roots growing out of dead ground." I made a face. "Not very good, huh?"

"You're comparing it to something else."

"What's wrong with that?"

"Nothing." He smiled at me, a warm, wide smile without opening his lips. "I brought you something." He searched his stuffed briefcase and then held out a brown paper bag. A flight of stairs was still between us, and for a moment, neither of us moved toward the other.

"Don't you want it?" He laughed, blushing a little above his collar, and I laughed, too, for no reason. We had never exchanged anything before, never offered anything to each other, and I was nervous for him, the gift-giver, who risked having his gift disliked. He came down the steps to me, and I took the bag quickly, thanking him. It was a tape of Toscanini's recording of *The Rite of Spring,* the one Stephen and I had talked about on one of our breaks. "Have you heard it before? How fast he takes the opening?" Stephen asked. He could compare almost every recording of every piece in the repertoire, but unless the oboe player was famous, I lost track of which recording was which.

"I haven't heard it before. Thank you," I said again, and promised to listen as soon as I got home. "Pretty soon there'll be recordings of all your works."

"Yeah, right." The corner of his mouth curdled into a frown. "Just give me a few more years and some money. And those." He pointed with his chin to the practice rooms beyond the stairwell.

"Don't you ever get lonely, working all day?" I said, but he shrugged, as if it hadn't occurred to him.

"You had your audition last week," he remembered. "How'd it go?"

"Pretty well." I told him about every piece, the slight unevenness in *Tombeau,* the judges' silence after the Brahms. His eyes, older than mine and surprisingly blue, stayed fixed on me, absorbing my every word. His close attention thrilled me, made me girlish and talkative, and I couldn't stop myself from telling him everything.

"You know," he said, "I can hear you through the walls."

"You can?" I wanted to know what he thought of my playing.

"I liked getting to know how you did things. It was like a study—the way you worked. There was this one piece you played, I don't know which."

"Sing it."

"I can't remember."

"Try." I held his eyes.

He tried the first phrase and then stopped. "I can't."

"That was 'Niobe.' The mourning song." I scanned his body once quickly: his sturdy chest, tucked-in shirt, the blond hairs showing through the top button of his shirt, the only one undone.

"This audition means everything to me. If I don't get it . . . ." I gripped my neck, and Stephen studied my face.

"What makes you happy?"

"What makes me happy?" I laughed, delighted by the question and his directness, though I prevented myself from talking so much again. "What makes *you* happy?"

He clamped his lips, thought. "The blues, Delta blues, I mean. And New York City. Ever since I moved here, I'm so wired I can't sleep." He lowered his voice. "And talking to you. I like that."

I laughed again from a husky, deep part of my lungs. I knew I should have mentioned Tom somehow and said something about my boyfriend, a native New Yorker like me, who loved the city, too. I knew I should have, but I enjoyed flirting too much.

Stephen nodded down to my oboe. "Will you play for me?"

"Play for you? I've already done that."

"In person."

"I don't play for anyone."

"You won't make an exception?"

"I don't have any of my own music with me."

"But you have your oboe. Your new oboe," he remembered.

"I'll play for you some other time. I promise," I said, but still I opened my case to show him my new oboe. The new silver sparkled and the wood was a raw brown. I held it out to him like a gift. He moved closer to me, and I breathed in the strong scent of tobacco on his shirt. He didn't smoke and I wondered whom he might have been with that did. I'd never seen him with anyone, a woman or even just a friend; he was always alone, working.

He stroked the inside of the case, feeling the lining, and then he touched, so gently, a shiny silver rod.

"It's beautiful." He folded his arms across his chest. "How does it feel to play?"

"Easy. Like cream."

"Sounds good." He laughed a little, arms still folded.

I gathered my hair over one shoulder in a way I thought he would like. Stephen looked into the case, which I held between us right beneath my breasts. His eyes moved from the case to my snug T-shirt, and then immediately I knew I was doing something wrong.

I shut my case, snapped it closed.

"I have my rehearsal now. The New Amsterdam Orchestra. It's a humiliation. I was expected to be here"—I showed a high and then low level with my hand—"and I'm here."

I complained about the money, only fifty for once-a-week rehearsals, but Stephen shrugged. He was living on just the grant he'd won, portioning it out to make it last longer than a year. "Pretend you're playing with Cleveland," he told me. "Or Philadelphia."

"If only," I prayed, looking up at the ceiling, but when we told each other good-bye, I knocked myself for being too unself-conscious around him. I rambled too much, flirted when I should not have. All rehearsal, however, I did what he said. I fooled myself into thinking I was playing with a great orchestra, and the more I played, the more I believed that soon I would be. We were rehearsing Beethoven's Seventh and I gave myself over to joy. In the beginning of the second movement, I shivered when the winds played that sad, clamoring chord, and then the cellos began their grave march. I dared myself to close my eyes and count measures in my head and to only look at the conductor at the last minute before my entrance. Sometimes I even dared myself to play that way, eyes closed, as if the music came directly from my body, not from Beethoven's page. There was nothing in the world better than this.

The night before his Prokofiev Quartet audition, Tom kept to himself. Arms pulled tight to his sides, he sat on the sofa, drinking bourbon in front of the Clinton-Bush-Perot debate. He ignored Betty Blue, who chirped along with the TV. The Prokofiev Quartet was one of the five best quartets in America, and it was the most prestigious group Tom had ever been recommended for. "As long as I don't make a fool of myself, I don't care if I win," he'd insisted the few days before. "What am I anyway, some schmuck from the Bronx?"

I had never lived with Tom through an audition before, and I hung around him, waiting to give my support. During Perot's turn to speak, he switched the channels to a cable fashion show where full-breasted models strode down the runway in sheer evening dresses.

"Tom." I laughed nervously, watching him watch.

"What?" He looked up, his black eyes anxious and remote, half-hidden by his curls. "I'm not allowed to watch this?"

"'Allowed.'" I laughed at the word, embarrassed by my jealousy. I wished he would change the channels without my having to ask. It was a whole line of skimpy dresses, the kinds of clothes I'd often worn before we moved in together, but now only rarely did.

"You wish I still wore clothes like that, don't you?"

"What's wrong with that?" He shrugged. Models in hot pants strutted to "Vogue" by Madonna, and a rage I couldn't explain made me turn away and face the fire escape. Tom watched and did not change the channel. "I don't understand why you're so upset. I just need to relax. I'll never get this opportunity again. Never. You're making me even more nervous, hovering like this."

I left him alone in the living room, and I lay on our mattresses, beneath the slanting shadows. Overlooking an alley, our bedroom was dark and quiet, shut away. The brick building across the alley blocked all light, all view of the sky. Before I met Tom, I used to play alone late at night. I wouldn't play anything written, just abstract notes filling the room and the empty space between buildings. I wanted to love someone so badly.

I touched myself over my stretch pants, but the feeling came and then went, as it always did. Three weeks had passed since Tom and I had made love, but for some reason, I was starting to feel safer this way, sexless. In the beginning, the thought of being with him made me twist with longing alone in my sheets all night. Our first time he'd pushed me up against the Juilliard basement wall, and I had never known how searing desire could be until I felt his hand, gripping my inner thigh. "Do you want it?" he breathed at me. "Do you?" He held my head back, covering my eyes. Crying out, I didn't have to exaggerate as I had done with others.

But I expected, already knew well, the despair that was to follow, even though he clung to my hair, whispering, "You know I like you so much. I really, really like you." I was glad he had not used the word *love*. Later, in the lobby, other players congratulated him on his snaking, daring solos in *Scheherazade* that afternoon.

"This is my girlfriend, Gala," Tom said, without hesitating to introduce us as lovers. He was a catch at Juilliard with his reckless, brilliant playing, and his rumpled, expensive clothes which always hung suggestively over his body. That evening, I worried we should separate and not rush things, but he insisted on cooking me a late dinner at his place. He spent the night showing me his stuff: his collages, his cartoon drawings, and his children's violin method, which he said he was going to try to publish next year. Cross-legged on the floor, he spread his work in a circle around him.

"I want you to like me," he told me. Wrapped in hand-painted paper was a gift for me: a drawing of a woman's face with Medusa-like hair. "A wild, strong woman. Like you."

"He's really cozy and sweet, but also a little dark," I told Pam later. "He's had a lot of losses. His father left, his grandmother who helped raise him died, but he's really ambitious, really driven, and I like that. He might be the one."

Only two weeks later, we planned for Christmas at Tom's mother's in the Bronx.

"Everyone loves my mother. It'll be great," he reassured me, and it was. His mother kept saying how glad she was that he had finally met someone like me, so intelligent and kind.

"Maybe this will be it," she told us, and when we blushed, she said, "What's wrong with that? You find someone, you make a life. That's it. The whole thing. You make a decision and do the best you can. I can trust him." She nodded to Tom's stepfather.

"She's so sweet." His mother gave me a fat good-bye kiss on the cheek. "Now you be sweet, too," she warned him.

Tom shook his head, waving her off, but I could tell when he looked at me, he was thinking only good things. We cuddled in the cab ride home, talking about families and how to make children either end up or not end up as musicians and what names would be perfect for a kid who was half-Jewish, half-Italian as ours would be. He told me all the rough stories of his childhood, how he was beat up at school because he was fat and the only white kid on the block.

"The miracle of my life was getting into Music and Art High School. Or else I would have ended up here." He pointed outside the cab to the desolate streets. His stories impressed me, his mother impressed me, his arm never let go of me, and I thought, yes, this was someone I could love.

On the day of Tom's audition, the sky was unsettled: chilly and gray and bright all at the same time. In his new wool Armani suit, Tom was uncomfortable, sweating all over, on his forehead, chest, and under his arms. We'd rushed in a cab and then had to wait outside the

cellist's house on Riverside Drive and Eighty-sixth, ten blocks up
from where my father had moved.

"I don't have a good feeling," Tom said, shaking his head. He
faced Riverside Park and then, beyond that, the highway and Hudson
River. "If I win this audition, this is where we could live. We could
have a river view. Three kids. A jungle for Betty Blue."

"You could cook for me every night," I told him.

"And you could clean every day."

"You gotta be kidding, my friend," I said, imitating his mother.

"Wouldn't this be great?" He squinted up at the old, elegant
building where he imagined our life together, and I tried to imagine
it, too, and to believe in the happiness he'd described. The thing I
wanted most was to win my audition, to never sink so low in doubt
again.

Tom checked his watch and let out a long, anxious stream of air.
His curls blew across his face. "I'm tired of being poor. There's nothing good about it."

I nodded, though I'd never truly known what it was not to have
enough. All my life I'd liked men who were rough and lonely and
struggling somehow, who, like my father, had pulled themselves up.

"I'm sorry I pushed you away last night," Tom said.

"I understood."

"I've always been alone."

"But now you have me."

"I'm not used to it. Yet." He laughed once nervously at himself.

"We're family now. I love you whether you win or lose." I rubbed
my nose against his to make him smile, and we held each other for a
long time before he said good-bye. Alone, I stood on the corner in the
gloomy, metal-colored day, not knowing what to do. At a payphone,
I called my father. He wasn't home as he usually was Saturday mornings, his reading mornings, and I had to leave a message: "I miss you.
Where are you?"

I drank three cups of coffee to kill time, waiting for Tom in the
Argo, the only cheap coffee shop in that area of Broadway. Behind the
counter, the girl with a tired face looked crammed into her jeans, and
the men called her "Delie" or "Dee" or "Dorothy" and once "Joan," as
if they'd all made up their own name for her.

I ate my Danish slowly until I felt Tom's hands on my shoulders.

"I might have been fantastic."

"Really?" I squeezed his hand. He was bleary-eyed, but smiling.

"I was wild."

"Wild?" I worried. His playing was bold and furious, but often careless, causing his second-place finishes at too many competitions. "You're scared now." Tom grinned. "You don't understand. It's my thing to be wild. That's what people like. I'm not the usual boring player. I'm raw."

I nodded, trying to erase my worry.

"At the end, the cellist pushed his chair back and stared."

"He must have liked it then."

"Or else they all thought I was crazy." He laughed, remembering, and wiped his hair away from his forehead, still damp with sweat.

Hand in hand, we walked slowly beneath the lush aisle of trees in Riverside Park to the Neighborhood Music School, where Tom taught four days a week. Women with babies sat on benches and joggers huffed by.

"A perfect day," I told Tom, swinging his hand, the way I used to swing between my parents when I was young and they were happy.

"Tom's wonderful," his student's mother said to me as we listened to a lesson together outside the studio door, and I felt wifely and proud of my life, which, just then, seemed lucky and settled and right.

At my New Amsterdam rehearsal, I was in control of the wind section. The other wind players followed my interpretations and leaned into my sound. In the second movement of the Beethoven, I closed my eyes, counted measures in my head, and sang out above the orchestra. The wind section shuffled their feet, applauding my solo.

"She plays as beautifully as she looks," the conductor said. All the strings turned to stare at me. I was wearing a short skirt, and I felt ashamed and pleased thinking of their eyes on me. We went back to the first movement and my articulation was sloppy in the fast, 6/8 solo, but the conductor didn't stop the orchestra. He only smiled at me as if he was sure I'd get it right the next time.

I tried to forget my mistake—it was small, small, I insisted to myself—as I struggled open our front door.

"They want to hear me again!" Tom shouted, jumping up from the couch. "Me and just one other person. Yakov Lutveczek! Can you believe it?" We hugged each other and his hands slid over my ass.

"Mmmmm. Delicious," he said. His eyes gleamed with his success, or maybe from watching something on TV that turned him on. The gleam seemed separate from me, but I tried not to think about that, tried instead to empty myself of my need to resist.

"I want you," he breathed into my ear, half making fun of his words, even as he meant them, and he pressed me against the wall, kissing my neck. His rough curls tickled and I tried not to squirm.

"You did it," I told him, and when he didn't answer, I tried to lose myself to the feeling of his lips and teeth and tongue on my neck. He pinned my arms above my head and I closed my eyes and imagined that his other hand, squeezing my breasts, was a stranger's hand and that I had no choice. He grabbed between my legs, the way I liked him to, as if what was there were his. I wanted so much to feel something, to feel myself warm and flush in his fingers, but every time the feeling started, it went away again. I felt Tom watching my face, waiting for my excitement, and so I exaggerated it as I used to do only with others.

"You like it?" He grabbed harder and I moaned again. He flicked off the lights and pushed me down on the living room carpet. I kept my eyes closed and pretended that he was not himself, but that he was still a stranger lifting my sweater above my head so it covered my face and eyes. The wool filled my nostrils and mouth.

"So sexy. Will you always be sexy for me?" he whispered into my ear. When I didn't answer, he worried and said, louder, "Gala?" His hands holding my wrists above my head loosened their grip.

"Yes," I said in a small voice. Tom turned me over again and pushed his way in and out of me. I looked up at his face and saw that his eyes were closed, his upper lip drawn up, as if he were in pain. I didn't ask him about what he was thinking, though. I received his body, plunging into me. When the tears came, as they always did, I wiped them away as if I were pushing aside my hair.

Afterward, Tom brought a tray of Heath Bar Crunch ice cream and Oreos, his favorite treats, into the bedroom, as we watched David Letterman, and he ran on and on about all the good things the Quartet had said about him.

"I just don't want to get too excited." He dunked the Oreo into the ice cream and scooped out a mouthful. "You never know what will happen."

Naked, his body sticky with dried sweat, Tom curled against me and laughed in my arms as David Letterman brought a dancing dog onstage.

"What's wrong?" Tom said because I stared at the ceiling. I shrugged, an angry, lonely part of me wanting to tell him how our sex brought me despair. I knew, though, that he would feel criticized, as he always did, when I tried to talk about it, and he would tell me what was true—that I had asked for whatever he did to me.

"Nothing's wrong." I kissed his shoulder, snuggled up closer, and I tried to pretend that the sex before had never even happened, that it was no part of us at all.

The next day I felt groggy for no reason and couldn't concentrate when I tried to practice. As I passed through the mail room on the way to visit my father, I wasn't even thinking about the audition notice. My mind was blank and dull, and I had to keep shaking myself awake.

The envelope from the judges was thin, too thin, and I knew what it said before I took it out of the box. I had not made it to the semifinals, not even to the second round. I crumpled the letter, stuffed it in my pocket. The creaking of the narrow steps drummed in my ears as I climbed back up the four flights to our apartment. I lay on the couch, facedown, my mouth open to the corduroy pillow. The sun through the fire escape soaked my back.

"When you're swimming, what makes you come up for air?" I had asked my mother on the beach when I was ten. Her hair draped her cheeks, and in her black suit, her skin looked extra-pale, washed away.

"Why can't people drown themselves?" I asked.

"Gala." She gave a short, exhausted laugh because I was always asking these kinds of questions, senseless, morbid, attention-getting. And she was always sad on the beach. The blanching sun made her cry. My father had gone off someplace, exploring, he said. He could do anything. She had to stay with me. Her book open, unread on her lap, she watched the women walking by.

"It's the skinny and lanky girls who come out the prettiest," she told me.

"You're thin," I reassured, just as she wanted.

"Your father pays more attention to you than to me. Now why is that?"

I blushed, my head dizzy in the hot sun.

"He kisses you all the time." She frowned at a passing woman. "Your father never makes love to me. I try everything, but he still doesn't want me."

I closed my eyes, a sudden exhaustion overwhelming me.

"Do you know what it feels like not to be wanted?" my mother asked, and I imagined that I did know, that there was no separation between what she felt and I felt.

On one of those weekend trips, she swallowed eight sleeping pills. A small amount really, but enough to get back at my father. As a child, though, I felt the act only in relationship to myself. It was a threat, an accusation against me. I had been the one to find her, mumbling on the beach. When they tried to take her away, I held on to her legs, sticky with dried salt water.

6

fter the glaring sun on Riverside Drive, it took me a few
moments to adjust to the darkness inside my father's building. His lobby was marble with thirty-foot, domelike ceil-
ings, and the air was so still and close it seemed if I spoke, my voice
would echo. On a mahogany table was an enormous bouquet of flowers, and I thought of stealing the pale white rose, but the elevator man
was watching. My father was living much better than my mother, I
thought. He should have had to suffer some, too.

By the corner pay phone, I smoked a cigarette, trying to work
myself up to call and cancel on my father. Two days ago, I'd told him
how well I'd thought I'd played, how sweet my sound was on the
Brahms. I'd exaggerated. I couldn't stop myself. My lies fed him,
made him happy and full. Even his voice changed, became easier and
more expansive.

"Sweetie. That's wonderful. I'm so proud of you. I was up all
night worrying. Isn't that crazy, up all night?"

It might have been crazy but it was our secret pact together; he
would worry, but I would always please him.

I lit one cigarette after another, watching the finished butts roll
into the cracks of the clean concrete. The rejection letter was still in
my pocket where I'd stuffed it an hour ago. It would be easy to make
up a lie and cancel on my father, but then I would return alone into
the day with nothing at all, not even his concern.

It felt like a defeat, though, riding up in the elevator and ringing his bell.

"My big love!" He opened his arms and I wanted both to bury my head against his chest in the thick wool of his old Woodstock sweater and also to get away. He kissed my forehead with dry lips, then squeezed my head against him. I braced myself, curved my shoulders inward so my breasts would not flatten into his chest.

"I'm so proud of you." He pressed my head tight and I inhaled him—the mustiness of his sweater and the pipe he'd smoked mostly when I was young, mixed with a fresh-smelling cologne, something I never remembered him wearing.

"There's no reason to feel proud." I cleared my throat. "I haven't heard anything yet."

"It ain't shit," he said in his old Bronx accent, "if the judges whisper like that after you play."

I'd lied about that, too, how in the silence after the Brahms, I'd heard the judges praise me.

I wheeled around ahead of him down the long white hall. My father's uneven footsteps were as familiar and distinctive to me as my mother's bright voice.

"Still limping, old man?"

My father laughed. "My little girl." He mussed my hair. "All grown-up. Do you know I'd do anything for you?"

"Yes."

"Climb the highest building? Leap the tallest fence?"

"Fly over the moon," I added, but then I came to the edge of the living room, his new life. Nothing in the room reminded me of my father. Talia, the woman he was subletting from, had my mother's taste. There were maroon Moroccan pillows all over the floor and Mexican tapestries on the wall. On the coffee table was my father's book on the Jewish Resistance, the same book my mother had been reading.

There were no signs that my father had a girlfriend—no photographs, cards, or clothing—and I thought maybe I'd been wrong all this time.

"Let me show you." He raised the linen blinds. Before us, the Hudson River wound far into the distance until it was just a thin gray strip between mountains. It was just a few days before that I'd looked at the same view with Tom, but that experience seemed small compared to seeing it with my father.

"Spectacular, isn't it?" he said, but then he squinted down the river at his new view with an almost baffled expression.

"You're sad." I felt almost triumphant; I hadn't expected him to be.

He gazed out over the river, his hands clenched in fists at his sides.

"I'm nearly sixty years old. Whoever thought life would be changing so much. I thought I'd be settled by now, content." He patted the air once with his hand. His eyes were milky and red-rimmed, lost in creases, and his hair was white; he was nearly old, like the man I'd seen at Columbia. The natural light showed the dried toothpaste in the very corner of his mouth and the dried, flaky patches on his face. I remembered how my mother would chase him around with moisturizer because he was too absentminded to remember himself.

"Dad." I tugged on the shoulder of his sweater. "Who takes care of you now?"

"No one," he said heavily, but then he began joking again. "Am I such a baby?"

I didn't answer, didn't joke back with him. I wanted him to stay sad.

"I guess the answer is yes." He laughed, his round stomach shaking up to his chest. "Twenty years of analysis and every day is still Yom Kippur."

"Isn't therapy supposed to make you happy?" I teased.

"I'm still in the misery phase. Five more years of discovering myself, being miserable, and then"—he raised his pointed finger— "I'll be sixty-five and nearly dead."

"Why don't you up your dosage?" I suggested, and my father laughed again. He had been on and off various antidepressants his whole adult life.

"Up it to forty milligrams. Come on," I told my father.

"Is that the kind of thing a daughter should say to her father?"

"You don't care. Up to forty. Come on." I nudged him.

"Have you spoken to Mr. de Laney? Has he heard anything yet?"

"I haven't called."

"Why not? If you can find out now, why wait?"

I shrugged, wincing at the humiliation of the note in my pocket.

"You could call right now." My father nodded to the phone. "Why don't you?" He pressed my back, the tender part between my shoulder blades, and I almost went to the phone.

"Dad." I rolled my eyes. "I'm not going to call in front of you."

"Why not?" Then he laughed his silent, red-faced laugh because he knew why not. He liked to push me though. "Tell me again what he said."

"I can't remember. It was a month ago."

"Please."

I sighed but gave him what he wanted. "Mr. de Laney said he was sure I'd make it to the semifinals."

"Sweetie." My father rumpled my hair again, but then his eyes lingered on my face for a moment, and I almost hoped he would know I was lying.

"I'll finish the tour." He pointed to the bedroom, and I blushed, being shown his bed where he did not sleep with my mother. The linen was obviously Talia's: the comforter was red with lace, and some pillows were heart shaped.

"I never thought I'd sleep in a bed with heart-shaped pillows." My father patted one of the pillows. "It looks like one of those afternoon hotels. A love nest."

"Dad." I giggled.

"In Japan they have them, places you can go for an afternoon. It's part of the culture."

"How do you know?"

"How do I know?" My father laughed, too. "Haven't you ever been to one?"

"Dad." I couldn't stop giggling. I concentrated on the clean white edge of his desk. There were stacks of books on European Jewish history and disorganized pages of yellow legal paper with his illegible handwriting scrawled at random angles. I didn't see anything to even hint he had a girlfriend.

On the wall, he'd taped his historian's award from Columbia, and two notes he'd written to himself. The first note said, "You always feel better when you jog. Just do it." The next one encouraged him with, "You always do everything right, don't worry."

"What's wrong with you, Dad?" I punched him in the arm.

"Nothing's wrong with me. I just need to remind myself sometimes."

"What are you so insecure about? You've got your success."

"Success, success." My father shrugged, bringing his chin down deep into his neck, hands up to his ears. He slid five typed pages of his memoir out from underneath the scrawled legal paper. The beginning of his book was about his boyhood in the Russian Jewish section of the Bronx and how his mother had burned to death in front of his eyes when he was three. *She had survived the pogroms in the Ukraine,* he had written. *But then while ironing, the most ordinary of activities, she had accidentally ignited her clothes and then herself. She had pressed the hot iron to a tie carelessly covered with flammable cleaning fluid.*

My father described working with his father in the candy store seven days a week—before and after school on weekdays, and twelve hours a day on weekends. On the second page, he wrote about looking at porno magazines in the barbershop, owned by a family friend. He wrote:

In the back room behind the stools, I would pore over every picture—a tall voluptuous woman with auburn hair. I stared at those large breasts pointed up at me. . . . Even writing this, I become aroused.

I kept my back to my father so he couldn't see me.

"Dad." Anxious giggles bubbled in me again. "I don't want to see this."

"Why not?" His body shook close behind mine. "Is a father not supposed to show his daughter his work?"

"Not this kind of work. It's inappropriate."

"I'm insulted." My father pretended not to understand what I meant. "You didn't like my writing."

"I liked it." I elbowed him because this, too, was part of our game. I felt a deep shame in my whole body: my face, my breasts, and even my fingertips.

My father stared at the pages of his memoir. "The wreckage of my childhood."

"Jesus Christ." I rolled my eyes. My father often cried at noon, the time his mother had burned to death. It had been part of my Sunday ritual to pass by his study and find his tears rolling onto his scribbled notes. "How ridiculous," I'd say sharply, though really I loved having a father who was so dramatic and intense. He ate up all the air in our home.

Never did I feel more alive than with my father. Never did life feel more dangerous.

"Only someone with a severe ego deficit writes notes like this to himself." I fingered his encouraging letters to himself. A face-down photograph was poking out from between a stack of paper. There was tape on the back as if my father had just taken it down from the wall.

"Sweetie." My father placed his hand on top of mine, holding the picture. Our fingertips were touching.

"Why can't I look at this?" I said, and then we were both smiling at each other, as if excited before the discovery and the smack of pain that would follow.

My face burned hot seeing my father's arm around another woman. She was slim and deeply tanned, with heavy, penetrating eyes. She looked to be in her late forties, younger than my mother, and in her angular black evening dress she appeared elegant and wealthy. Sexy. My father's arm latched her waist.

I felt stupid, slapped in the face. "What's her name?"

"Let's put this away." My father pulled at the picture, but I jerked it back.

"Just tell me."

"Marissa," he said as if the name were foreign to him, too. He told me she was from Argentina and that she was an art dealer who had lived all over the world: France, Spain, Italy, and even Hong Kong.

"Sounds exotic." I laughed again, staring at the picture of the sophisticated woman in my father's arms. My father had always talked about women's looks, about faraway, unreachable, beautiful women. Legs and breasts. Mostly breasts. My mother would get this twisted, peaked little smile as he spoke.

The picture had been taken at a party. On the trimmed lawn, in front of freshly flowered dogwoods, was a crowd of unfamiliar people, a whole world I didn't know about.

"Who's that?" I pointed to a silvery blond woman on the other side of my father.

"She's German. The first time she met me she wanted to stick me in the oven."

"I saw you and Marissa together. At Columbia. Three weeks ago."

"Three weeks ago?" Caught, my father's voice rose high as he pretended to be searching his memory for the date. I stared at the picture, and I had to adjust to it all over again. It was like looking at something too bright, too sexual, and chaotic. Marissa, my father, and the woman were laughing easily together, as if they were all good friends and had known each other a long time.

"Dad"—I shook the picture at him—"how long have you known these friends?"

"Not very long," he said quickly, as if unconcerned.

"How long is that?"

"Marissa and I have been friends for a long time. She's sold paintings to Columbia. But we just began seeing each other," my father said in the same distracted tone, and I thought he might be lying, but I didn't hold, couldn't hold, that thought in my mind for long. It had only been three months since he had left my mother.

"Gala . . ." He gathered himself to speak, but then didn't seem to know what to say. "Gala, I always loved your mother. There wasn't one moment when I didn't want our relationship to work."

"Why didn't it work then?"

"We were mean to each other. We couldn't stop. We tried again and again but we always ended up unhappy. I could never be what she wanted. Nothing was ever enough for her."

"You made fun of her, mocked the things she liked."

My father spoke from a deep part of his lungs. "She went from one thing to another. She could never commit herself, not even to music."

"You failed," I told my father because I couldn't stand to hear him say those things about my mother. "She did everything to please you. Visited you every day at school, even brought you your lunch. Every hour she spent trying to make you happy was an hour she didn't give to herself."

"I loved your mother. I still do." My father cleared his throat. "We could never simply accept each other. Forgive everything."

"What was there to forgive?"

"At a certain point, you have to just say this person is enough for me. Your mother and I could never do that. She threatened to kick me out every year. Every year. Who can live like that, with someone threatening you constantly? Remember all the times she told me to leave?"

I did remember—both her anger and what he did to provoke her. Memories of his flirtations smarted in me. Once at a faculty party, years ago, he had absorbed himself with a tall woman in high-heeled boots for nearly an hour before returning to my mother, shy and alone in the corner, left to take care of me. The woman was the new star of the Slavic studies department, and I remembered exactly the way she had tossed back her hair, drawing my father closer, and how attentive he was to her, nodding at everything she said.

"You never treat me that way," my mother said, trembling in the cab ride home.

"Oh, Roberta." He waved her off. "I was just talking. I can never do anything right."

"Just wait," she threatened. "One day you'll walk through the door and I'll be gone. And then, all of a sudden, you'll realize what you had."

At the next light, my father jumped out of the cab, leaving us. My mother hunched into herself, both fists pressed against her mouth as she stared out the window at the other lane, the traffic moving against us. I knew not to say anything, to make myself small, looking out the opposite window.

Marvin Gardens was a quiet Upper West Side restaurant with uncomfortable, country-type wood booths and menus painted with flowers and squiggly stems. When the manager showed my father and me to our table, my father brushed his arm and said, "I'll have the usual table in the back."

I sank down too hard on the uncushioned seats. "Is this where you and Marissa come?" It was difficult to say her name without laughing a little bit.

"She doesn't live around here." He wiped his mouth with a napkin though we hadn't eaten anything yet.

"Where does she live?"

"Central Park South."

"Oh." I raised my eyebrows to insinuate something about her wealth.

He squeezed my wrist on the table. "Sweetie, let's not talk about this anymore. This is upsetting for you."

"It's not upsetting."

"It must be. It upsets me. Let's talk about you." My father dropped his corduroy jacket in a heap on the seat beside him. I remembered how my mother would have said something about that, something about how he was so absentminded she always had to take care of him. Of course, it was true, but my father would have felt criticized and a huge fight would start and end with one of them leaving the restaurant.

"Everything okay? You seemed low as soon as you walked in." He usually noticed if I was sad or happy. My mother usually did not.

"I'm fine." I gulped my water, crunched loudly on the ice, the way I would do only around my father.

"Money's okay?" My father patted his wallet beside him on the booth, ready to give me some.

"Dad . . ." I rolled my eyes to make him feel bad for even having offered.

"Have you been getting any playing work?"

"I got two new students. Sixty dollars more a week."

My father did not look impressed. "Let me try to understand something," he said in his teaching voice. "If you at least get to the semifinals, will that mean that more people will hear about you and therefore will you get more calls?"

"Probably." I made my voice indifferent. The waiter came over to take our orders. My father ordered a diet Coke and a house salad with no dressing.

"If I could just lose ten pounds, my life will be a success."

"Dad," I groaned, and then told the waiter, "I'll have a diet Coke and spaghetti."

My father chewed on his ice the same way I had. "How many auditions have you taken?"

"Eight, ten, I don't know," I lied, keeping my eyes focused on the stained wood of the table. "Not too many."

"How many did Keisuke take before the Boston Symphony?" Keisuke was Mr. Barret's prize student. Before Merkin, Mr. Barret had always said to me, "I'm hoping you'll turn out like him." I'd leave my lessons high on the dare. If I had played well at Merkin, anything might have happened. Mr. Barret was the principal of the New York Philharmonic; he'd let his best students play beside him. From there, they'd gone on to the top orchestra positions in America.

"I don't know how many Keisuke took," I said to my father, even though I knew it was only four. And he'd gotten something even before Boston.

"What is the average amount that people take before getting something?"

"There's no such thing as average." Though I was telling the truth—there were so many various and unpredictable ways oboists I knew from Juilliard supported themselves—I felt sure, just then, that I was failing compared to everyone else. I had my students and bad-orchestra gigs. A few people had nothing, but the majority, I was convinced, had more.

"It will be hard to go on, won't it, if you don't get this one?"

I stared at the wood, the dark stain bleeding through the surface.

"I just mean it's hard to keep losing. You need—one needs," he corrected himself, "one needs some success."

I said, without believing it, "If I don't win this one, I can simply try the next time. I'm giving myself till I'm thirty."

"Thirty?" He thought thirty was way too old for me to continue as I was going. By the time he was my age, twenty-six, he had a position at Columbia and his first book contract.

The waiter brought the diet Cokes and my father raised his glass.

"Let's toast. I want to make a toast to my lovely, talented daughter, and to the beginning of a new phase in her career."

I clinked my glass against his.

"I haven't done so badly." He clasped my hand. "I wasn't so bad, was I?"

I held back, made him wait.

"Come on, honey." Fleshy and needy and warm, his fingers pressed mine.

"No," I squeezed out, "you were the best father in the world."

"Sweetie." His face flushed with happiness and relief.

I thought I would feel freed, kissing my father good-bye and then watching him start to his new home. But as he walked away toward Riverside Drive, heaving his bad leg, I wanted to call him back, to tell him how I'd lost so he could somehow make it better. Instead, I remained alone at the corner, facing the clot of cars.

It was Saturday night, and I was supposed to meet Pam, Kurt, and Tom for drinks to celebrate the end of these two weeks of auditions. From the corner pay phone, I called Pam and Tom to cancel, but it was too late, neither was home. Walking up Broadway, I looked ugly in the sharp mirrors of Love's. My skin was blotchy and I wasn't thin. Marissa was thin, even thinner than my mother and Pam. Her body looked so small that on top of her I thought my father might crush her.

I was twenty-five minutes late by the time I reached the Abbey Pub. The jukebox was playing the Rolling Stones, "Just My Imagination," and the pub was dim and woody, faces lit in flattering candlelight. Pam, Tom, and Kurt were at a table in the back. Pam was radiant, laughing, blowing the smoke luxuriously up into her blond bangs.

"Gala." Tom gripped his beer glass and nodded in my direction. His handsomeness struck me all over again; his white linen shirt loosely draped his chest, the rolled-up cuffs revealing his muscled forearms still tan in the beginning of October, and his strong fingers were callused at the tips from the strings of his violin. For a moment, I was overwhelmed with relief and gratitude for having him to share my life with. He looked me up and down and raised one eyebrow, just slightly, so no one in the restaurant would notice. He was drunk. So were Kurt and Pam. Kurt had taken off his long-fringed red scarf and was wrapping it around Pam's neck. She posed, batting her eyelashes over one shoulder and puckering her red, shiny lips, and then the two of them laughed, tilting down to their wineglasses. They were a striking couple, his rich, dark skin against her whiteness.

"Hey." Tom kissed me slowly, his tongue pushing between my lips, and then he stroked my palm, which lay between us on the booth. I let my hand go limp, but his thumb continued its stroking.

"Guess what?" Pam's breasts swelled over her leather halter top as she leaned forward. I tried not to stare. I drew my arms to my sides, hiding in my thick wool sweater.

"Guess what I found out today?" She held my eyes, made me wait. "I made it to the second round."

"Congratulations." I stretched over the flickering candle to kiss her cool, powdery cheek. "You did it." It was the first time I had failed so completely compared to her.

"Gala's been checking the mail four times a day, right?" Tom squeezed me to his side. He smelled of beer and Pam's strong tobacco. "Every time you go downstairs, I get nervous for you. Did you know that?"

He slid his hand down my back to my ass. He wanted me to move secretly against his hand as I would have done many, many months ago before I'd messed up at Merkin Hall, before we'd moved in together. I felt disgusted with myself, remembering how I'd always tried to please him, slithering against him in my short skirts and push-up bras.

I moved away from him, leaving inches between us on the hard wood booth.

"What's wrong with you?" he said, his voice high and pinched.

"I'm fine. It was just a long day." I addressed Pam not Tom, though I knew he was hurt. I felt his hand withdraw from behind me. "You're pitying yourself. Just start playing again," he had said impatiently after Merkin, and now I hardened myself against him, kept my distance on the booth. Pam was telling Kurt and Tom about the schedule of the second round, and Tom was running on about his second audition next week; they leaned in close to each other, their faces radiant in the candlelight.

I sipped my white wine quickly though it was cheap and pungent. I missed my father and wished I had told him everything so he could comfort me.

"You want?" Pam dangled her tobacco sack for me, but I shook my head, not wanting to take anything from her, even her strong, pure tobacco, which I loved.

"So you'll die of lung cancer and Gala won't," Kurt told her.

"I'm immortal. Didn't you know that?" Pam sucked in deep off her cigarette, joint style. Her manicured nails were deep red. Mine were jagged and I remembered all the times she'd wanted me to do things like that with her: manicures, pedicures, facials. I'd refused, thinking it was a waste of time to be so frivolous. Better always to stay home and practice, I'd thought, but here she was, winning.

"The thing is I knew I played well as soon as I left. Remember, Gala? And you did, too."

"I messed up the very last measure."

The glumness in my voice silenced everyone for a moment.

"I met someone who knows you," Pam said, changing the subject. "This composer who writes at Manhattan."

"Stephen. He's a very good friend," I said, hoping Tom would be jealous. I had been spending more and more time with Stephen. Every day during our practice breaks, we talked of everything about books and music and which, words or music, was purer and whether it was possible to describe one with the other.

"He seems very gentle, very thoughtful," Pam said. "He said he can hear you practice every day. He told me how beautifully he thinks you play."

"Really? He did?" I acted even more cheered than I was, but when I glanced over at Tom, he was polishing off his beer, paying no attention to me.

The waitress organized Kurt's cheeseburger and fries on our table, crowded with drinks.

"Men are always eating. Look at him." Pam pointed with her fork as Kurt smeared on both mustard and ketchup.

Kurt bared his teeth at her, but then said, "She's so full of herself. I love her." He kissed down her neck and Pam giggled, shimmying away from his lips.

"We should be more like that," Tom said under his breath, and I gave him the same blank, mean look I'd given my father at the restaurant.

"What?" Tom pulled back from me, and though I heard the hurt in his voice, I could not make myself tell him what I was the most upset about.

Tom defended himself against my silence. "The truth is that you're always angry at me. If I don't touch you, it's wrong; if I do touch you, it's wrong."

"What's going on over there?" Pam said.

"Nothing." I smiled at her. I finished the last of my wine and then ordered another. My head was swirling already, but swirling alone in its own liquid haze. Pam was laughing with Kurt, her red lips vivid and alive against her white skin, and occasionally Tom joined in. My mother had once said that there was always the adored and the adorer. "It's better of course," she said, "to be the adored." Of course, she was kidding, but it made me sad to think of it. She was alone again in her apartment tonight. I did not know if she would be okay, if she would make it through so many lonely nights. I am like her, I thought. In sadness, I was with my mother, not alone.

"Most of the time," Pam was saying, "I feel blah. Just dulled. But now I feel so happy." She shimmered her hands in the air like tambourines.

"It's so rare, isn't it? Pure happiness," she said to me. "One minute it's here, the next it's gone. And then you can't even remember you ever felt so good. Life!" She raised her open hands to the ceiling, but then said, "I'm worried I won't have a good reed. That's my biggest fear." She looked at me for encouragement about reeds, which I always gave her. I said nothing.

"Gala's in a bad mood tonight. For some reason," Tom told her, coldly enough so that Pam checked both our faces.

"It's hard waiting. You're nervous, aren't you?" She nodded at me with real sympathy, and for some reason, the idea of her pity made me sure I was going to start crying right then and there, ugly tears.

"Excuse me," I said, then left the table.

There was a phone outside the bathroom. I would have to wrap the wire around the corner if I wanted to call my mother without Tom, Kurt, and Pam seeing me by the phone. Instead, I hid in the bathroom and locked myself in a stall. I covered my face with my hands because I could not call her. I would not be able to bear her disappointment.

"Gala? Are you in there? Are you all right?" Tom called ten minutes later. "I'm sorry. For whatever I did." His voice had tightened, lost its drunken sway. He banged on the door with his fist.

I thought I could just shout it through the door, without having to admit anything to his face. I didn't want to see him think, adding up this loss to all the last.

"What did I do?" Tom pushed the door open a little. "I haven't been in a women's room in years." He had an awkward smile on his face, and for a second I thought, I'm not going to tell him. He is not someone whom I can trust to know what to do. There was no tenderness between us. No real love.

"What's wrong?" He wrapped his arms around me and I buried my head on his shoulder, my cheek against his linen shirt. His chest was padded and soft even after all the weights.

"I didn't make it to the second round."

His arms loosened around me as he took in my words, then he held me tighter again. "Aw, aw." He patted my back, unsure of exactly what comforting sounds or gestures to make, but I could feel how hard he was trying.

"Why didn't you tell me before? You could have called, Gala."

He stuck out his lower lip in a sad clown's face "You don't trust me."

"I trust you." As soon as I said that, I knew it wasn't true. I didn't trust anybody. "How do you learn to trust? I have no idea." I searched his eyes, but they fidgeted away from me.

"That's a silly question," he said, laughing a little. "You just do it." His hands were still clasped around the back of my neck, but I could feel he wanted to get away.

"But how?"

"You take a leap. I don't know."

"I want us to talk more, Tom. We never talk."

"How can you say that? All we do is talk." With a funny, toothy smile, he wagged his finger at the doorknob. "We're in the ladies' room."

"It's true what Pam said. Happiness goes like that." I opened my hand as if releasing magic into the air. "Just like our closeness."

I'd been cruel, I knew immediately, but I didn't apologize.

Tom forced out a laugh, absorbing the blow. "Maybe I'm an idiot. I thought things were good."

"I want there to be more. We don't understand each other."

Hands on his hips, Tom avoided my eyes and glanced around at the bare bulb on the top of the mirror, the Magic Marker breasts on the wall, the cracks in the ceiling.

"You're always so critical, Gala. You judge every moment. Maybe you're the one who makes us distant. Did you ever think of that? I can't even touch you the right way." He swiveled around as if he'd heard someone at the door. "This is the ladies' room. Let's go."

"You don't want to talk?" I sounded needy like my mother and I cringed.

"I'm not like you. I didn't grow up where people discussed their feelings. People got killed on my block. Maybe I'm stupid. Maybe I can't give you what you need." He hung his head. I waited for him to tell me more, to give me more. I didn't consider that I was being selfish.

"This is all there is, baby," Tom said from the corner of his mouth in his gangster's voice, then he laughed painfully, his shoulders caving in as he turned to the door.

Part Two

The New Amsterdam Orchestra met on the top floor of Manhattan School of Music in the large room with the percussion instruments and extra music stands. Outside the window, the angles of rooftops and incinerators almost distracted me from the violins scratching through the first movement of Beethoven's Seventh. They had not adopted the concertmaster's fingerings, and their bows moved up and down at different times. They were so out of tune that the conductor rehearsed them stand by stand for almost the full two hours. I vowed to myself I would quit this orchestra.

I had not practiced for four days, my longest break ever. Even though my lips longed for the reed and I craved that moment of release when my sound vibrated through the wood, I would not allow myself to play.

"There's always one thing wrong with your playing," Mr. Barret had said a month after Merkin when I played the dotted eighth–sixteenth rhythm in the second movement of Beethoven's Third like triplets. A beginner's mistake.

"Can't you hear it?" He clapped the subdivisions of the beat, three sixteenths in the first note, one on the last, and told me I should hear them when I play. Of course, I'd been hearing rhythms this way since I was six or seven, just starting the piano, but then in my lesson, I felt nervous and muddled, and halfway through the solo, I lost track and couldn't hold the subdivisions in my head.

"It's all off," he told me. "If you can't play this, you can't play anything. What's wrong with you?" He pinched the sides of his reed, frowned at it, then at me. I had no answer. I never had answers for his insults, which had come with varying intensity since Merkin Hall. My playing disintegrated, but still it took me months to leave him.

"It doesn't matter who you study with," he told me, my last lesson. "There'll always be something wrong. Some mistake. Always."

"You were less nervous this time. That's an achievement," Daphne said as we jogged in Riverside Park beneath the yellowing trees. Leaves fell around us on the muddy path, and the damp air was palpably soft against my face. "Why won't you let yourself feel good about that?" Sweat shined on her forehead and the tiny creases at the corners of her eyes, and her tight blond ponytail swished at the top of her head.

"I never feel good," I said. "That's not true. I feel good with you."

"I've known you all your life," she reminded me, and looking into her familiar clear green eyes, I remembered my long history of successes and rejections. For a moment, this one didn't seem so bad. We ran under a short tunnel and then into the gray daylight. A drizzly weekday afternoon, the pavement path along the Hudson was nearly empty except for the guy who was always there, carving his six-feet totems, which he chained to the bench.

"He works solely for himself. For his own pleasure," Daphne said, admiring him, but when she waved, he gave her a nasty look.

"I should be like him. Unconcerned about the world. Mean. Solitary." I sped up to try to get rid of the meanness in me. I had almost felt glad this morning when Tom told me his final audition hadn't gone well.

"Don't you ever miss dancing? Professionally, I mean?" I asked Daphne carefully.

"If you'd told me when I was with Balanchine that I could have a life without dance, as a profession, I never would have believed it. I had no other identity." She swerved out of the way of a man, another Riverside regular, who tossed a red brick for exercise as he walked.

"But how did you decide to stop?"

"When it was truly over, there was no going back. There might have been other times I had thought of quitting, but then something broke me. It had become only torture. Every movement should have been godly, a gift to Him, but it wasn't."

I had always been a skeptic, unable to speak about God without feeling awkward, but I nodded, never wanting her to see me doubting her faith. She had traded one devotion for another, and she led a strict life alone, eating only certain foods and working on any project the Baba Center in India sent her. She claimed she was happier now, teaching and making her yearly treks to Meher Baba's retreat where she said she had found herself. But I could not fully believe her, could not help but share my father's cynicism and believe that she had settled, resigned herself.

We jogged back uptown past the clanking boathouses. In the distance, the George Washington Bridge stretched magically through mist across the river. Daphne's strides seemed to float. I chugged along.

"The most important thing is your own process. You can't judge yourself after every audition. This time you weren't as nervous. You should feel good about that." Daphne reminded me that when I was a child, four or five years old, I used to spend hours alone composing different piano pieces. "And you loved Stravinsky, even at that age. Do you remember dancing to *Petrouchka?*"

I remembered. I was delirious with joy, spinning around and around the living room. The cymbals made me leap, the piccolo sent me turning in the air, and the crashing of the brass left me crumpled on the floor, but not for long. A moment later, I would start the record from the beginning once more.

"Don't lose that love," Daphne told me. "It took me years to find it again."

In the dark auditorium of Manhattan School of Music, Stephen rehearsed a cello, violin, and piano for a performance of his music. Spotlights flooded the stage, and he listened critically, standing slightly out of the light, his eyebrows knotted. This piece, which I'd heard him work on for months, slowly adding one note to another, was abstract and complicated, and the violinist slopped haphazardly through chords Tom would have nailed cleanly on the first try.

"Shit." The violinist slumped in her chair. "I had it before. You should have heard me."

"Don't worry." Stephen strained, his voice even quieter than usual. "It's like this." He conducted with well-schooled, concise wrist loops and sang the rhythm in a high, sweet tenor, which sounded incongruous coming from him, someone so tall and reserved in his wool blazer and plain gray tucked-in shirt.

"Letter B." Stephen counted the group in, but the violinist played a wrong chord immediately. The other players fell back in their chairs. The violinist glared at her music.

"It's a D-flat dominant seventh with a sharp nine. You have the root and the fifth," Stephen explained, but she didn't understand what he meant. "Just play a D-flat," he said, simplifying.

When the players packed up, Stephen stood alone at the edge of the stage, lost in thought. He did not see me sitting in a far aisle, and I did not want to shout out, to hear my solitary voice echoing in the huge hall. He was gentle, as Pam said, and I longed to talk to him, to feel his quiet concern. My chair squeaked as I rose, and Stephen glanced around the empty auditorium, shielding his eyes from the light.

"Gala," he exclaimed, saying my name as if it was something special as we came down the center aisle toward each other. It had been a week since I'd lost the audition, a week since I'd seen him.

"That was a great piece." I couldn't help smiling into his eyes, so serious and blue.

"Thanks." He nodded, taking the compliment, believing it, as Tom would have. "If only that violinist learns the notes. I only have four more rehearsals and then the concert. At Town Hall."

"Wow," I said, but I didn't feel jealous as I would have with Tom or Pam, people I knew well. I was fresh with Stephen. "You must be so excited."

"If I could bring myself to do it, I'd fire that violinist. Everyone in the group keeps expecting me to."

"She'd remember it for the rest of her life."

"I know." Stephen's lips curled down at the sides. "That's why I can't do it." He tapped the velvet top of a seat lightly with his closed fist, worrying.

"I've been carrying something around for you." I dug into the bottom of my bag, messy with broken cigarettes and change, and held out the tape I'd made of Mr. de Laney playing Mozart. For a moment, Stephen stared down at my hand, as if the tape were too precious a gift. Giving it to him hadn't seemed to mean so much before—he was my practice-room buddy, as Pam had once been—but now the tape felt dangerous between us.

"Because you gave me the Toscanini," I explained nervously.

"Mr. de Laney." He held the tape up to the light, regarding it from all angles as if Mr. de Laney meant everything to him, too.

I suggested I walk him home, which I knew was nearby on Manhattan Avenue, and we headed uptown in a strangely dense, intimate silence, our inner hands knocking together occasionally. On a stoop, two girls with purple lipstick were listening to a slow Spanish love song, and the maroon projects and the aboveground subway tracks looked almost serene against the pale violet sky. I hoped we would not run into Tom.

"So where have you been?" Stephen said finally. "I was so used to seeing you every day."

I concentrated on the broken-up pavement squares and tried to speak without emotion. "I lost the audition." On the corner, in a newsstand window near a Lotto sign was a giant poster of a glossy girl in a red thong. It seemed to mock me, to belittle anything I might feel. I checked Stephen's eyes to see if he was looking at it, but they were fixed on me, taking in all I was feeling.

"Why do you play?" he asked me. I repeated the question back to him, as if it were a question that didn't need an answer.

"Do you love music?" he persisted.

"I've been a musician since I was five. I've put my life into it. Ever since I can remember, my dream has been to play all of Beethoven's symphonies with a great orchestra."

A subway squeaked to a halt on the tracks above us. Footsteps clattered down the metal stairs, and then Stephen and I looked at each other again.

"I wish you had more confidence," he said, and then he stroked my face, right there in the wide-open day.

His block was deserted except for a stripped car on the curb. The once-luxurious buildings were boarded up and crumbling inside. I wondered if he felt like apologizing for himself for living here. I surprised myself by expecting him.

"I better get home. It's getting late," I said. My hair blew across my face, and when I pulled it back, I felt Stephen's eyes sweep down my bare neck. Though I knew it was wrong, I held my hair up a moment longer so that he would look

"Do you want to come up?" He gripped his briefcase tighter.

I was in a fragile mood, craving care, and I knew that going upstairs with him would be foolish, but I ignored my own better judgment and said yes.

Even in the daytime, his studio was dim until he flicked on an old lamp by the upright piano, which took up half the tiny room. The only three shirts I'd ever seen him wear were folded at the foot of the bed. Stacked wood cartons contained old hardcovers: Nietzsche, Heidegger, and Schopenhauer, the kinds of books my father read.

We stood side by side, our sleeves touching, in front of his kitchen cabinet, filled with a large assortment of tea and jars of grains and granola. His home felt familiar to me, as if I belonged.

"I could cook you dinner sometime," Stephen offered.

"That would be great." I blushed, both because it could never happen and because I wanted it to. As he passed me on his way to the stove, his fingers grazed my lower back. It was a light, intentional touch, but when I checked his face, it was the same, quiet and reserved, fixing our peppermint tea.

I sat down on the piano bench, the safest place. On the stand was his music, some of his notes erased and rewritten so many times the page had almost worn through.

"That's my string quartet." He stood above me as I tried with cold, clumsy fingers to sight-read all four quartet parts on the piano. His harmonies were so intricate I had to strain to get my mind around them.

"Pretty impressive," I said.

"Over here." He learned over my shoulder and touched my fingers on the keys. His hands were large and sensual, the nails clean and cared for. He wore a faint spicy cologne, something I wouldn't have expected.

"Much better." I smiled up at him. "I love this piece. You're a genius."

"I don't know about that," he said, but I could tell he believed he was something close.

On the floor by the piano was an open carton with a stack of unframed watercolors of flowers and fruit.

"My ex-wife's," he told me, and I hid my surprise. His past life in Mississippi, a place so foreign to me, had not really seemed to exist.

"She must be a cheerful person."

Stephen humphed and then sipped his tea. I studied them again, the flowery, decorative colors, an exaggeration of girlishness. I could easily see how Stephen, with his intensity and seriousness, would be drawn to someone like the woman who drew those sunny pictures. It occurred to me that he might miss her, and I wasn't sure why but I felt jealous.

"Was she an artist?"

"An artist." He frowned, implying the worst about her talent. I imagined that he had put her down a lot and that their fights were familiar ones, but then he surprised me by saying, "She was a nurse. A far more respectable profession." He set his tea down on the top of the piano. "I've told you as much about myself as you've told me. You can trust me now."

"Trust you?" I laughed.

"Play for me."

"I can't."

"Please." He nodded to my oboe on the floor. "You promised," he said, and I gave in both to please him and because I suddenly wanted to play. I was nervous just unpacking my oboe and dipping my reed into my film-container filled with water. Stephen had taken off his shoes and was sitting on the bed against the wall, his hands in his lap. He didn't say anything, but he observed all of my movements, all the sounds I made moving on the bench, twisting my oboe together. Tom was never so watchful, and I didn't know whether I liked being so observed, Stephen's gaze traveling my body, or whether I wanted to get away.

I had to wait a few minutes for my reed to soak, then I had to start playing right out of the silence. I was afraid even to begin, afraid my sound would be ugly. It was different when we were in separate rooms and I wasn't sure if he was listening to me or not. Now I even worried about how ugly my face looked, playing.

I made myself look straight into his pale eyes. "I'm scared I won't sound good."

Stephen laid each word carefully between us. "I already know
how you sound. And I already know it's beautiful."

I turned away from him to face the grimy window overlooking
the boarded-up buildings and deepening sky. I dared myself to do it;
I played the Brahms with everything I had inside of me, without the
critical voice that judged every note, suffocating my own singing voice.

Stephen hung his head until I finished. He started to say something, then stopped.

"Thank you."

"Thank you." I laughed a little, nervously. The room was suddenly too quiet. Above the piano, the same schedules Tom and I had
of Carnegie Hall, Lincoln Center, and the Film Forum were taped to
the wall.

"Play something for me." I patted the bench beside me, but didn't
move over. The seam of Stephen's jeans touched my thigh, and I let
him reach across me, his shoulders rubbing mine.

"Do you like this one?" he said softly, barely over the chords of
the Scriabin prelude.

"Yes," I said, and he stretched by me to the high register, his
upper arm moving against my breasts.

"What's your favorite piece by him?" He sat still, neither playing nor moving his arm away. He knew what he was doing, and I
couldn't tell if that should make me hate him or not. Or whether I
should hate myself for letting myself be touched.

"I like this one."

"I can play you another."

"I like this one." I stared at the keys and leaned forward, pressing my nipples into his arm.

He played until the end. When he stopped, we turned to each
other, and his lips pressed mine briefly, just long enough to tempt me.
I remembered the urgency of desire, and I told myself it wouldn't be
so bad if we kissed just a little longer. Our lips met again, and I felt
his hand on my back, so gentle, barely touching me at all. He knew
how to tease me, how to make me play for him and then to make me
want him. He knew how to circle my back with just his fingertips
until he found my breast, and then he knew how to cup his fingers
around it so tenderly that I was the one who pressed into his hand,
asking for more.

"I want to make you happy," he whispered as he kissed my neck, behind my ears, feeling for my every response. I could not resist as he lowered me down to the piano bench. But then the wood was hard and narrow against my back, and his bulky weight was too much. I opened my eyes. Over his shoulder, I saw the dirty, chipping ceiling and he became real and what we were doing became real and I could not imagine what else besides a shameful desperation had brought me here, to a stranger's house, his hand roaming up my thigh.

"I better go." I stopped his hand.

"What?" He didn't move. I pushed him away, sat upright on the bench, my bra loose under my arms.

"What's wrong?" He blinked at me, stunned by my quickness. I mumbled something about the dangerous late hour and ignored him when he offered to walk me home. I hurried my reeds back into their box, clasped, then zipped my oboe case. Stephen sat forward on the bench, his hands perched on his knees, as if he were about to get up and make some kind of grand gesture or statement, only he didn't. I fumbled, hooking my bra.

"Always happens," I joked stupidly.

Stephen walked me to the door. His lip was puffy from our kissing; I couldn't look at his face.

"I'm sorry," I told him, then took off quickly down the hall.

Warm, damp wind filled my mouth, blew back my hair. The moonlight shined on the metal of the ripped-up car, and drunken voices clamored inside a boarded-up building. Stunned by what I had done, I sped faster and faster toward my apartment, hoping to escape what had just happened and make the whole afternoon suddenly vanish.

At the corner of 124th, I stopped. I was too close to home. The aboveground subway tracks looked dark and abandoned, threatening.

I went into Ralph's deli on the corner where I always bought Tom his favorite treats: Heath Bar Crunch ice cream, Devil Dogs, and Chips Ahoy. Every night, we would snuggle together under the covers, giggling and eating and listening to music until after midnight. It was what I looked forward to all day.

I blinked in the harsh, fluorescent lights of the deli, bag of cookies hanging in my hands. Stephen's dim room, his books and music, were serious, too serious, I told myself. But when I imagined his fingers cupping my breast, gentle in a way Tom hardly ever was, I made a sound of pleasure, a giggle, a cry, right there between the rows of Twinkies and toilet paper.

Behind the counter, Ralph stared up at the Spanish soap opera on the tiny television beside the shelf of toilet paper. His eyes were glazed as if he'd just received bad news.

"Are you all right?" I laid my ice cream on the counter.

He shrugged. "It's okay. It's okay," he said, but he seemed heartsick.

An angle of light stretched out under my front door into the hallway and a recording of the Tchaikovsky Violin Concerto boomed inside my apartment. I remembered climbing these narrow stairs the first nights Tom had moved in and how grateful and lucky I'd felt seeing the light under the door, knowing he was waiting for me. "Hello, my fortune cookie," he'd greet me with a new sweet name and a new dish for dinner every night.

I leaned back against the front door to collect myself, but Tom opened it behind me.

"You're late." He grinned, his eyes bright. The old white T-shirt he always wore around the house was scraggly at the sleeves, and it showed his dark mesh of underarm hair, reminding me of sex. I blushed, thinking of Stephen. It seemed all over me, how I'd let myself be touched, but Tom noticed nothing.

"Guess what," he said.

"I bought you some presents." I stuffed the bag in his arms, but Tom only glanced down for a second before putting it on the stereo.

"Guess what happened today." He clasped my hands, his fingers trembling around mine. "I'm going to be in the Prokofiev Quartet."

"That's wonderful," I said, but as Tom pulled me to him, I backed away, afraid he would somehow smell Stephen's kisses on me. There was only a flicker of doubt and questioning in Tom's eyes.

"Why don't you hug me?" He kept grinning, too happy to notice more, and I clung to him as if between our two bodies I could squash both my jealousy and my guilt, and the selfish voices in my head that kept telling me what a failure I was. The Tchaikovsky Concerto sang triumphantly through the speakers.

*   *   *

"Can you believe it! All these years," Tom's mother cried to me over the phone. "You know I love you, don't you? You're my best girl."

I clutched the phone, not wanting to say good-bye, until Tom wrestled the receiver away. He paced, dragging the phone along the floor behind him, as he told his mother the conversation he'd had with the Quartet. She wanted to hear the story again and again, and each time he repeated the story for his mother, his voice grew louder and happier and the compliments the Quartet had given him became greater and greater.

"Ha!" I laughed out loud after he'd told her the Quartet was going to adopt all of his interpretations and fingerings to the Schnittke.

"Gala's laughing at me. She doesn't appreciate my greatness." Tom laughed over something his mother said. "Our best girl." Tom came over to the couch, the phone trailing behind him, to kiss me on the forehead.

"My best girl," he whispered, and I wrapped my arms around his back.

"What's going on over there!" I heard his mother shout.

"You're my family," I whispered to Tom before he pulled the phone into the kitchen and rummaged through the cabinets for a glass. In the moment he disappeared from my view, I saw Stephen's face, poised to kiss me, and I felt desperate, as if I were already losing Tom.

I hugged Tom from behind and would not let him pry himself away to drink his water. He was telling his mother all the concert dates—the first one at Alice Tully was in less than a month—the tours next summer, to Aspen, Tanglewood, Fontainebleau in France, and then to Italy.

"My whole life is going to change. Italy! Can you believe it? Florence, Rome, Siena . . . My mother's never even heard of Siena . . . ignorance." He shook his head and I heard his mother laugh, one of her deep belly laughs that could make almost anyone happy.

8

obin's sound was still a beginner's, squawking and strident. But I didn't need to tell her how to feel the music, when to give more or when to pull back. She had already developed a critical ear far beyond her playing level. She winced at her own sound, which became even more harsh when she crescendoed.

"That's okay," I told her. "You're hearing the phrasing."

Robin's brown eyes widened, grew solemn when I complimented her. She gripped her plastic oboe, a Bundy, with both hands. Her legs were slightly apart, her feet firmly planted on the Persian carpet on top of which the old iron music stand teetered. (The apartment was cluttered with beautiful, impractical antiques.) Robin's mother was washing dishes with the kitchen door open, so she could hear the entire lesson. This made Robin even more shy with me; she was twelve years old and hid her body under an oversize black sweater that went down to her knees.

"That's what's most important now. That you understand the music."

She nodded slowly, without believing me.

I dug out of myself my confident teaching voice, a voice with authority, and I said to her, "We can work on your sound, Robin. But no one can teach you to feel the music. You play very musically." I wasn't sure if it was the best thing to exaggerate, but her eyes widened even more with the praise.

"No, I don't." She tried not to smile.

"You do."

She blushed, and I thought of how thrilled I was whenever Mr. de Laney said something nice.

"You're very musical." I placed my oboe on the mahogany coffee table, expensive looking with its shapely, carved legs, and I felt a flicker of rage at her mother and then at myself because I hadn't been able to ask for more money for traveling to Robin's lessons.

This morning, to avoid seeing Stephen, I'd practiced at home instead of at the school. Playing for the first time in a week, my lips felt flabby. I missed all my low attacks and my lips blew out after only an hour. But still, I felt I was coming home, back to what was most natural to me. I played through all my favorite pieces—"Niobe," "Pan," the Brahms—but then I lost the feeling. I had no goals, no audition coming up, no gigs, my next lesson with Mr. de Laney I had canceled again, and I couldn't think of what to play next. I tried long tones, scales, but my defeat came back to me, not in specific thoughts but as exhaustion, weighing my eyes and the back of my head.

I showed Robin physically how to control her sound. I made an embouchure and pointed to the sides of my mouth. "If you hold the reed with the sides, your sound will be more centered." I wanted her to see how strong the sides of my lips were. "Feel."

She giggled, but I said in my firm teacher's voice, "Feel the muscles."

She quickly poked my mouth, not really feeling anything. This wasn't the right way to demonstrate my point.

"Listen." I played with my mouth purposely not rounded enough, my lips straight across. "Did you hear that? How unfocused my sound was?"

She nodded, but I wasn't sure if she'd heard the difference.

"You try."

Her sound was as squawking as ever. "Uch." She dropped her oboe to her side.

"No 'uch.' Try again."

She grimaced at the effort. A part of me felt cruel for a second. If everything was so difficult for her, maybe she should not be encouraged.

She touched the sides of her mouth. "With these muscles?" she said, fighting herself to try again. And when she did, her sound was just a bit more resonant and focused. It was just a little better, but she heard it.

"There. I did it," she said with wide eyes, and I wished I could tell her something to make her feel confident always. She was like George, my only beginning piano student, who constantly needed my approval even though he was in his thirties, older than I. Another student of mine, Adam, barreled through everything whether he sounded good or not. He took criticisms easily, as if he knew his mistakes were either inconsequential or natural, a part of the processs. Though anything could happen, it seemed he would find himself much more easily in this world.

At the end of the lesson, I went through my reeds to find two for Robin. I gave my other students my bad reeds—they couldn't tell the difference anyway. But I gave Robin reeds that had once been good but were now too old for me to play on.

"Pretty soon I'll have to start you making your own reeds," I told her. "That's a whole other story."

I tried my reed in her oboe, which was so bad I had a hard time getting much of a sound.

"You should think about getting a new oboe."

Her mother, Florence, peeked in from the kitchen, her hands in rubber dishwashing gloves. "You think Robin needs a new oboe?"

"Well, I mean . . ." I hesitated, not wanting to give a careless answer. "Right now, there's only so much you can improve with a plastic oboe."

"Can I try your oboe? Please," Robin said. Even though nothing could really happen to it, I didn't like watching my students who hadn't developed enough care handle my new oboe. But Florence was watching and so I handed it to Robin. First, she ran her fingers down the keys, new and shiny, just as I had done when I first bought it.

"I love the way it feels." She fiddled with the second octave key, a key her oboe didn't even have.

Her tone was much darker, and she had less trouble playing it; the sound came out easily.

Florence planted her rubber-gloved hands on her hips. "Even I can hear the difference." She asked me about the cost of new oboes and if I advised getting Robin a Lorée, the best, most expensive kind. I skirted her real question about Robin's ability and talked only about comparative costs. I wanted to have time to give her a thoughtful answer. When my mother asked my first teacher if I could get into Juilliard Prep, he'd said, "A life in music is too difficult. If Gala can do anything with her life besides music, that's what she should do." But he'd told my mother that, of course, I could get into Juilliard. As we left the lesson, my mother had squeezed my hand: "There isn't anything else you want to do, is there?"

There wasn't. At twelve, I lay in bed at night listening to records of oboists: John de Laney, Joe Barret, Elaine Douvas. All people I had now studied with. I'd memorized John de Laney's recording of "The Flower Clock" by Francaix. Every articulated note was perfect. The notes were separated, tongued, but also seamlessly legato as if the breaks in between were incidental. I practiced for hours trying to articulate that way. My mother didn't understand what I was doing. On the piano, she'd understood everything I practiced, but on the oboe I could tease her.

"You can't hear the difference?" I played her one way and then the other.

"Your ears are better than mine. You're better than me." Her voice wavered between pleasure and regret. Music was our joy; it was what bound us together, but she worried, too.

"Someday you'll surpass me," she said. "And then what will I do?"

But we both knew I had to be better than her. In all ways. I had to have better ears, better rhythm. I had to be a better sight reader, less anxious and liable to get confused. I needed to be tougher and more determined. I needed to be able to take rejection and then let it go.

Even at her best, my mother had never possessed enough technical brilliance, but her music was expressive, every note extracted from deep inside. Sometimes when I heard her old tapes, I would almost confuse our playing. She did with the music exactly as I would have done—hesitated, grew darker or showed a sudden brightness just where I would have. It was frightening and mesmerizing to listen to her music, like losing myself, staring too long at my own reflection.

That evening, I bought Tom thirty dollars' worth of flowers from the Korean deli on 104th Street.

"Lucky boyfriend," the young, handsome owner said, and along Riverside Drive, all the mothers and eccentric neighborhood characters seemed sunny, smiling at my bundle of bouquets. I arranged them in vases all over the apartment: the snapdragons on the windowsills, the sunflower beside Betty Blue's cage (she peered right into the black face of it), the iris on the stereo. Then I cleaned. I mopped the floors, scrubbed the counters, and when I was finished, our apartment was fresh and hopeful with cleanliness and colors. What had happened with Stephen seemed almost wiped away.

For the past three days, Tom had been so excited he had not been able to sleep. All night, he stared up at the ceiling, his white undershirt glowing in the dark, asking again and again, "Is this real?" His curls rustled on the pillow as he turned to me. "I'm so happy I'm scared. What if something bad happens? What if they change their minds?"

The contract could take weeks, and so he traveled to the cellist's house in Brooklyn to get his Bartók part even though he already had a copy at home.

"I want something concrete," he said. "I want them to see me again so they'll feel too guilty to fire me."

On the phone, he ran on in breathless circles to everyone he knew, and he told me he was going to invite his father to the concert. "What? You think he won't come?" he guessed from my worried look. Two of their last three dates, his father had not shown up. "He'll come to Alice Tully Hall," Tom assured me. He never stopped hoping for his father, no matter what.

"What will your mother feel?" I asked. She had not seen Tom's father for twenty years.

"You always worry about my mother. What about me?" Tom spent two hours on the living room floor making his father's invitation: a blue, gray, and black melancholy watercolor, the colors melding into each other, though in the middle the black looked like a pummeling hole.

"It's about loss," he said easily as if he spoke so openly about himself all the time. "Remember that drawing I gave you when you first came over? I couldn't believe you liked me. You were like those Upper West Side girls at Music and Art who never used to speak to me."

"I don't believe that." I could not imagine Tom as he described himself in high school: fat and in the worse half of violinists. "I was stoned and depressed all the time." His lips quivered into a funny smile, which he tried to hide.

The night I bought the flowers was our celebration night. Tom was supposed to be home from his very first rehearsal at seven, and I debated wearing something special, which I hadn't done since he moved in. I hardly ever did anymore the things that pleased him, and I felt it was my fault we had not made love since his first audition, weeks ago. In the bedroom mirror, I judged myself naked. My stomach stuck out a little and my breasts were uneven. One was still scarred from where I'd picked and dug at a cut years ago. I hadn't been able to stop myself once the bleeding started; I kept wanting to see it bleed a little more.

"You know that's crazy, don't you?" Tom had said when I confessed the reason for the scar to him. He gave me the same look as when he would point out some mess I'd left behind. "Disturbed."

I lay on my back on our bed, arms and legs spread. The half-lowered vinyl shade rapped against the window overlooking the alley. The slight breeze washed up the scent of me. I touched myself, searching for feeling. So often I couldn't find it, even with Tom. I'd move one way and then the other, but the feeling kept going away. Sometimes I pretended it was there when it wasn't. Stephen had been so tender, testing for my every response, and I imagined for a moment that, with him, I would feel everything I'd always missed, but then I made myself erase those thoughts immediately.

"Ain't it great?" Esther said to me over the phone. I clamped the receiver under my chin while I cooked Tom's favorite pasta sauce. "In my whole life, I never thought this would happen. His father left him with nothing. Not one thin dime."

I nodded as I ground pepper onto the sauce.

"He didn't give two shits for him. I had to come after him for the money, and after a while I said forget it."

"It wasn't worth it anymore."

"And then I married Harold, and Tom saw a good marriage. A happy one. I taught him what's important. Family. The rest don't matter one iota. You, my dear, are too serious. You worry too much. When you're young, you gotta be happy."

I believed her completely and vowed to myself that I would change. I would not be jealous of other people's successes. I would not be someone with such flimsy loyalty that I could break boundaries with another man so easily.

"You know, darling, I'd be a very happy woman if I could see you and my son together. A very happy woman. You know I love you."

"I love you, too," I told Esther for the first time, before we hung up.

The table was set with candles, roses, and a bottle of wine. The sauce was ready on the stove. I sat on the sofa, completely dressed in my silk blouse and leather skirt, flicking television channels, but by nine o'clock, two hours after his rehearsal was supposed to have ended, Tom still hadn't even called. I paced the apartment, reapplying lipstick and resisting cigarettes. Scenarios, one worse than another, flashed through my mind: Tom was hurt, beaten in an alley, shoved onto the subway tracks.

At ten o'clock, he was three hours late, and I lay chain-smoking on the couch. I'd seen the Quartet's album covers with Glenn Cooper, the glamorous pianist with the shiny blond hair. At twenty-eight, she was already famous, and I became convinced she was at this rehearsal and that was why Tom was late. It was easier than I'd ever thought to cheat and lie to someone; there seemed nothing that would hold Tom back.

The old shoe box that he usually stuffed away in the closet was by the bed, and I poked off the lid. I searched the box for signs of other women, but there was only one photograph of Annette, Tom's girlfriend before me, and I'd seen it before. In the photograph, taken in her kitchen in front of stacked dishes, she wore a man's shirt, unbuttoned low enough to show her breasts, and she had a strained smile, one hand in a fist. She was "wild" in bed, Tom had once said, but then wouldn't tell me any more. I imagined that together they'd had the kind of sex Tom always wanted with me, the kind that both frightened and lured me.

At eleven o'clock, Tom's keys finally rattled in the lock.

"Where were you?" I jumped to the door. His curls were mussed by the fall wind and his eyes were bloodshot.

"I messed up. I was terrible." He fell against me, his body heavy and sad.

"What happened?" I stroked his hair, forgiving his lateness immediately. I knew so well the humiliation of playing badly. "Tell me," I said, but he twisted out of my arms and set his violin down in the corner where he couldn't see it.

"I just want to be alone." He shut himself up in the bedroom, not even noticing all the flowers. I stood outside the room, my hand on the knob, the anxiety of the past hours still swarming in me.

"Tell me what happened," I called through the door. "I always leave you alone."

There was silence in the room.

"So I should talk to you because you need me to," Tom said finally, "not because I want to myself."

"Please," I pleaded in a tone I regretted immediately.

"You only ever think of what you want," Tom snapped.

I let go of the door handle and quietly, very quietly, sat down on a small space on the couch. On the table, the beautiful center rose had already opened up to its deep, tunneling heart. I had spent the whole day preparing the dinner. I had not practiced well for a week.

In the next room, Tom laughed on the phone with his friend Noah.

"So-so. Could have been better," Tom said when Noah must have asked him how his rehearsal had gone. "They said my Schnittke was sloppy. 'Unfocused.' " Tom laughed with only a slight strain in his voice. "You know that part?" He sang the section he had skimmed over, practicing yesterday. I'd nearly warned him to be more careful, but he'd gotten away with recklessness all his life. It was his thing to be raw, he would have argued. I was almost glad now that I had been right.

"Next time I'll kick ass. Just wait," Tom said to Noah, and then I heard him joking about some bad violinist who was overrated by everyone in the press. "And he sounds like shit, too." Tom laughed again only a bit too loudly, as if he had not just been upset minutes before. He shared himself only in bits and pieces with me, with everyone.

9

"'d like you to meet Marissa," my father told me on the phone two days later. It was the middle of October. My favorite soft breeze blew in through the fire escape window, and Betty Blue hopped from perch to perch, singing.

"Why?" I asked my father in that snotty tone that usually made him laugh.

"Because I'm your father and she's the woman I'm moving in with." He informed me that Marissa had a sixteen-year-old son, and I tried to pretend that none of this news meant anything to me.

"What if I don't want to meet either of them?"

"It's just one evening. You're my daughter. You can do this for me."

Simple as that, I thought. My father could play at being childish, pushed around, though in the end, he always got what he wanted.

I tried to determine exactly how I felt about meeting Marissa and her son. The situation seemed both remote and interesting and not quite real yet. I could not imagine my father hugging another child with the kind of love he'd shown me, and I could not imagine what it would be like to see my father with someone other than my mother. I thought Marissa would try too hard around me and that I would dislike everything about her. In the photograph, she seemed perfectly at ease at the cocktail party, tucked under my father's arm, laughing with rich-looking people I'd never met before. My mother had never fit in. She'd given up her own world, but never become a part of my father's. At his faculty parties, everyone talked about books she'd never read and theories she'd never heard of. In a low mood, my father might hide and complain about how much he disliked everyone, but when he was up, he could devour all the attention, lecturing and telling his jokes, while my mother remained at the edges of the room, watching everyone flock around him.

Waiting for the light to change on Broadway near Lincoln Center, I scanned the crowd for Marissa and my father. It was seventhirty, concert time. There were dozens of women in designer clothes, furs, and Hermès scarves who might have been Marissa. The yellow taxis streamed ahead of me to Lincoln Center and I panicked, worrying that my mother might be in one of them. She would see me and then jump out of the cab, her long skirt and Mexican bag flapping at her sides. "What are you doing here!" she would exclaim brightly, always excited to see me whenever we ran into each other on the street. "My daughter, of all people, in the middle of the city!" She would open her arms to me, and I would try, as usual, not to let her feel me flinch when we hugged each other.

The restaurant my father had chosen was not like the Upper West Side Chinese restaurants where the tables were less than a foot apart and you had to shout to be heard. Shun Lee had huge brass art deco doors, which a host, a young white man in an expensive suit, held open for me. The mahogany bar was shaped in voluptuous waves, and well-dressed older women and dark-suited men leaned into the inner swells, stirring their drinks.

I saw my father at the bar, alone, nudging past a woman with sprayed gray hair and three strings of pearls to meet me.

He grabbed my arm, spilling some of his drink in his other hand. We didn't kiss each other hello. His round face was already flushed from alcohol, which he hardly ever drank. He had on his favorite silly feathered felt hat, which my mother had given him years ago. The hat, along with his bristly, never-brushed hair poking out the bottom, made him stick out among all the conservative men at the place.

"Does Marissa come here all the time?" I raised my eyebrows at her wealth, but my father was motioning to the bartender for another drink.

"You don't drink." I punched him in the side. He didn't laugh this time.

"This is a fantastic restaurant." He waved his finger at me, lecturing. "They serve delicacies from all regions in China. Marissa knows how to order. She speaks six languages. Including Chinese."

"Does she speak English well?" I asked, but my father was bouncing on his tiptoes, searching for her over the heads at the bar. The woman with pearls looked him up and down.

"What's wrong with you? Calm down," I told him.

"Marissa's late. Maybe I should call." He pushed through the crowd away from me, but I grasped his arm.

"Don't leave me here. What if she comes?"

"Sweetie." My father hugged me suddenly as if he were afraid of losing me. Then just as quickly, he let me go. I turned around and there she was: a tan, fragile-boned woman with heavy eyes and a slick, neat bun. Her silver earrings glimmered, and she had on a tight, green wraparound dress.

"Gordon! Introduce us," she told my father.

My father laughed into his drink and so she stuck out her hand. "I'm Marissa." Her fingers were bony and long like my mother's. "I'm finally meeting Gordon's favorite topic of conversation." Her voice was quick and unmusical, foreign. "There's no father I know who talks about his daughter so much."

I smiled dumbly at her, and she looked me up and down. I felt too fat in my tight velvet top and leather skirt, which I'd chosen to wear because, an hour ago, it seemed like the sexiest, most expensive outfit I owned. My father squeezed Marissa to him, his hand on the slim curve of her waist.

"My son, Jason, will be a little late. Why don't we sit down?" She wheeled around and led the way from the bar. I stared at her legs, skinny between the high slit in her dress.

Marissa, not my father, negotiated with the host for the table she wanted. Her bracelets jangled on her thin wrists. She looked so much like my mother—that same thinness, delicateness, the same way they ornamented themselves. Only Marissa did it better; she was more chic, more decorated than my mother. My mother always looked mismatched, off somehow, in her funny, floppy hats with flowers that she thought were "fun" or "joyful," or maybe she would wear all purple one day, purple blouse, skirt, shoes, all the shades slightly different.

Nervous perhaps, Marissa strode way ahead of us to the table. My father smiled at me, his lips closed, as if he meant to explain something, but then couldn't think of what it was. We couldn't find what to say to each other. I wondered if he'd been staring at the slit in Marissa's dress. My mother would never have led the way; she was too dreamy, stopping to look at things. Here, I could see her pointing to the art deco bathroom doors and then at the black carpeting that covered everything in the dining room: the steps, the booths, the waterless fountain in the center. I could hear her voice—its brightness, its richness, its lilting—commenting on everything. My father, though, would have gotten impatient and implied the worst about her.

"Look at your mother," he would say impatiently. "She could lose herself anywhere."

I felt like my mother, dreamy, half-here, drowning.

"I think this is a fine table." Marissa planted her hands firmly on the back of the wavy wood chair.

"A perfect choice." My father pulled out the chair for her, something he'd hardly ever done for my mother, and Marissa readjusted her jacket on the chair three times before sitting down.

"Marissa has a visual sense," my father said, his hand on her naked shoulder. "She's very careful about how things look."

"I'm not so careful. It's just that you're so *un*careful. Why do you think," she said to me, "your father insists on wearing that hat all the time?"

"It looks very silly?" He touched the rim. "I'm famous for my looks and for my brains," he said, his favorite line, but his voice had no confidence this time. He looked back and forth between us, his hands on the back of his chair. I pretended to be studying the silver design on a fork. Each place was set for a feast: two china plates, china saucers, china bowls, and three silver forks and spoons.

"Are you more visually oriented than your father?" Marissa caught me looking at the plate design.

"Not really." I felt her nodding at me, waiting for me to speak more.

"A musician must have some visual, artistic sense. Don't you think?" She leaned toward me, her silver bracelets ringing against the china. She was more stylish than me, prettier, too.

"I'm a slob." I took a drink of ice water to wake myself up and say something better. She looked over at my father and I saw him pat her leg under the table to reassure her.

"Your father tells me you just took an audition for the New York City Ballet Orchestra." She nodded at me. I stared at her face, her tan cheeks, maroon-painted lips. This was the face my father kissed now.

"Yes," I said.

"And what a success your boyfriend has had!" she said nervously, clapping her hands together.

The waiter was an older man with a long, gentle face. Marissa tried to speak Chinese with him, and even stumbling over her words, she seemed lighter, more animated, and relieved to be talking to someone besides me. My father looked back and forth from me to her.

"So?" he said, and I made my most glum face for him. Another, younger waiter came over to talk to Marissa, and then the two of them laughed together over something she'd said.

"It ain't Yiddish," my father tried joking, but his voice was sad as he imagined, I thought, the world of differences between him and Marissa. "Remember the rabbi with the guitar?"

I remembered: the rabbi in Woodstock who played Joan Baez at my aunt's wedding years ago and how my parents had danced on Magic Meadow, my mother waving her scarves in the cloudless sky, my father doing his silly fifties box steps—extra-silly in the high wild grass. I was so happy, dancing between them. I had long braids, which I loved to feel flopping on my back.

"Life passes." My father looked away, sucking his lips in.

"You could go back, you know," I said, not caring that we were both being cruel to Marissa.

"What were you talking about?" Marissa pressed back into the conversation. "Gordon." She pulled his sleeve, needy, like my mother.

"Nothing important." He took her hand to make up to her, but when he told her that we were speaking of Linda's wedding, she seemed to know every detail.

"You mean in Woodstock with that crazy rabbi?" She touched the base of her neck to show where the rabbi's beard ended. It kept happening like that. She intruded on my memories, seeming to know all about them. She ordered for us—because "she's the expert," my father said—and every time she knew things about me, even small things such as that I was allergic to shellfish, I felt as if something huge were being taken away from me.

She told me about the trip she and my father were taking to Argentina. She was trying to organize exhibitions of contemporary American painters in Buenos Aires, the most cosmopolitan city in South America, she said.

"I own paintings by Mark Rothko, Edward Hopper, and one by Jackson Pollock." She named the million-dollar paintings on each of her fingers.

"Marissa's a real businesswoman." My father massaged her shoulder with his thumb. "She built her business out of nothing," he said with a respect he'd never shown my mother. "She's tough."

"I'm not tough." She elbowed him.

"Marissa's like me. Both of our parents had nothing."

"What a miracle you are, Dad," I teased, as I always would have, only this time I meant to hurt him. My father didn't notice, and he laughed his silent, jelly-roll laugh.

"Your father still sees himself in his candy store," Marissa told me. "He hasn't grown up yet."

"Everyone likes to make fun of me," my father said, pleased. "Nobody takes me seriously. Marissa's strict. When she says something, she doesn't fool around."

"Gordon." Marissa punched his shoulder, the way only I did. "Your father always tells me how strict I am." She laughed girlishly, intimately for the first time.

"Her son is well trained." My father bobbed his finger at me, teasing. I looked at him, trying to wound him with all my sense of betrayal, but he was paying no attention. Instead, he motioned to the waiter to direct him to our table with our food.

The waiter placed a huge fish on my father's plate. The fish looked alive with its eyes wet and open and all its scales glistening.

"I don't know if I'm old enough for this."

"So squeamish." Marissa elbowed my father. "Just like a boy. You have to learn to try things. Underneath it all your father is very meek."

"That's me. Meek as a mouse."

"I think I'm going to use the bathroom," I said, wanting to breathe alone for a minute, but Marissa decided to join me.

"It's good. Before we start eating," she said as if it had all been planned out.

Without speaking, we walked side by side toward the ladies' room. I was bigger, taller, and bulkier than her. I felt dizzy on my high heels, as if the ground weren't real or stable beneath me. I thought people should be staring at me, wondering what was wrong with me, but they weren't.

Marissa snapped open her red sixties-ish pocketbook and leaned up to the bathroom mirror to apply more maroon lipstick. On either side of her were waterfalls that came from the ceiling and dripped over the mirror.

"Isn't this bathroom great?" she said, her lips still in a tight O, and then she smacked them together. "This color might look good on you."

I nodded and then realized she wanted me to try on the lipstick. She wanted us to be friends, like girlfriends. I wiped on some lipstick. I always did what people told me to do.

"You look great." She nodded at me. "Really, it's perfect."

"Don't you think it's a little too purple?" I tried for that girlish banter I was never good at. She watched me look at myself in the mirror. I hated being watched. It was like performing. I adjusted my hair. It was French-braided and I pretended the sudden need to stick in all the flying wisps.

"I always wanted to have a figure like yours. I was the boy-sister in my family." She looked down her own body in the tight green dress. "Flat," she said easily. "You're lucky."

I slumped, wishing to cover myself.

"My sisters were considered the great beauties. I was considered the brains."

The opposite of my mother, I thought, whose father called her stupid again and again until she believed him. What a relief for my father, I thought, to be with someone who needed him less, who would never suffer so much without him. Marissa was easier. She would be all right no matter what.

"Do you think your father seems happy now?"

I stared at her reflection. She had her hands on her hips, and there was a plainness, a frankness, about her. Still, I evaded the question. "I don't know."

"People say that he seems more relaxed now than they've ever seen him."

I patted a wisp of hair back into the braid. I didn't look at her. I was afraid I would say something mean and then later regret it.

"I think he'll enjoy the trip to Buenos Aires." She snapped her purse back up.

I flopped my hands at my sides as if I'd finished my hair and was ready to go. But I regretted suddenly that I hadn't said something to her, that in my constant passivity I had not defended my mother. My mother had no idea how loyal I was to her in my heart.

Jason was tall and gangly and narrow like his mother. His hips seemed only as wide as my thigh. He wore glasses and a young boy's haircut. He stood rigid and unhappy at the edge of the table while Marissa circled her arms around him, her face buried in his polo shirt.

"This is my son, Jason." She held his limp hand and said something to him in Spanish about introducing himself, but he only nodded at me and would not look at my father.

"Jason." My father rubbed his shoulder, but Jason kept himself stiff.

We formed a tight foursome that might have been mistaken for a family. My elbows knocked Jason's as I went for my glass of water and he recoiled, inched farther away from me. I wondered where his father was, far away or close, and if, in time, my father would be his father, too.

My father made efforts, asking Jason question after question about the piano lesson he'd just come from, and Jason took each question like an assault.

"I'm not ready yet for a new book." Jason gave a self-conscious, wet, adolescent laugh, then looked down at his plate, which was empty.

"What are you playing?" I asked.

"Just some easy pieces." He laughed again toward his plate.

"Jason needs to practice more," Marissa told me, then explained how even though Jason wasn't planning on becoming a concert pianist, she wanted him to continue his education at least another year.

"Just another year so he'll always have it. Right, Jason?" She reached across the table to brush his hair out of his eyes.

"I'll probably never touch the piano again after next year," he said.

"Jason has the same attitude about music as his father. His father is American." She frowned. "I'm hoping some of your music, Gala, will rub off on him," she said, smoothing down Jason's hair again, and I cringed for him. I was at least as self-conscious, especially with my mother, when I was his age. I tried to ask him questions gently. He went to a boy's private school on the Upper East Side. He had five hours of homework a night and had to wear a jacket and slacks, no jeans, to class.

"It's not as bad as it sounds. I don't think about it. I'm conditioned." He laughed and I laughed with him.

"Jason's just started his SAT preparatory course," Marissa told me. "Two days a week to bring his scores up to seven hundred. He wants to go to Yale or Columbia. Your father is going to write a letter to the dean."

"Gala failed the SATs," my father teased. "That's why she's a musician."

"You didn't really prepare for them, did you?" Marissa questioned me. My father must have told her my scores, which were only average, in the five hundreds. Kids of his Columbia colleagues got at least six hundreds.

I spoke as if I didn't care, though suddenly, ten years later, I did. "I was never good at those kinds of tests. At Performing Arts, they didn't stress them anyway."

"Gala was a musician from a very young age," Marissa explained to Jason. "She started piano at Juilliard Preparatory division when she was six or seven. Isn't that right?"

I nodded, trying not to let myself feel proud in front of her.

"It's like being a ballet dancer or a gymnast," Marissa continued. "As long as you have one thing you're good at, that's what counts. Fifty percent of the students from Jason's school go to Ivy League colleges," she bragged with no self-consciousness at all.

"The other fifty percent go to hell," Jason said. I imagined that at school he straddled two groups; most of the time, he was with the lonely, hectic intellectual boys, but he was sharp enough, funny enough, to be allowed to tag along with the more popular, physical boys for whom he would have dropped the other group in a second.

"What's your favorite subject?" I asked.

"Computers."

"All day," Marissa said. "All he does is sit in front of his computer playing these games."

"I like computers, too." I told him about the E-mail system at Manhattan School of Music, and I pretended not to understand it so he could feel good about explaining it to me.

My father and Marissa linked hands under the table. For them, it was turning out to be a good dinner after all. This was their new family, me and Jason and them. My father wore that sentimental smile of his, and Marissa liked me. I tried not to feel happy or relieved about that. Only two weeks ago my father's voice had broken, telling me he still loved my mother.

"Maybe one day Jason could show you his new program," she said between the last bites of her fish.

"Maybe," I said politely, and I gave my father a cruel look beneath my smile, but he didn't notice. Instead, he put his arm around Marissa and leisurely massaged that naked part of her shoulder. Jason looked down at his plate, at the eye of the fish. I wished he would do something—shove that fish onto the table or send his plate crashing to the floor. But he wasn't the type and neither was I.

Marissa helped my father on with his coat, made sure it was buttoned all the way to the top, before letting him leave the restaurant. He lumbered, that uneven, strained walk I knew so well, but his hand was on Marissa's hip and he kept it there, guiding her, caressing her, as he had never done to my mother. At least not in many years. I imagined that right now my mother was home alone, still waiting for him, and it seemed to me that he had ruined her.

Well-trained, Jason let me pass ahead of him between the last table and the host's stand. I couldn't think of anything to say to him.

The four of us left the restaurant. Crowds from Lincoln Center rushed into the street for cabs.

"Someday you'll be playing there." Marissa pointed to Avery Fisher and then, with that same hand, drew me to her and kissed me on the cheek. Her lips felt thin but warm, and all of a sudden I wanted more. I wanted to be loved by her. I kept myself distant, contained.

She tightened the scarf around Jason's neck. Her touch was quick and economic. She chided Jason for not dressing warmly enough, and my father took my arm.

"My only daughter. Everything okay?" His eyes were milky and baffled, as they were so often lately. The traffic rushed behind him. His wisps of hair, all white, blew out the side of his feathered felt hat.

"Fine." I tried to pull my arm from his, but he wouldn't let go.

"Not too difficult?"

I wouldn't look at him, but his arm holding mine felt like the only firm thing supporting me for a long time.

"My big daughter." My father tried to hug me good-bye, but I jerked away from him. He ran out into the middle of the street—as he always did, dangerously—to hail a cab. I watched as the three of them boarded the cab and headed to Central Park South, to Marissa's house, where I guessed my father was already living most of the time.

I bought a pack of cigarettes at the nearest street stand and smoked and walked up Broadway, past Fairway, past Zabar's, past the Thalia Movie Theater where my last boyfriend, Wendel, and I had our worst fights. I imagined that with every step I was leaving my father further behind.

But I still had my mother and she still had me. A few nights later, a week and a half before Tom's concert, my mother called at midnight. I knew it wouldn't take long before she found out about Marissa, now that my father was moving in with her. My parents lived only ten blocks apart. They knew the same people and went to the same places: concerts at Carnegie Hall, readings at the Y or Symphony Space. Anyway, she must have had the knowledge of Marissa tucked away someplace for a long time, just as I had.

Though I didn't know when it would come, I dreaded her phone call. Boundaries had always been blurred and sometimes broken between my mother and me, but now they seemed gone. Anything could happen to her. First, she'd relinquished her music world, and then she'd lost my father and their mutual friends. I was the only one who called to check on her in the middle of the day.

The night of my mother's phone call, Tom was in the living room, practicing, and I lay in bed in darkness, half-listening, half-watching TV. Tom and I hardly went to sleep together anymore. He practiced late, long after I had gone to bed, and his playing was no longer reckless; it had become exact and polished. More like that of the conservative players at Juilliard he'd always scoffed at.

"I have to be tough. If I fuck up, that's it. Every day of my life is different now," he said, and it was true. His life had changed all at once. He'd stopped working on his violin method and making his collages, the things that used to relax him and bring him closer to himself, and he'd had to drop most of his students at the Neighborhood Music School. He didn't have time anymore. He had rehearsals every day for the concert at Alice Tully, and he had to relearn all the Bartók quartets for the recording dates in December, only one month from now.

The phone rang constantly. The Quartet called at least once a day, and he was offered new high-paying gigs all the time. Two magazines, *Opus Magazine* and *String Player,* wanted to do articles on him. To get away from the phone, he took walks alone in Riverside Park, listening to various recordings of the Bartók quartets on his Walkman. Once, coming home with groceries, I saw him crossing the street about a block away. His headphones flattened his curls, and his eyebrows were knotted, his lips pressed tight. He looked grim and determined and unfamiliar to me.

At night, he couldn't sleep. I made him hot milk or Sleepy-Time tea to try to calm him down.

"You're going to be fine," I'd tell him, but he never wanted my comfort. He practiced over my words, barely nodding over his violin. Sometimes I would tread into the living room in my long, unsexy cotton nightgown and ask him when he was coming to bed.

"I miss you," I would say sheepishly, foolishly.

Exasperated, he'd drop his violin to his side. "You're making me feel guilty for practicing. Why are you doing that?"

I shook my head.

"Why are you so needy all of a sudden?" he said, his bow dangling in his hand.

"Am I needy?" I wasn't sure. I thought maybe I was justified; our most intimate times used to be before falling asleep. In bed, we ate our treats, snuggled under the covers, watching our nature shows or listening to Bach.

The world seemed an unsteady place, I told Tom to explain myself. There was my parents' separation, Marissa, the audition loss . . . My voice sounded false, as if I were making things up as I went along.

"Your parents separated five months ago," Tom told me. "Are you going to be depressed about it for the rest of your life?"

"I'm just a little shaky." I showed him my shaky hand, trying to make a joke, and then I made one of my sad-cute faces, lower lip pushed out. I always used to make this face for my father.

"All right." Tom slammed his music down on the table. "I'll stop practicing. I'll be in there in five minutes."

He banged his violin case closed to show how much he resented coming to bed with me. It was on the tip of my tongue to tell him about Stephen and that I had someone who wanted me even if Tom didn't. My heart slipped, thinking of Stephen's fingers gently circling my back. But I told myself there was nothing between us but the attraction of something new. It had been like that with Tom, too: those wild, reeling nights beneath the concert hall that kept me up, alone in bed, longing for more.

Now, though, Tom and I bickered over everything. He shared little of himself and only seemed to want to know about certain parts of me, too: the parts that were not needy or struggling.

"We fight because we haven't had sex in so long," Tom said, and I thought that might be true, too. If we could just break through, make love to each other again, but in a different way.

"Let's just be tender with each other," I whispered, wrapping my naked body around his back. Stiff, he faced the wall. "You're never tender with me anymore."

"Is that what you think?" His voice was high and pinched, and he took shallow, quiet breaths so I wouldn't see or feel him beside me. His body was curled away from me in a tight ball.

"I didn't mean to criticize you, Tom." I stroked his side, but he shuddered.

"I'm sorry," he whispered. "I don't feel like being touched any-more."

The night my mother called, I was lying in bed, watching an old *Partridge Family* rerun. I remembered how my first best friend and I had been in love with Danny, and how we had acted out all the episodes so many times that even now lying in bed twenty years later, I could mouth the lines along with the actors. In the next room, Tom was practicing the Debussy. His sound was sweet and ephemeral, perfect for Debussy. Before, I'd have had to tell him to alter his tone color more and not make it so consistently flashy.

I lay on my back in the dark with the TV up loud over his playing. I was relieved when the phone rang, though I didn't know who I hoped it would be.

"How are you, sweetie," my mother said, her voice trembling and shrill. I flicked on the Mute button, balanced the receiver on the pillow beside me, and told my mother I was all right.

"Guess who I saw today at the Y," she said. There were loud cars in the background on her line, and I imagined she was alone in the kitchen, the only noisy room, sitting at the table in her bathrobe, clutching the phone.

She told me she had seen my father with Marissa. As my mother was coming out of the gym, they were buying tickets for a poetry reading, Adrienne Rich.

"He had his arm around her."

"I'm sorry."

"Well, I was very good. I just nodded and went on. Just like that. Right past him. After twenty-eight years. But I kept saying to myself, 'You're okay, you're okay. Just walk right past.' But you know what?"

I shook my head and then I waited in the wide, empty silence for her to tell me what would change my vision of my father forever. The blue and gray lights from the TV streaked across the ceiling. In the next room, Tom was slinking up to a sugary high note.

"It was the same woman from ten years ago," my mother said, and her breath came sharp and wheezing. "He's been seeing her all this time."

Tom plunged back down to a resounding chord. The wind felt knocked out of me and it took me a moment to find my voice again.

"Mom, Mom . . . it's okay . . . ," I told my mother over and over again. I couldn't say the right thing. Nothing would stop my mother from crying. She was inconsolable even when I told her I loved her. Something I didn't remember ever having said before.

10

The next morning Tom was up early practicing scales, but by ten o'clock, I still hadn't gotten out of bed. The shadows from the alley weighed like bars across my chest, constricting my breath, and my heart raced, though I only lay there. The phone, our old black rotary, was on the floor by our bed. When I dialed my mother, she didn't answer until it had rung ten times. Her voice was groggy and distant as if the receiver were lying on the pillow beside her.

"I can't hear you, talk louder," I ordered as if this would make her snap out of it.

My mother mumbled something back, the words confused and out of order. A rush of panic washed over me.

"Did you take anything? Any sleeping pills?"

She didn't answer. I heard only crying sounds.

"Should I come over?" In her silence, I imagined her head falling to the side into sleep again. "Mom, Mom, should I come?"

"I have nothing. My hands are empty."

"Do you need an ambulance?"

"Just you," she cried.

As I dressed, I kept thinking this is it, this is it, my mother has tried it again, and I seemed to be moving in slow motion, watching myself as I put on my clothes, shoes, and purse. I couldn't find the keys to my mother's house. I spilled my desk drawer filled with papers and practical things onto the floor. Because what if she couldn't come to the door? Blood spun in my head and I had to stop for a moment to regain my balance. With one sweeping arm motion, I shoved all my jewelry boxes and framed photographs off my bureau. The glass shattered, earrings rolled under the bed. My mother's keys pointed up on the floor by the radiator.

"What the hell is going on in there?" Tom shouted in a joking tone, but did not stop playing even when I entered the living room. "Perfectly in tune. Pretty good, huh? What happened?" He was facing away toward the fire escape and I could tell he didn't really want to know the answer. Under his white T-shirt, his shoulder blades moved with his quick bow motions.

"My mother's very upset." I tried to make my tone hold the gravity of the situation, but somehow I sounded theatrical and light, like someone else, and Tom did not turn around.

In the cab, I chastised myself for not having called an ambulance. I remembered all the times I had feared my mother's death, her hurting herself, but then also fantasized, too, about the attention it would bring me. After so much suffering, anything I did, win or lose, would be acceptable. There was a traffic jam at Broadway and 110th Street. A green gypsy cab with tinted windows and a scraped side stopped sideways in front of us, trying to turn. In the middle of the intersection, a fireman leaned out the window of his fire engine shouting, "Move it, move it."

"Shit, man," the cabdriver said, pounding both hands on the wheel.

I leaned forward to the divider. "Is there any way you can go around?" I said in a cheerful voice, but then I surprised myself and the driver by starting to sob. Retching, heaving, ugly sobs. The driver cut around the fire engine and then we sped down West End along the series of majestic prewar buildings that I knew by heart, the setting of my youth.

The elevator dinged slowly up to ten. I jammed the key into the lock.

"Mom!" I called, and found my mother standing in a white cotton nightgown right inside the door. She gripped the foyer shelves for support and held a strong-smelling mug of coffee in the other hand. Her face was white, her pale lips trembling with bitterness.

"I hate your father. He destroyed my life."

My arm around her, I helped her into her bedroom.

"I have nothing," she cried, her saliva and tears mixing together on the pillow. Sitting on the bed beside her, I focused all my tenderness into my hands, massaging her shoulders, bone thin under her nightgown. I made sure she didn't fall back to sleep. Outside the shaded window, the light changed from a bright high noon to faded gray. I wanted to disappear, to bury myself and this whole day in a hole where we could be forgotten.

11

*M*y mother gathered evidence. She spent the next few days and nights, raging and sleepless, calling every one of their old mutual friends for information. Before, ashamed of being left, she had let no one but me see her sorrow. Now she no longer cared. Her voice was bitter and she no longer spoke of my father coming back to her.

"The past ten years of my life have been a sham. Utterly meaningless," she told me over the phone. We were speaking five times a day. I called to make sure she had not tried anything again, and she called with every new fact. She spat them at me as if she were angry at me, not my father. The woman he had seen ten years ago was Marissa. My mother had discovered her name through a mutual friend. And five years ago, my mother said, she had called my father at his hotel on his book tour and a woman had answered.

"You don't know it was Marissa. You don't even know he was having an affair," I argued.

"Someone saw him," my mother snapped. She claimed a friend of hers had bumped into him with a South American woman and that Gordon had denied everything. (I was beginning to use my father's name, Gordon, as my mother did, when I thought of him.)

"I believed him," my mother said. "So stupid."

She had more evidence, unexplained weekends away that now ("stupid," she kept calling herself) made perfect sense to her. She called Hannah, an old friend who owned a gallery in SoHo and who was one of the few people who had been both my parents' friends, equally.

"And you know what Hannah said? She told me she knew. She knew all along because your father used to bring Marissa to her gallery to buy art."

"How do you know Marissa wasn't just a friend?"

"Well," my mother laughed at the ridiculousness of my question, "if your father had a friend who he hid from me for ten years, there must have been something pretty suspicious going on."

"I don't believe it."

"Hannah told me it was clear that she wasn't supposed to tell me about Marissa. One time they came in, your father and Marissa, and he said they were on their way to Club Med. Club Med!" My mother laughed again, shrilly, then continued, "I figured it out. That they went right when his second book came out, eight years ago. Every single one of our friends must have known."

I stayed in bed for three days, not practicing, only watching TV and speaking to my mother.

"It's your mother again," Tom would tell me, shaking his head when the phone rang. When I told him how she had swallowed pills, he had been absorbed, cutting out the photographs in an *Opus Magazine* article about himself: the bright new star of the famed Prokofiev Quartet. The article talked about how he was raised in the poorest section of the Bronx and how his mother had sold their furniture to buy his first good violin. That part made Tom laugh and he wanted me to laugh with him, to be the woman he had first fallen in love with, who had inspired that strong Medusa-like portrait, and who had been loud and fresh and silly with him. He didn't want someone who needed him so much.

"That's really crazy," he'd said with an awkward smile, magazine and scissors in his hands. My mother's desperation unsettled and embarrassed him. "She didn't really mean to hurt herself though, did she? I mean, if she had, you would have known. Lots of people get divorced," he told me to prove she should not be so upset.

"Not everyone discovers their whole life was a lie." I used her words and spoke in her angry tone. "Her hands are empty. You don't know what that means. To wake up with nothing." I opened my hands, empty, for him to feel it.

"There are people who are a lot worse off," he argued, and I shut myself back up in the bedroom. It had been a mistake, I was sure, to have been so drawn by Tom's darkness, the hard-to-get-ness of his emotions. He was shut down, bottled up, I decided. The only time he let go was when he played.

I didn't want to talk to him anymore, even though what he'd said about her not truly meaning to kill herself was true. Alone in the apartment she had once shared with my father, my mother's loneliness had finally become too much to bear. She had swallowed pill after pill, tempting herself to do it, to get back at everyone and take the whole bottle. But she had not done it.

I told Tom I was sick and that was why I was in bed, but really I was too angry to look at him. Too angry to speak to anyone. Except my mother. I called her before I went to bed and then right when I woke up. Then, in the morning, if it took too long for her to answer, I lay on my back in the relentless light, Tom sleeping beside me, tears bubbling in my chest until I finally heard her voice.

She had never been asleep when I called. It didn't matter what time it was. At 5:00 A.M., she was in the bath or listening to music, a cloth over her eyes to shut out the light.

"My life is wasted," she said. "Everyone knew I was being fooled, but me."

It was a sudden sixty-five-degree day in the last week of October, and blank with rage, I marched around the city, sweating in my black sweater, looking for a dress for Tom's concert. Everything I tried on proved my body had gotten worse. I spent half my money on a short black dress from Charivari (it showed off my legs, hid my stomach) and spent the other half on a new haircut in the West Village. I did not think about how I had no money left for rent. I did not toss my hair to feel its new lightness, but instead went to Washington Square Park to call my father. He was not going to come to the concert.

Under the arch at Washington Square Park, a crowd had gathered around a fusion band. A white guitarist with long dreadlocks blasted distorted chords through his too-small amp. A few feet away from me, three girls in thrift-shop miniskirts were swaying to the beat, lazily smoking clove cigarettes. I had never been like them. Time without music had always seemed aimless and wasted to me. No hour was free. If I wasn't practicing, I worried that I should have been. One of the girls, dragging in off her clove cigarette, turned her face to me, and I saw that her face, college-aged, looked much younger than mine; the whole scene beneath the arch had become too young for me. And I seemed ridiculous to myself, at twenty-six, still calling my father from the street to whine and battle him, still made helpless by my mother's anger and her despair, which loomed above me, insurmountable.

"It's the big G! It's my big daughter!" my father shouted into the phone. "Did you see the polls today? Bush is dead!"

I squeezed my eyes shut against his voice. "You can't come to Tom's concert."

"Why not?" he said happily, shuffling one of his messy piles of papers on his office desk. I'd thought he would immediately be upset. He was sentimental about concerts, graduations, and birthdays. He'd gone to my Juilliard graduation even though I hadn't—I hated those things and had an important gig—just so he could imagine me there.

"You can't go because Mom told me what you did."

"What did I do?" he said, still playing, as if he really didn't know. "Something terrible?"

Ten feet away from me, the skinny guitarist strummed his guitar as if he were making love. I huddled into the phone.

"You had an affair with Marissa for ten years. You lied to me."

His silence was stunned, kicked-in. I gave him my evidence, the sighting on the book tour, the weekends away. I sounded like a wife, like his, and my face beat with shame.

"What are you talking about?" he said as if it were him and not me who had been slapped in the face. Right now, my mother was alone in her apartment with her rage while he had a whole new life.

"Ten years ago. Even I remember."

He was silent for a moment, and taking that as proof, I hung up on my father for the first time in my life. The guitarist played a Jimi Hendrix riff and the crowd whistled and clapped. My two-hundred-dollar dress in a bag over my shoulder, I walked past them to the number 1 train.

I could not piece my father together. He was the brilliant man who mesmerized his students and had written three successful books,

famous in his field; he was the father who had always loved me and
taken care of me, the one I'd called in the middle of the night. And
now he was also the father who my mother said had deceived his family for nearly a decade.

He sent me a note: *None of this is true. I'm sorry your mother is
involving you. She's been telling this to all our friends. Please call. Your old
dad needs you.*

A part of me wanted to call him up immediately and slip back
into that warm, anxious net of his love. I needed him, his love, his
comfort, and he needed me so badly, I thought, that if I did not call
him back, something bad would happen. He might die of a heart
attack or maybe he would be hit by a car (he always ran so dangerously into the middle of the street), and I would feel guilty for the rest
of my life.

I thought maybe if I told him what my mother had threatened
to do, he would come home to her and rescue us both.

The next day he sent me another note, begging me to let him
come to the concert: *Let me come. Don't shut me out. Your old dad lives for
these kinds of things. I'm not so terrible.*

By the end of my father's fifth phone message to me in two days,
I started to believe him and not her. He was denying everything so
earnestly. He said my mother could not accept that she herself might
have done something to damage their relationship. "Your mother is
not such a victim," he said into my machine. "She can be pretty cruel
herself." He told me it was easier for her to blame him than to recognize her own destructiveness.

I wanted to dismiss my mother's evidence and to discount what
their friend Hannah had said. "Your mother is cold," my father said
in his next message, and for some reason, those words stuck with me,
made hot tears nearly break through my anger.

There was no space, I thought, for my father to have been leading a double life. It was truly an outrageous story. Ten years ago I was
still living at home and my father was always there: in the evenings
when he'd sit in the living room for hours listening to my mother and
me play, and in the mornings when he woke up early to write. I
remembered traipsing into the dining room at 6:00 A.M. and finding
my father already at the table, his pen working furiously on his yellow legal pads. (Always yellow legal pads. His ideas, he said, didn't

come forth onto other kinds of notebooks.) He would talk to himself as he wrote, and he would not feel me behind him until I laughed out loud at his hands waving in the air.

"Fat, old Dad," I'd tease, startling him out of his solitary conversations, then I'd sit beside him at the table, my eyes full of sleep, as he told me about his struggles with his book. He never knew if he would finish. With every one, he said, "I'm beginning to believe it takes something I just don't have."

He always doubted himself and I adored him for this, too. I loved to watch him flip through those scattered yellow pages and then explain how they might all come together.

My father hadn't had the chance to lead a ten-year affair. He was always at home, I argued with myself, but then threw facts at myself from the other side. Obviously, he'd been seeing Marissa for longer than two months, which was what he had told me. They were too intimate, knew too much about each other. Even that picture in my father's house was dated.

The argument went on constantly in my head. I tried to weigh which relationship I could more easily lose, my relationhip with my father or my relationship with my mother. I thought if my father died, I would know he had loved me and somehow that would make it better. But if my mother died, I thought my grief would overwhelm me.

Please let me come to the concert, my father wrote in his last letter. *Don't shut me out of your life, you are my only child.* I left him a nasty message on his voice mail at Columbia, telling him not to come, although a part of me hoped he would anyway. He would surprise my mother and me and show up with roses for us both.

I called my mother to tell her I had disinvited my father, then I called my father again. Neither was home and I began to think they were together. This crisis had made them break through what had kept them apart. My father did not really love Marissa, who was so bony and practical. She was mild, compared to my mother, father, and me. She would never truly move him as my mother did. I remembered it: how evenings my father would stand for hours in the curve of the piano, listening to my mother play.

"Beautiful," my father would say. "As beautiful as the day we first met."

"If only." She would open her eyes but not stop playing, her fingers rising and falling gracefully on the keys. Music was her power over him. He didn't understand it, couldn't even sing in tune. My mother was mysterious to him when she played. If she had never quit, I thought, he would have loved her still.

Three days before Tom's concert, I had plans to visit my mother, but when I arrived at her apartment, she wasn't there. I rang the bell, shook the door by the knob, dizzy with panic, as I had been so many times. After five minutes of ringing, I used my own key. Stella met me at the door, meowing hoarsely, her old head cocked to the side.

"Baby, I love you," I cooed loudly to wake my mother in case she lay sleeping in her bedroom. Stella trotted ahead of me down the hall, leading me, it seemed, and I prepared myself, telling myself that this could be the biggest moment of my life. The moment I crossed into my mother's bedroom, I might enter the world of irrevocable sorrow.

Her empty room seemed to yawn in the bright afternoon sun, lazy on the sheets, tumbled and twisted on her bed. As my panic drained out of me, it was replaced by a familiar anger at my mother, who was famous for being outrageously late, for being so absorbed or distracted that she forgot dates.

She had not, however, let the room remain as it was; she had altered it, made it more her own. Her perfumes and jewelry boxes covered both bureaus, and two new paintings hung on the wall: one of the field in front of her childhood house in Bearsville, and another of a swami my father would have mocked her for liking. On the floor were torn-open cartons of old family photographs, half of them strewn on the carpet. Separated from the rest was a faded picture of my mother alone at Lincoln Center. The fountain was turned off, and the square was blanketed with a quiet snow. My mother wore a big, unstylish parka which marked her as a newcomer, and her eyes were dark and nervous, but hopeful, peering out from beneath the hood. She must have been around twenty-five, still practicing during the day and ushering at night. Her life was ahead of her. Looking at the girl in the picture, I felt a kind of endless regret over the future she'd never had.

I searched my mother's bathroom cabinets, lined with her makeup and lilac soaps, and finally I found her sleeping pills,

Halcion. Half the pills were still there, and for some reason, this filled me with rage and self-pity. She had never really wanted to die. This time or the last. But here I was again, still overwhelmed, still lost to her despair.

I left two pills in the bottle and stuck the rest in my pocket. In my old bedroom, now a study, I lay down on my back on the sofa bed. Overlooking an alley, the room was lightless and quiet like my room in my apartment, and all of a sudden, it seemed significant and horrible that I kept choosing such gloominess and things that were shut away.

I got up quickly from the sofa bed, wrote my mother a note, an angry one, about how I'd been waiting for her, and then I rushed out of her building to make sure she did not catch me. At home, there was a message from her on my machine; she was so sorry, she had been confused about the time. . . . I erased her voice before she finished speaking.

That night, I dreamed that I was alone, drowning on the beach where my mother had once before given way to sadness. On the shore- line, the waves washed over my legs, and seaweed twisted up my thighs, dragging me farther into the ocean. The water filled my nos- trils, sucked me under. Screaming, I woke myself up beside Tom.

"What's going on?" He bolted upright.

My heart raced and my skin was hot. I breathed from deep in my abdomen to calm myself.

"Nothing. I just had a bad dream."

Tom stared down at me, waiting for me to tell him more.

"About my mother," I said, and in the darkness I could feel his eyes settle on my face, straining to understand.

"I love you," he whispered for the first time since he'd won his audition, then he stroked my shoulder with his sleepy hand. I wanted to tell him how afraid I was that my mother might hurt herself again and that I would never overcome her sadness. I would fail at music, at everything. I wanted to tell him of this immeasurable despair weighing on my chest, suffocating me, my voice and my words, even as I lay there.

His hand slowed on my shoulder and I knew he was falling asleep.

"I have to be free of this," I murmured. Half-dreaming, Tom mumbled something, but I did not repeat myself. It was enough to have said it once, just for myself.

12

"*I* know your father loved your mother, no matter what else he did," Daphne said. Our sneakers thudded on the pavement path to the boat basin. Below the park, along the West Side Highway, the traffic made lulling, churning sounds. "Your mother may surprise you. She's been so overshadowed by your father. This is her time to find herself. To grow."

"I can't imagine it."

"Sometimes you have to hit the absolute bottom before feeling better."

"She's starting therapy again. Three times a week. So what's new." My parents had been in and out of therapy their entire adult lives. Their enormous swinging cycles of happiness and unhappiness didn't seem to end. I asked Daphne again if she had known anything about Marissa.

"Your father never told me anything," she said, but then added carefully, "But I know that he was always provoking your mother. Like with that woman from Columbia. The Russian scholar."

"Jen Tallent." I remembered her clearly, her wispy blond hair and thin wrists. She and my father had spent months writing a paper together on Russian Jews. My mother was jealous at first, but then something transformed, and Jen and my mother became friends, telling secrets and laughing conspiratorially around my father. Now though, like most of my father's friends, Jen stuck with my father, her original alliance, and no longer made the effort to be in contact with my mother.

There had been other female colleagues whom my father had admired too much, but I had never heard anything about Marissa. That was the difference. She was his secret.

"My mother says that my father used to bring Marissa down to their friend's gallery. She says he took Marissa to Club Med." I laughed as I said this, just as my mother had done. I could no longer distinguish my feelings from my mother's. It horrified me to think of my father on a beach with Marissa, and how he probably had to sneak off to call my mother and lie to her.

At the Ninety-sixth Street light, two women in Lycra outfits jogged in place beside Daphne and me. I scowled down at my tattered white undershirt, Tom's really, but when the light changed, Daphne and I took off effortlessly faster than the other women.

"Good." I grinned, but Daphne looked at me neutrally. Pam would have been glad to be faster, just as I was.

"You know, Gala, just because your parents were unhappy doesn't mean you have to be. Meher Baba says that marriage is a confrontation with the self. You meet with everything that is difficult about yourself."

Later, as I was going to my New Amsterdam rehearsal, the guard at the front desk gave me a package from Stephen: ten tapes of Toscanini conducting all of Beethoven's symphonies, which I'd told him I'd always dreamed of playing with a great orchestra. *I miss you,* he wrote in tiny, meticulous handwriting. *Where have you been?* I jotted, *Thank you,* on a torn-off corner of manuscript paper and stuck it in an envelope on the desk. "I appreciate you giving this letter to him." I blushed in front of the guard, then stuck the tapes in the bottom of my bag even though Tom, who was never jealous, would have thought nothing of them. I climbed quickly up the stairs to avoid bumping into Stephen, who was probably just beyond the stairwell in the practice rooms. Knowing he was so close to me, though, I couldn't help imagining his sturdy arms around me, holding me, soothing me. I was sure his gentleness would allow me to feel things I'd never felt before, and for a moment, as I passed Stephen's floor, I thought I might be passing up on love, too. But I did not seek him out. I was determined to keep myself clear and out of confusion.

* * *

Tom didn't sleep the night before his Alice Tully Hall concert. Curled to the wall, I felt the rise and fall of our bed every time he swung his legs onto the floor and then disappeared into the bathroom. Each time he came back, he would sneak quietly into bed and I would wrap my arms around him, my naked breasts flattening against his cool back, my face in his curls. Being comforted embarrassed him and so I said nothing, just held him the way I would have wanted to be held.

At around 3:00 A.M., he stayed in the living room for what seemed like half an hour. Unsure of whether to intrude, I stood in the doorway, watching him. He was slumped on the couch in his scraggly T-shirt, watching the TV with the sound off. His penis was small, curled against his thigh. A beer was balanced between his knees.

"Do you need anything?"

"No, no." He grimaced. "I don't know what's wrong with me."

"There's nothing wrong with you."

"I'm like a maniac."

"You're just nervous."

"Nervous." He rolled his eyes. "I'm always nervous. I haven't been good to you." He looked down at his beer. "I should have been more sensitive. About your mother."

I kept my eyes kind, neither affirming what he said nor denying it.

"There's just been so much pressure," he said. "And maybe I don't know how to be good. I haven't felt loving."

I hung in the doorway, waiting for him to tell me more, to reassure me.

"It's okay," I reassured myself instead. "Everything will be all right."

Tom looked down, fingering the top of his beer bottle. "My father isn't coming. He called me this morning."

"I'm sorry," I said, careful not to push at his feelings.

"What if I really fuck up? In front of all those people."

"Won't happen."

"Sit with me."

I realized how little he asked of me and how few were the times he ever said he needed me. It was always me needing something more from him. His voice was hoarse from sleepiness and the effort of asking.

"Just a little while?" He reached out and I took his hand, clasped it between mine. On the muted television, a woman in a magenta lace bodysuit was rubbing her nipples with a telephone receiver. A nine hundred number flashed on the screen.

"This is what you're watching?" I tried to sound teasing, light.

"I don't know." Tom pressed his fingers down the side of his cheek. I had never seen him this anxious. Gently, I pushed his head down to my lap and stroked his cheeks and rough curls. On the screen, a woman in short shorts and a halter top was rotating her hips. I flipped the channels and tried to settle the anxiety I felt but didn't understand.

I bent forward and kissed Tom's forehead.

"I love you," I said.

Tom spent all morning playing slow scales in the bedroom. At noon, he emerged, dressed in his new cashmere sweater, one of his celebration gifts to himself.

"Andrew just told me he's sure we'll get a *Times* write-up," he said with a jittery grin. "I'm going crazy, I'm going to take a walk."

In front of the door, he held me tight. "You've been so good to me. I promise I'll be better. I'll give you so much more."

"I'm happy already." I kissed his lips.

"Maybe you'll come to Eastman with me. We haven't had a vacation together in so long."

Tom was teaching a master class, his first one, at Eastman in two days.

"Maybe that's all we need, to get away."

"We should take a big trip together. We should go to Italy."

"And Morocco." I swiveled my hips to an imaginary beat. Tom jerked his body in his silly dance motions, and then we hugged each other again. When he came back from his walk, he had a bouquet of red roses for me.

"I'm supposed to buy you those today." I buried my face in the bouquet, soft and wrinkled against my cheeks.

"We promised when we first moved in together that we'd always have fresh flowers. You're the only one who's bought any."

We lay on our bed, facing each other, talking about silly things (anything but the concert) and giggling together, just as we used to do when we first met, when we always felt like kids together. We compared ourselves, the lengths of our bodies, our kinky hair, almost exactly the same, and then the bit of extra flesh on both our stomachs.

"We're made for each other," Tom said.

At three, he left for his final run-through with the Quartet, and I felt hopeful, walking alone down Broadway to the polls in the 109th Street public school where I pulled the lever for Clinton. At the voting booths were crowds of Democratic mothers with Clinton and pro-choice buttons, and I imagined that my mother might soon be like the happiest of them, wearing big, colorful clothes, gabbing loudly with her friends. My mother would come through, as Daphne had said, stronger, happier, better than before.

"Beautiful!" Ralph said when I laid my cigarettes on his counter. I was in my new black dress, which fell just right on me—low-cut and slinky but not too tight. He turned from the European soccer game on the TV on the high shelf next to the ScotTissue.

"I never seen you looking so good." He made the curvy shape of a woman with his hands. Coming from him, that didn't bother me. I didn't believe he sold drugs. Tom was just trying to be tough when he said that, to impress me, I thought, smiling to myself. "Where you going? Why dressed up so pretty?"

"My boyfriend's playing a concert. That's why."

"Where is he playing?"

"Lincoln Center."

"Lincoln Center." Ralph shook his head, impressed.

I was impressed, too, and proud, walking into Alice Tully and seeing Tom's face printed over and over a hundred times on the brochure. The picture was of the whole Quartet. The other members, whom I'd never met, were much older than Tom. The violist, the player Tom most respected, was in his seventies and had only wisps of white hair. The second violinist was the only woman. She looked angry, as if she didn't like the person who was taking the picture. Against the other three, Tom looked intense and alive, exactly like the kind of man I'd always wanted to be with. His black eyes flashed, his springy curls were untidy and wild, and he had a mischievous but wide-open smile.

He was handsome and talented, and though he'd suffered many losses, he'd driven himself to become the new star of one of the best quartets in America. I knew if I met him right now, I would fall in love with him again.

An older, well-dressed couple studied the brochure beside me, and I wanted to tell them that the new violinist was my Tom. My very own Tom.

"He looks very young," the woman said.

"And very Greek," the man said for some reason. The woman glanced briefly at me, and I wondered if they could tell by my expression I was the new violinist's love.

Two girls with long skirts and long hair, music-student types, perused the brochures. They studied the picture of the Quartet, registered nothing in particular about Tom, then dropped the brochures indifferently into their bags.

I stuck five brochures in my purse.

"It's over an hour before show time," the usher at the inner lobby door told me. I gave him my name. He checked a list—not that important-looking on a scrap of yellow legal paper—and then let me in. My heels clicked across the empty lobby floor, and I remembered that walk across the dark stage at Merkin, how long it had seemed to take me to make it to the podium. My fingers were already trembling so much I worried my oboe would slip from my hands. Nothing in the world had prepared me for how scared and unprotected I would feel, standing in front of an orchestra, the spotlights on me.

Near the backstage door, behind the water fountain, Tom kept adjusting the nub of his tie and then peeking out around the fountain to see if I had arrived yet. His curls were pulled back into a loose ponytail, and he wore his new silk Armani suit. It made me nervous just to see how dressed up he was with his shined shoes, lapis cuff links, and Charivari tie. He was trying too hard, I worried people would think.

"My baby." I kissed him on the lips.

"I'm fine," he said, a laugh catching in his throat. The backstage door opened behind him and the knob hit him in the back.

"Watch out, kids," Andrew, the cellist, said. He was fleshier than in the picture. "Is this the girlfriend?" He raised his eyebrows.

"This is Gala, this is Andrew." Tom laughed again, pulling at his tie.

"Calm down. Relax. You play great. The next prodigy," Andrew said. "Are you a musician, too?"

"I'm an oboist." I thought of myself more as an oboist than a musician; I spent my days studying grains and shapes of cane.

"A beautiful oboist." Andrew made a point with his finger. "A beautiful, beautiful oboist."

Tom checked his watch. "Maybe the building will collapse and I won't have to play."

"Will you look at this guy?" Andrew said. "He's been like this all night. We couldn't even do a run-through."

"In the cab, I kept hoping for an accident," Tom said. "Just a broken leg. Nothing serious."

Even the memory of those hours before playing—at Merkin, before any audition—made my heart buzz with nerves. Before I had a chance to stop myself, I thought how glad I was that I was not playing tonight.

"There's your mother." Tom pointed to the ticket booth in the outer lobby. I expected, as always, to see my parents together. My father would be guiding my mother by her elbow, and every so often, he would whisper an observation to her and they might laugh together, I thought, but then I couldn't picture it. I couldn't conjure the image of them happy anymore; more likely, my mother would be annoyed at my father's distraction. She would be watching his eyes, anxious whenever an attractive woman stole his attention, even from across the room. She would accuse him of all he had not given her, just as she had the night they told me about the separation, driving him away when she meant to draw him closer.

From a distance, near the ticket booth, my mother was lovely. Her burgundy silk blouse and flowing skirt blew back against her body, against her small breasts and bone-rippled chest—the kind I always wanted to have—where her jade stone hung. As soon as she was close though, I could see the effects of all her sleepless nights. Her lids were swollen and mascara was blotched below her eyes. Uneven maroon ovals were painted on her cheeks.

"Darling." She brushed my cheek with her lips and then kissed Tom. I looked at Tom and Andrew to see if they saw something off about her.

"Very nice to meet you." Andrew shook her fingers with both hands. Neither he nor Tom noticed anything. She had tried to hide a bouquet of roses in her bag; some petals had fallen on the carpet, making a sort of garden around her. Tom pretended not to see them.

"Well! Look at you!" My mother glanced up and down Tom in his Armani suit, and Tom laughed self-consciously, pulling his shoulders together.

"I'm trying to fool everybody," he said.

"Why do you need to fool?" My mother smiled brightly at him. "I'm sure you sound beautiful. You know, I've never heard you before."

Tom laughed again. "I don't know."

"You'll be wonderful. Just relax. Take deep breaths, close your eyes." My mother closed her own eyes, and Tom stared at her, unable to stop smiling. "You don't want to hear it."

"I do," Tom said, but he had gotten too nervous to reassure her enough.

"Nobody listens to my advice." My mother pouted like a child to make everyone laugh, but I was the only one who did.

"Do you think Clinton will win?" I changed the subject to something my mother usually liked to talk about, but she only nodded, drawing in a breath. Tom ran his hand through his hair, glanced back at the outer lobby where ten to twenty people were already waiting.

"I better go," he said. His body was stiff when I hugged him good-bye, and I felt my mother observing how Tom and I held each other. When he disappeared backstage, she and I were alone in the lobby except for the ushers at the snack bar. Next to her, I felt too large and fleshy. That morning after she had swallowed the pills, I had seen her startling boniness under her nightgown. Her ribs rippled and her shoulder blades cut sharp angles. It was hard for me ever to imagine that my body had come from hers, that I was of her flesh.

"Are you happy with Tom?" She squinted at me.

"Happy?" I stumbled. I wasn't sure what the right answer was.

"Well, that's the important thing, isn't it? Don't be like me. Don't waste your life. If you're not happy, don't stay."

I nodded. All of a sudden, I couldn't remember whether I loved Tom or not.

"You have to watch out with these handsome men." She gave a short laugh. "He's successful like your father."

"He's nothing like Dad." I turned red.

"Do you know that all our friends knew about Marissa? I can't speak to them anymore." She pointed her finger at me and I stepped back as if I had been accused. "Do you know what it is like to be fooled?" She screwed up her face and I couldn't bear to look at her. Across the lobby, the ushers had begun tearing tickets. In half an hour Tom would be onstage. I was almost as nervous as if it were myself. I touched my stomach to show my mother where I was nervous.

"Now you know how I felt." My mother laughed. She was about to tell me a story of one of my early performances. I kept my expression blank to discourage her.

"Well, I was just worried about you." She laughed even more brightly. "You're my daughter, you know. Even if you wish you weren't."

"Mom . . ." My face reddened again and I clenched my teeth against the rage that suddenly pounded in me.

"It's okay. It's natural. I wished I had a different mother, too," she told me, her thin lips twisting horribly. "My mother never loved me."

"Of course she did. Don't say that."

"Parents don't always love their children. Mine didn't. Someday you'll realize how difficult it is. It's terrible to be a mother and watch your children perform. Remember when you played that nocturne?"

I shook my head to ward off any conversation about that performance. I was eleven, performing at Juilliard Prep, and it was the first time I learned what it was to be so nervous I felt like crumbling onstage. I quit the piano soon after that.

"You remember, you locked yourself in your room all night?"

"I don't know." I shrugged. In the outer lobby, a small line was forming in front of the ticket booth, and I kept hoping to see my father with his flying-around hair and funny felt hat, coming through the door, his arms open to both of us. "My big loves," he'd shout, not caring who heard. He would deny everything my mother accused him of. He would hold her until her sadness was gone, and then he would hug me, soothing away my tangle of anger.

"Dad was really hurt when I told him not to come." I said his name tenderly so my mother might feel tender, too.

"I saw him two days ago."

"You did?" For a moment I was hopeful. They had been together the night I called them late. "What happened?"

"Your father denies everything. He doesn't know what the truth is."

"How do you know he's not telling the truth?"

"Your father lied to me for ten years. Everyone knew," my mother snapped. "He told me you met Marissa."

I shook my head, denying it.

"What was she like?" My mother still had that twisted smile and her face was slightly flushed. "Tell me."

"I don't know." I shook my head. "I don't remember."

"You remember."

"I don't. I was in a daze."

"Tell me about her."

"I don't know anything," I said through my teeth.

"Was she pretty?"

I covered my eyes. "Don't do this."

"I want to know what's so good about her."

"There's nothing."

"Why did you decide to go out with her?"

I couldn't answer. A thin crowd of mostly women in long dresses and suited men milled in the lobby.

"All I can say is, never get married," my mother said with a short, brittle laugh.

I wouldn't. I was sure.

"Is Marissa still tough?" my mother asked.

"What do you mean?"

"I knew her a bit ten years ago."

"You did?"

"Even before your father. In fact, I introduced them. If you can believe it. She was in a meditation class with me, and I had her over with a bunch of friends, the ones your father always made fun of. She was different from the rest, though. She was hard, you could tell. She had just started in the art business. And she seemed like someone who would get exactly what she wanted."

I was not that sort of person. I would not get what I wanted. I was muddled and without confidence. The person who had been so proud and clear and happy for Tom just a half an hour ago did not seem like me at all. In the outer lobby on the ticket line, Pam and Kurt looked stunning and theatrical together. Kurt had on two dashing scarves, one red, one royal blue, which dangled to the floor.

Against the deep colors of the scarves, his skin was an even richer brown. Pam had on her long Versace black dress that flared at the bottom. I waved even though I knew they couldn't see me.

"Aren't they a pair. He's good to her, too," my mother said when Kurt touched Pam's shoulder as they moved up the ticket line.

Tall and fashionable, Kurt and Pam parted the crowd on their way to my mother and me. I kissed Pam hello and told her how glad I was that she had come even though she had to leave right afterward—her audition was the next day. As soon as the words were out of my mouth, I realized the mistake I had made. I pulled Pam to the side so my mother wouldn't ask her about the audition and then discover that I had not made the second round.

"Don't say anything to my mother," I whispered like a child.

"Poor Gala." Pam touched my arm. "Kurt! Stop it!" She spun suddenly, her flared dress twirling. Kurt had squeezed her by surprise. "What a menace." She rolled her eyes. I could tell how impressed my mother was by Pam's good looks and confidence, and I felt mean and jealous all over again.

On the ticket line were Noah and Rick, Tom's friends. I knew my mother would not like Rick, so I turned my back slightly so they wouldn't see me.

"You guys can go in," I told my mother and Pam, fearing something awkward would happen when Esther arrived. The last and only time my mother and Esther had met, Esther had gotten drunk and loud and too eager to please my mother, who appeared to her so much more moneyed and "cultured." My mother was in one of her cold, lonely moods when she had difficulty speaking, and she had made no efforts to be warm to Esther.

Esther appeared in front of me in her huge gold dress, and for the first time since I had known her, she was unable to speak. She clutched her glittery purse in her trembling hand.

"Will you look at this?" She let out a loud stream of air, taking in the luxurious lobby with expensive-looking people waiting to hear Tom play.

"I'm sorry for my rudeness." Esther shook my mother's hand, which appeared even more bony in Esther's thick fingers. "That I didn't say hello sooner. That's not like me, right?" she said to me.

"You must feel overwhelmed," my mother said stiffly. "This is quite an occasion. The first of many, we hope."

Esther let go of my mother and then didn't know what to do. "I love this girl." She locked my arm in hers and I let myself be pulled close. "I always tell her I'd be a very happy woman if I could see her and my son together."

"Not to move too quickly though." My mother waved her finger in the air.

"I'm Pam." Pam stepped in, offering her hand. "And this is Kurt. Kurt!" She yanked his red scarf. "My father was going to come, but then he wasn't feeling well."

"Your parents are divorced, too?" my mother said, and I cringed.

"My mother died," Pam said. "A long time ago. I'm used to telling people by now. Don't worry." She touched my mother's wrist. They both had red, manicured nails. My father had always put my mother down for her manicures, perfumes, and beauty treatments as if they had been the reason why she hadn't succeeded. "Frivolous," he'd said of her, and I believed him.

"Tom is so striking," my mother said, flipping through the brochure.

"A chip off the old block," Esther said, though really Tom looked exactly like his father, who was Italian, dark-eyed, and olive-skinned with the same rugged features as Tom. "How much more time do we have?"

"Ten minutes," my mother said, watching Esther size up the line for drinks.

"We better just go in," I said.

"I could use a good Stoli," Esther said. "He's not coming, is he?"

"He called two days ago," I said.

"I knew it." Esther shook her head. "That piece of shit. I can't tell if I'm relieved or what."

"This is Tom's father?" my mother said politely.

"He sired Tom. He ain't his father," Esther whispered loudly to my mother, who had taken another step back from her. "I don't know why he invited him in the first place."

Pam chattered with Esther about how talented Tom was as they walked ahead of my mother and me into the hall.

"Esther's out of control, isn't she?" my mother whispered to me.

"I don't know." I shrugged. I had never thought of Esther that way; I'd seen her as overbearing and loving. Ultimately loving.

"What do you think?" My mother locked her arm around mine just as Esther had. I had to force myself not to recoil.

"I don't know," I said, my most common answer to my mother.

We sat in the fifth row: Kurt, Pam, my mother, me, and then Esther. Our crossed legs made a neat row, our high heels hanging off our ankles. The hall was packed all the way up to the top. The stage was still lit. From behind the slim pillars of wood, Tom would soon emerge. I remembered how I'd huddled into the musty curtain at Merkin, knowing I would not be able to play. I was so faint and shaky that I would have done anything to stop the curtain from rising. The dread was almost as great now as I waited for Tom to play.

"I can't bear this," I said out loud without meaning to, and Pam and Esther glanced over at me. My mother was immersed in the program notes

"Everything okay?" Esther asked, fanning herself with a brochure. "Tom always tells me how worried he is about you."

"He does?" I tried not to sound surprised. I had felt only his impatience, not his worry.

"You're too sensitive. You can't worry so much over every little thing," Esther said.

Pam yawned into her program. "How nervous is Tom?"

"Tom was always a performer. A natural onstage," Esther answered. "Ever since he was little. He had the gift. Like his father. A trumpet player." She told me about how he and Tom used to put on shows together, a memory Tom had never shared with me. He'd said he couldn't remember anything about his father except that he gambled away all his mother's money and then that he was gone. The last time I'd asked about his father, he'd shrugged his shoulders and gotten annoyed when I pressed him. "You don't want to tell me?" I said. Which made him more distant, more remote from me. "You want me to give you whatever you want whenever you want," he told me. "I can't give you feelings on demand. Sorry."

It all became a knot.

I flipped through the program to find every mention of Tom's name and tried to remember the hopefulness I'd felt just a few months before when we first moved in together. Simple things I loved, like coming back from practicing in the evenings and finding Tom in one of his scraggly T-shirts, cooking one of his secret recipes, singing along to an Oistrakh or old Heifetz recording as Betty Blue chirped in the background. "You're my home," I'd say, coming up behind him, squeezing his soft chest.

My mother pointed to a man with gray, wavy hair in the front row. "He's from the *New York Times*. Your father knows him. Tom must have really practiced."

I nodded, though that wasn't really true. Until recently, Tom had only ever practiced three or four hours a day, which wasn't much for a violinist.

My mother placed her curved fingers on my arm and then whispered in my ear, "I wish it were you up there. You need to push yourself more, Gala."

I refused to look at her.

Her fingers pressed my forearm. "You didn't make the second round, did you?"

I shook my head, stared at the shiny wood floor of the stage, and the four music stands waiting. My mother's eyes were traveling my face, my neck, my shoulders, my breasts.

"Well," I told her, trying to sound snotty and unemotional, "maybe it will never be me up there."

The lights dimmed, the audience quieted. The backstage door slid open and the applause clattered through the hall. Tom looked misplaced and young onstage in his slightly large Armani suit and his hair splaying out of his ponytail.

"I don't know if I can watch this," Esther whispered to me.

Violin under his arm, Tom bowed and smiled at the audience amiably, as if he had done this a hundred times before. He did not look like the person who had stayed up all night, who needed to be coaxed to sleep. Carefully, without hurry, he adjusted his chair and music stand. When his music slipped a little off the stand, he smiled at the cellist and then took as much extra time as he needed. The audience was silent.

As the first violinist, Tom had to beat in the opening. He glanced at the rest of the quartet, then raised his bow to begin. As I watched his bow, ready to descend on the strings, I thought, What if he couldn't play, what if his fingers were shaking and he fell apart? What if he had not practiced meticulously and his playing was reckless, as it used to be? Or what if, I worried, he had tamed his playing so much that he had lost what was special about it? There was so much that could go wrong, but Tom's grin was huge, as if he just couldn't wait as his bow plunged to the strings.

The opening of the Bartók was pounding, rhythmic, and electrifying. Tom tossed his head, almost rose up off the seat. Every note was charged with energy and life, but there was no more sloppiness. He made no slips. Only once did he hit a high A way sharp, and I worried that would throw him—it would have thrown me—but Tom didn't even seem to have noticed. He'd learned how to forget mistakes and go on, a skill I'd never acquired. And for a moment, I blamed my failure on that lack—if only I'd learned not to hate myself over mistakes.

I looked sideways at my mother. Her face was tired, but her lips were tight, holding back a smile.

"He's wonderful," she whispered to me. She studied my face, and what had once been her smile turned anxious and small, and I could see no love or warmth in her eyes for me, only disappointment.

It would never be me up there, we both knew. I slumped in my seat and called myself all the ugly names I could think of.

At intermission, behind the crowd swarming around the snack bar, I saw my father. He was in back of the bar beside the table of glasses where nobody but the ushers were supposed to be. He had on his favorite green felt hat with the feathers, a faded blazer with a hole in the shoulder, and he squashed a brownie in his hand. The usher serving the drinks kept knocking into him and then glaring at him, but my father didn't notice. He was distracted, moving his lips, talking to himself, as he often did when unhappy.

It was not that he had shown up that stunned me; it was his loneliness, so much like my own, which I saw clearly for the first time.

"Is that Gordon?" My mother craned her neck over the crowd. "It's him," she exclaimed as if he might save her, as if all her anger and all the lies between them could vanish if they simply spoke the right words. For a moment, I hoped, as I had always relentlessly hoped, that my parents would fall in love again and I would have my family back.

My mother's burgundy skirt flowed against her body on her way to him, and my father's mouth twisted somewhere between sadness and longing, but when they finally came close enough to touch, they stayed a few feet apart. My father's head was pulled back, away from my mother, and his eyes looked bewildered and sad. My mother was trying to be charming, tilting her head, touching her long neck, which he had always adored.

I shouldered past a group of older women in velvet on my way to my parents, but something had changed between them in just that moment or two as I approached. My mother's fingers grazed her bone-rippled chest, stopped at the place where her jade necklace hung, and she said something, blinking quickly at my father: "For ten years, you betrayed me."

I stopped three feet away from them, waiting to hear my father's denial.

"You kicked me out," he hissed, slicing the air with his hand. "You kicked me out every year. That's not love. You think that's love?" He waved his finger in her face. The older women stared at him and moved away. My father had not denied anything.

"You ruined my life. I gave up everything, and for what?" My mother's voice broke, and my father stared up at the ceiling as if he were trying to make tears fall back into his eyes. When he looked back at her, he saw me from the corner of his vision.

"Sweetie." He opened his arms.

I let my grief overcome my face.

"I'm sorry," my father said. I took the apology to mean for everything, and I could have cried at the recognition. But I told him the opposite of what I felt.

"I don't want you here. I told you not to come."

I turned around to storm off but instead bumped right into Rick, Tom's friend.

"Tell me that wasn't amazing." He cornered me just as my father lumbered out the lobby doors.

There was still the second half of the concert, the Beethoven. My mother and I both sat still, not touching each other, our hands in our laps. Her flowers for Tom were crumpled on the floor, the fallen petals surrounding her feet. She squinted at the stage, her eyes nearly shut, either blocking out the music or hearing every note intensely.

When the concert was over, Tom dropped his bow to his side and sank back in his chair. His face shined with sweat and his loose curls stuck to his forehead. The audience clapped so hard the Quartet got three curtain calls. Tom bowed as if the whole audience were for him alone. I tried to catch his eyes, but he wasn't looking for me as we had planned. I stretched above the man in front of me, tried waving, but then quickly gave up. Tom's gaze swept grandly over all the rows of people clapping, taking it all in.

"Backstage is going to be a mess," Pam said to me. "Do you think Tom will mind if we go now?" She nodded to me instead of mentioning her audition the next morning.

We waded through the audience, funneling slowly through the exits. Esther, Pam, and Kurt were discussing the Bartók, the second slow movement, how beautiful and mysterious and sad, how perfect Tom's sound had been. My mother stood silent and apart, watching the seats emptying out, the rows abandoned.

"Mom." I touched her shoulder. The silk bagged over her shoulder bone, so thin I drew my hand back quickly.

"Let me wait a minute." She stared at the empty stage, the chairs pushed away from the stands. Performances didn't seem finished until everything had been put away.

In the backstage hall, a crowd of musicians and patrons swarmed the Quartet. I did not see Tom at first. The violist, second violinist, and cellist were packing up, teasing each other about that missed attack, that surprise fortissimo, the unexpected G-sharp from the violist—all the mistakes they'd had to recover from.

Behind them, Tom was with Glenn, the pianist who had recorded the albums with the Quartet. She had on knee-high leather boots, and her blond hair splashed all the way down her back to her suede miniskirt. She wore a shiny top as low-cut as the necklines I used to wear but hardly ever did anymore. The high swells of her breasts were scarless and creamy white. Tom was laughing, catching her eyes.

"I was nervous. You didn't see me shaking? My hands were like this." He showed her his trembling hands. His face lit up, dark eyes contagiously happy, happier than I'd seen him in months with me. Glenn tossed her head back and laughed.

"Oh, come on. You were great." She brushed his arm, letting her fingers linger on his wrist, and he did not move his hand away. He was watching her, the changing shape between her thighs as she shifted her hips.

"I just loved the first movement." Glenn shook her long hair off her shoulders and it flapped down her back. Tom's eyes swept down to her breasts.

"You're working that stage presence," she teased. "Those roguish looks. The ponytail." She tugged on the nub of hair and her fingers rested on the nape of his neck. Tom didn't move his head away. They were in suspense, daring each other, seeing how long the touch could last.

"I can't wait to see you perform," he said, breaking the moment, and suddenly they both laughed, their faces flushed.

I turned around, pushed past two fur-coated women and then past my mother, who was discussing the Bartók adagio with the cellist. My mother was expert in her musical understanding. This was the world she belonged in, and I could not bear any longer to think of all her disappointments and how similar mine seemed to be. She noticed me and waved, smiling brightly, and then she glanced over at Tom and Glenn, flirting with each other. Hand over her mouth, my mother gave me a shocked, conspiratorial look, as if the duplicity of men was a horrifying but inevitable fact of both our lives.

I found the EXIT door to the street. It was a one-way door, locked on the outside. Through the crowd of musicians and critics, Esther, Glenn, and Tom formed a tight circle, laughing together. Esther had her arm around Tom and was waving her hands, telling Glenn a story about Tom. "Really," Glenn said, and laughed, and Tom shrugged with mock bashfulness, and they all laughed again. They were already a family, I thought. Tom was leaving me behind.

I pushed open the EXIT door and it closed in back of me. The street was empty, lit in a gauzy yellow light from the Lincoln Center parking lots. Above me, the overpass hid the sky, and the sidewalk was new and white and endless-seeming. I started walking, then running toward the fuming buses and taxis and the broken traffic light on Broadway. Faster and faster I ran until my whole body felt tingling and free, and I thought what if I just didn't stop, if I just kept going.

At Tower Records, I had to catch my breath. I knew if I were to go home now, to simply leave without telling anyone, that my relationship with Tom would be over. The cold was biting, and my shoulders were bare. I hid in the half-shelter of a phone booth on the corner near Alice Tully. I wanted to call my father, I longed for his voice, his reassurance.

The last of the crowd trailed out of Alice Tully and hailed taxis in the street. The orange sign of Tower Records glared in the night. Neither my mother nor Tom came. I shivered and pressed my forehead against the cold metal of the phone booth.

It was Esther who found me.

"Where were you? Tom was looking all over. He didn't even say hello to anybody." She had her hands on her wide hips and was angry at me. Critics and important people, she said, had wanted to speak to Tom, but he was too worried about me. She asked me what I was doing here outside on the corner and I had no answer.

"No reason and he's all upset." She wouldn't meet my eyes again. "Now I have to go find him." She argued with the guard at the lobby door to let her back in.

A few minutes later, my mother and I were stepping to keep warm beside the tall Plexiglas advertisements in front of Alice Tully. "I can't take this." She clutched herself with her arms. She had only a shawl over her silk blouse. "I'm going to go. You know how I am. I'm too fragile for this. Are you sure you're all right?" she asked for the second time, and I nodded, facing away to the line of yellow taxis halted at the light.

"There's nothing more difficult than love. Except maybe music," she added with a short laugh to make me laugh, too. "Either way you have to confront yourself. Something I was never good at."

The broken light changed, and the traffic lurched forward.

"You don't mind if I go?" My mother shivered.

"No," I said, though it wasn't what I meant. I needed her suddenly, just as she was leaving.

My mother brushed my cheek with her cool lips. "Maybe you'll be better than me. At all things."

Up Broadway she went quickly on the heels she hardly ever wore. Her walk was stiff, her feet hardly leaving the pavement, and she stumbled. Alone, she stopped to steady herself. She hugged herself, glancing up at the moonless sky, and then began walking again. I had the urge to follow her, to beg her to hold me and also to let me protect her from anything that might happen to her in this night alone. Instead, I stayed separate. I watched her until I could no longer distinguish her in the night, the streets, the rest of the crowd.

I leaned against the Plexiglas and watched the yellow taxis press down to the hub of Lincoln Center where I'd taken my audition, a month ago. The bright lights inside Avery Fisher, where Mr. Barret played, were being shut off floor by floor, leaving a labyrinth of shadowy escalators inside the glass walls. I thought it for the first time then. Maybe I could not go on.

Tom hung his head, coming down the long sidewalk outside the parking lots. Noah and Rick were speaking emphatically, waving their hands on either side of him, but he didn't look up. His black hair was loose, and his jacket blew open. When he saw me, his mouth strained open as if he were about to say something important to me. I touched my neck, bare in the darkness and streetlights.

"That's it." Tom flopped his hands at his sides. He avoided my eyes and then kept a few feet away from me as we crossed Broadway to Mc Guills, our old Juilliard hangout. I was sure he knew why I had left. I kept expecting him to apologize to me and I only vaguely considered that I should apologize to him, too.

I followed Rick and Noah into Mc Guills, which was packed with college students. Girls at the bar sang "Respect" along with Aretha Franklin booming on the jukebox. On the television above the bar, Clinton supporters were cheering, waving their signs, waiting for Clinton to give what must be a victory speech. I motioned for Tom to look at the TV, but he had stopped in the entrance of the bar and would not follow me in. In the splashing white light above the doorway, his face looked harsh, eyes hollowed and circled in darkness from so many sleepless nights.

I gave him a stupid, playful flick of my wrist signaling him to come in. Tom shook his head, his hand cupped above his eyes to block the light. "Why'd you leave?"

"You know." My face reddened at the thought of him and Glenn, her fingers on his neck, his gaze sweeping over her body, and then the extra humiliation of my mother seeing it all. I stared into Tom's tired eyes so he would understand.

"I can guess. Knowing you," he said, gathering anger. "But it's so ridiculous, so selfish, that I don't even want to believe it's true."

I spoke through my shame. "It's ridiculous that I would get upset at you flirting with someone?"

Tom muttered something and looked up at the bald light, then back at the door to Columbus Avenue as if he were considering leaving.

"This was the most important day of my life. You only think of yourself."

"You were flirting with Glenn. She touched you." Hearing how ridiculous I sounded, I laughed. "You have everything. You're leaving me behind."

A guy with a crew cut knocked Tom's violin on his way into the restaurant. Tom hissed something at him and then looked up at me for the first time that night. "You know what? So what if for one minute, one moment, I was flirting with Glenn. I didn't mean anything by it. I was just happy."

I tried to swallow his honesty. I repeated his words over and over to myself—so what, so what—I had done worse than flirting. Much worse. Let it go, I told myself, but my pride wouldn't let me.

"You humiliated me," I snapped. His eyes searched my face for signs of love, but I refused to give him any. "I wish you'd never won."

Tom looked back at the door to the street. "You know what? I don't need this." He shook his head. "I really don't. Let's go. I want to go home."

That night in bed, I apologized over and over for what I'd said. I'd been selfish, I told him. I hadn't shown him how proud I was of him for this night and for everything he had accomplished.

"I'll make it up to you," I said, but he curled away from me and faced the wall. When I woke up in the morning, he was gone. He'd left me a note on the refrigerator. "I just went to practice. I'll call you later. Love, Tom." I knew he had weighed those words. He didn't want to say anything he couldn't take back later.

13

*M*r. de Laney always spoke practically. From his immaculate reed-making desk, he'd squint up at me through his black reading glasses. "It's a matter of getting from point A to point B," he'd tell me. "If I can do it, you can do it." He described himself as someone with minimal talent who'd worked hard and, with some streak of luck, ended up as one of the world's most famous oboe players. He'd start out his stories with his back to me, staring out onto his patio, the ordinary white table and chairs. Gradually he would face me, his arms folded when he finished his point. "I was not especially talented. Not like some other people. I always had to work."

I nodded at him as he wanted me to do, never correcting his assumption that I had neglected to practice hard at some crucial point.

It was the first week in November, the day after Tom's concert. He had not called me all day and I thought he was leaving me. Every hour the phone didn't ring confirmed that belief. Robin's mother, Florence, called and I jumped, hoping it was Tom. She told me they had chosen a new oboe and couldn't wait to play it for me. Then she thanked me for how much I had inspired Robin.

I *was* a good teacher, I reminded myself.

In the late afternoon, I taught George, my only beginning piano student, in a practice room at Manhattan School of Music. He was a burly, good-looking guy who worked in the Thirty-fourth Street post office and took night classes at John Jay College of Criminal Justice. He wanted to learn to play well enough to be in a band with his friends, but his fingers were stiff and uncoordinated, and truly, I thought he had no ear. I'd attempted to make him recognize harmonies, but they all sounded alike to him.

"I'm hopeless."

"Don't say that, George. You play very well. You're not hopeless at all." I patted his shoulder with as much professional affection as I could, but I wondered if it was as clear with me as it was with George—that I was simply not good enough.

Later that day, I sat on the piano bench for a long time before playing, listening to the intricate, abstract harmonies of Stephen's symphony in the next room. The wind blew in through the window, open to the subway tracks wrapping up into Harlem. I shivered, feeling the cool against my face and chest, but I did not brace myself. I made myself feel it—whatever the cold wind brought. On top of the upright piano, my oboe looked small and abandoned, and I felt bad for it, lying in the cool air, which could crack the wood. When I'd first bought it, I would never let it go from my sight, and I couldn't wait to play every day and hear the sound of my own voice through its rich, sweet wood.

I soaked up a reed in the water, which had turned cold (I had to squeeze the reed over and over to make it open enough), and I played without listening to myself, without judgment, without that critical ear between myself and my sound. I did not think about what notes to play. I let my fingers move, releasing keys as they wanted, as if they were receiving signals from the very source of my music and needed no intervention from my mind. I did not listen to the music as if it were separate from me; my music came from that buried place before words, before thought.

Stephen had stopped playing in the room next door and I knew he was listening to me. I closed my eyes and began another of Britten's *Metamorphoses After Ovid*, "Pan," *who played upon the reed pipe which was Syrinx, his beloved*. I called out, trying to cut through the walls to him. My sound whipped and coiled, then was warm, so warm I felt as if I were reentering that place again where Syrinx had been.

When I was through, I opened the door to Stephen's practice room but found it empty. Of course, he would not want to see me. I had stopped practicing at Manhattan School, and I had not even attempted to contact him to explain why I'd run off.

In a nearby practice room, a pianist was playing the somber opening chords of the *Pathétique* Sonata, the piece my mother loved, and all of a sudden, I missed our afternoons together, how we'd sit together at the piano, debating interpretations of Bach or Chopin or Beethoven. She would get so huffy over how much to bring out the bass line or what fingering to use. "I just know. Don't argue," she'd scold, but then neither of us could help from bursting into laughter as we pounded the keys louder and louder to prove who was right.

Inside the practice room, the pianist played the tragic opening of the *Pathétique* once more. I tightened my grip on my oboe case. It seemed strangely weightless.

"That was beautiful before," Stephen said from the other end of the hall. In the shadowy corner, his face looked grave. He spoke in a whisper. "I don't think I've ever heard such playing."

"I just remembered how much I love music."

We faced each other without speaking as the pianist's runs darted down the halls. Stephen was even taller than I remembered—I came up only to his chin—and bulkier. His chest was sturdy, pulling at the buttons of the navy blue shirt I'd seen neatly folded on his bed. He wore his old blazer and penny loafers, which I imagined he'd bought quickly, without thinking.

"Did you like the Beethoven tapes?"

"They were wonderful. Thank you," I answered, but I had behaved badly with him, too, thanking him only with that fast note on a paper scrap.

Stephen clamped his lips, digesting the situation, all of my lapses, and I prepared myself to tell him about Tom.

"I was thinking of leaving you another note," he said. "Either that or letting the whole thing go." He leafed through his music in his worn briefcase, then handed me a blank, sealed envelope. Inside was a letter in his tiny scrawl. *I enjoyed being with you so much the other day. I think we have something, but I don't know why you left. A drink, coffee, tea? Soon?*

I held the note in both hands, rereading it, and Stephen smiled at me, almost apologetically. He needed me—more than Tom, more than Pam, more than my father, who had his new life, and I felt such a tenderness for him that I broke all my vows to myself and ignored my good sense.

"Yes," I said, but then regretted it immediately.

Sure that we would bump into Tom, I could not relax as we headed to the bar on Amsterdam. I had always been a slow, dreamy walker, but Stephen was even slower, tapping and catching the sidewalk ahead of him with his black umbrella. He was telling me about his grandfather, about how badly he'd felt leaving him behind, first to go to the University of Virginia, then to come to New York.

"I was closer to my grandfather than to anyone in the family. He wanted me to spend my life with him playing blues guitar."

I nodded, only half-listening. A gnarly-haired woman, a mother of one of Tom's students, was hurrying up the sidewalk toward us. She grunted as she passed, her eyes shifting from me to Stephen, and I thought for sure she would say something to Tom. Something about how she'd seen me on the street the other night with someone else.

I'd chosen the New Amsterdam Bar because it was out of the way of any walk Tom might take home, but when Stephen and I got there, I remembered why I hadn't gone there in years. It was huge and cafeteria-like with low tables, and the jukebox was playing a Whitney Houston hit. The waiters all wore red and black. Except for a few Columbia students at the back tables, there were hardly any people.

"What'll it be?" A fiftyish waitress with a rough, square face rattled off a wine list, which I forgot immediately. I copied Stephen, ordering the Merlot.

"You've been nervous ever since we left school. What's wrong?" Stephen clasped his hands on the red tablecloth, and I stared at the little blond hairs, the cared-for nails, and soft tips, which had traced my back so gently.

"I'm always nervous."

"That's not true. Only now and when you left my apartment. Who was that woman?"

"You mean that woman on the street?" I laughed again. "Just someone I knew from a long time ago."

I drank half my wine as soon as it arrived, even though it was cheap and watery.

"Tell me about your ex-wife. What was she like?" I blurted out, then apologized, but Stephen said he didn't mind talking about her. He wanted to, in fact. It had been so long since he had spoken intimately with anyone.

"She's the complete opposite of me. Outgoing, bubbly, always in control."

"That's sort of like you," I put in, remembering how he'd touched me so secretively in front of his stove. "Quietly in control."

Stephen laughed out loud, then wiped his mouth with his napkin.

"Have I discovered your secret?"

"I don't know." His neck was a little red above his blazer. "That's what my ex-wife used to say. That I kept quiet but then always found a way to get what I wanted."

"Is that true?" I raised my eyebrows. It had come out more flirtatiously than I'd intended, or maybe that was just what I told myself as an excuse. Maybe I had meant to lure Stephen closer again and for him to catch my eyes and say: "I don't know yet. I hope so."

I drank my wine to the very bottom. "Tell me more about you."

"Ask me something."

"What's your favorite color?"

"I don't know. Blue maybe."

"Your favorite part of New York?"

"My apartment. My home . . ." He pulled at his chin, rough with blondish stubble.

"Why did you break up with your wife?" I asked him cautiously.

"We were lonely together." He cleared his throat. "And she left me for someone else."

"That's terrible."

"I shouldn't have told you that. You may get the wrong impression."

"Why would I?"

"If she left me, maybe she had good reasons. You might think that."

"I'm sure it was complicated."

"I wasn't good to her."

"I can't imagine that."

"I seem so good?"

"Yes." I nodded.

"I'll be much better next time." His eyes dug into mine, melting any distance between us, and I forced myself not to look away.

Between our new full drinks on the table, Stephen spread the score of his new piano piece, for which he'd just won $5,000 and a performance at Merkin Hall.

"Wow," I said. "You really will be famous."

"Maybe." He smiled his slow smile without opening his lips. "What do you think?" He nodded to the intricate, meticulously notated music. I could imagine the overall structure and I could hear some of the phrases in my head, but much of it was vague to me. I needed to play it.

"My ears aren't good enough," I admitted. "I bet you could look at any new score and hear every part."

"There are different kinds of talent."

"Good, bad, and mediocre." I listed the first two on my fingers and then, with the last, pointed to myself.

"You put yourself down too much. I wish you wouldn't." He set down his drink and then hummed the melody of his new piece in his sweet, incongruous tenor. I tried to make my way through the complicated harmonies and hum along with him, but we hit a tritone by mistake.

"Oh my God." I covered my ears the way I used to at my father's out-of-tune singing, and Stephen laughed and said something about how we were almost, but not quite, ready to take our act on the road.

"Tell me about the South," I said. "It's so foreign to me."

"Maybe I could take you sometime," he said, a nervous flutter in his throat. "Have you ever taken a road trip before?"

"Not a long one."

"We could make it to Mississippi in two days."

For a moment, I believed it might happen. I had never done what wasn't expected of me. Free. I'd never felt free, but I imagined I might in a car heading south with Stephen. He would drive, telling me stories of the country I was seeing for the first time, and we would talk in a way I could never talk with Tom. I would be grateful that I had not spent my life unhappily, afraid to leave. It was not that I had difficulty loving, it was that I had not found the right person to love. As if he knew my thoughts, Stephen gave me such a warm, full smile that I said to him to set distance, "You're such a romantic. So earnest."

"Earnest?" He set his wineglass down hard, spilling a little. Tipsy, I waved my arm, joking, to the waitress to order our third round. Stephen laughed as if he'd thought I was funny even though I wasn't.

"You have to understand, I don't trust romance," I explained in a false, theatrical voice.

"Why not?"

"I don't trust promises. You must feel the same way."

"No." He shook his head. "I could trust someone again."

"My parents were really in love at first and look where that got them."

"What made them break up?"

"They were mean to each other. Neither of them fully believed they were loved. And my father did something." I stopped myself. I always gave too much away with Stephen.

"What did your father do? You don't want to tell me?"

"My mother said my father had an affair for ten years." I laughed a little, embarrassed, but Stephen winced, feeling it with me.

"You must really feel betrayed."

"I can't even explain how much." Tears filled my words, as if they had been there all along, just waiting. "You're so easy to talk to. Too easy. I tell you too much."

"What's too much?"

"We've only known each other a few months."

"I feel like we've known each other much longer than that."

I finished my wine, afraid to meet his eyes, which I knew were searching for mine.

"It's my mother's despair that's the worst." I worried if I told him my mother had threatened suicide, he would see me as shamefully sad.

"I'm sorry you're having such a hard time." He stroked my wrist briefly, and at that moment, I would have done anything to feel his hand again. His touch was just as I'd remembered it, just as I'd longed for, so confident and tender, but I kept telling myself no, just sit here, don't do anything, because I was always going too far with men, needing their touch too much, and I liked being pushed against walls, eyes slammed shut, and I could fool around and slam around and love it and need it, but when it went too far, I disappeared and stopped feeling anything.

"Are you drunk?" Stephen asked, because I must have been hanging my head too long.

"A little." I sat forward on the table, pressing my elbows together. My breasts rose over the top of my sweater. "Do you want me drunk?" I said, mostly mocking, because I knew I could get away with this and almost anything.

"Not so much," he said carefully, "that I don't know if you're really here with me or not."

"How would you know anyway?"

"I could tell." He pressed his leg against my inner thigh.

"And what if you couldn't tell? I like to perform. I'm a good liar."

Our waitress interrupted us.

"Get another round," Stephen said.

"I thought you were so sincere." I cut him down again. "No more for me," I told the waitress. I felt embarrassed excusing myself to go to the bathroom in front of Stephen, but it was all the wine. Beside the empty bar, the waiters all stood at the cash register, and I was ashamed to be swaying on my feet. I hoped no one was watching as I held on tight to the banister, down the steps.

By the pay phone and bathrooms, I let myself stumble because it was lonely and ugly with dirty red wallpaper. I looked at myself in the mirror, and first I thought how pretty and then how plain I was. I was wearing my tight red sweater, and I ran my hands over my breasts, wishing my hands were Stephen's. I thought of how lonely I'd been with Tom lately, and that if Stephen kissed me just one more time, it wasn't so bad, so inexcusable.

Leaning against the pay phone outside the bathroom, I felt heavy and drunken and as if I had to go to the bathroom again. I dialed my number, but Tom wasn't there.

"It's me," he said in the message he'd left for me. "I'm sorry about our fight last night . . . I'm really sorry . . . it was my fault, too, I should have been more understanding. I love you."

I listened three times, and I repeated to myself how much I loved Tom and that the only reason I was with Stephen was because I was upset and not because I really cared.

When I hung up the phone, Stephen was right behind me.

"Who were you calling?" he asked, though he must already have known. Instead of waiting for my answer, he leaned toward me, kissed me gently, his stubble tickling my cheek.

"This is right," he whispered, guiding me back against the wall. His spicy cologne tingled in me, surprising me again. His fingers circled my nipples, and I let go of my resistance and arched my back. He was so good, so knowing, I didn't know if Tom had ever touched me with such care.

"You're so tender." I caught my breath as he rubbed his finger over my panty hose, and I thought I had been waiting my whole life for such tenderness.

"We're right for each other. Believe me," he whispered, and I embraced him, bunches of his wool blazer in my hands.

"Come home with me, Gala. Please."

"Yes." I nodded as his hand found its way under my panties. He held it there, still, making me wait. I wanted to feel this and everything else.

"Tell me how to do it." He pressed his hips against me, then he moved my hand down to his long, straight-up cock. He wanted to be inside of me, as close to me as only Tom had been for the longest time, and suddenly I pictured Tom, who, at this very moment, must have been opening the door to an empty apartment, to the home we had made for ourselves only a few months before. He trusted me.

I pushed Stephen away slightly. "Someone might see us."

"What are you afraid of?" he whispered.

"I have to tell you something." I hid my face from him, my footsteps loud and clumsy up the stairs, and I gave him some money so he could handle the paying.

Outside, on Amsterdam Avenue, the occasional car lights glistened on the wet, sleek tar. The drizzle chilled me and made me feel raw and less drunk. I shivered and hugged myself the way my mother had hugged herself outside Alice Tully the night before. I remembered how she had stumbled disappearing into the night, and suddenly, I didn't know what I was doing, leaving her alone for so long, neither comforting her nor keeping her safe.

Stephen pushed out the restaurant door, buttoning his blazer with one hand and popping up his umbrella with the other. I said it quickly. "I have a boyfriend."

Stephen's fingers stopped at the buttonhole, but his voice was firm and barely wavering. "I thought so."

A car sprayed gutter water beside us. It felt cold and grimy on my tights.

"Always happens," I said.

"So what are you going to do? You can't keep running away from me. We have something special." Stephen reached for my hand, but I pulled it away and kept space between us under the umbrella. We were only a few blocks from my apartment; Tom was always out at this hour, buying his favorite treats.

"It's not real. I already have a home and a life." I faced the steep hill to Broadway, toward my home, but I thought if Stephen were to touch me, if he were to place his hands gently on my shoulders, beneath my hair, I would not refuse him. Holding him, just moments ago, I had felt so sure.

A skinny man with red pants swerved toward us, his tongue hanging out. I jumped a little, but Stephen was squinting off into the distance. His loneliness in New York and his wife's abandonment tugged at me.

"Listen. I'm worse than you think. I'm horrible, in fact." I tried a little laugh. "You need someone who can really be there for you."

"If we were together, I'd give you so much, you'd never doubt yourself again."

"No one can solve me but me," I told him, but I wanted so much to believe him, to give myself over.

"You need support. I can give you that."

"You'd get bored."

"We're right together," he repeated, stroking my hand as if he knew that it was his touch that tempted me most. "You're not happy."

"Yes, I am."

"I know what it's like. You can't stay if you're not happy."

"Are you so happy now, alone?"

"At least I have the hopes of it. You could spend your whole life settling for something, but never being truly happy."

I thought of my mother and how much better off she would have been if she'd had the courage to leave my father years earlier. She had let her life slip away, I thought, but I said to Stephen, "Maybe happiness doesn't depend on other people. Maybe it's all here." I pointed to my heart, but Stephen ignored me.

"What are you afraid of?"

"Nothing." I gave him a quick, feeble good-bye kiss on the cheek. Hurrying away from him up my block, I half hoped he would call me back. The elevated subway raced into the night, and I dropped my head back, opened my mouth to taste the cold, clean rain. I imagined suddenly that it might be easy to make a break, to escape everything and take a chance with Stephen. The pain of leaving Tom would be quick and sharp, like ripping off a bandage. I would hold my breath, and then it would be over.

"I missed you." Tom jumped up from the couch, from his Oreos and David Letterman and Betty Blue chirping above him. "I don't want to fight anymore." He fell onto me heavily, his face moist and warm against my neck, right where Stephen had kissed me ten minutes before. The cheap wine soured my breath, and I shrank from Tom's arms.

I stalled, hanging my wet jacket carefully on the coatrack. On the way upstairs, I had practiced the words that would end everything between us.

"Where were you?" Tom made his sad clown's face, an expression he'd gotten from me. His curls were still gelled back from his concert, and I remembered how we had stayed up together the night before he played and how I'd stroked his forehead in my lap, trying to soothe away his worry.

"Out with Pam," I explained breezily, then sat down on the couch and fumbled through the messy pile of music for my cigarettes. My confusion and ability to lie shocked me, and my fingers trembled, pressing the match to the box. I was imitating my father, but deception did not feel sly or powerful as I might have expected; it felt weak.

"You could have called or something. Or just left a message."

"I did call. About an hour ago."

"I was home an hour ago."

"No, you weren't," I said, and then for some reason, I laughed.

"You're drunk."

"No, I'm not," I said in a stupid, drunken-sounding way.

"I can smell the wine. I don't know why you're denying it. I don't care if you have a drink. I don't." The growling beat of a slow, sexy rap blared by in a car on Broadway. When the car was gone, it seemed too silent, bright, and cluttered in our apartment.

"I keep trying to give you what you need. But it's never enough," Tom said. His eyes were dark and muddied with feeling, and suddenly I saw the person I'd first fallen in love with: soulful, sweet, and a little sad. I thought I might be like my mother, a bottomless well, demanding and exhausting to people.

"This should be the best time of my life," Tom said. "I don't know what's wrong with me. I'm like a mute. A deaf, dumb mute and I don't know anything." He wiped his hand across his forehead. "Sometimes it's like you said, I wish I'd never won."

"You don't wish that. I can't believe you would. You're playing with some of the greatest people," I said. "Like you. You're great, too."

"I don't know." He shook his head, but I could tell a part of him thought it was true, and my envy of his confidence, and the affirmation he'd gotten from the world, burned in me.

"I'd do anything to be in your place."

Tom looked straight at me, for the first time taking me in with all my jealousy.

"You'll get something, too," he said, but I could tell he wasn't sure about that anymore.

I lit a cigarette, pretended to enjoy it. Even Tom no longer believed in me.

"Aren't you making a tape for Boston Pops?"

I flushed with the disgrace of it "I'm not sure if I should try. I was thinking of doing Oakland instead."

Oakland was a small, barely decent orchestra upstate.

"Go for Boston. You have to. Come on." His encouragement had too much effort in it, and I hid my face beneath my hair. In the corner by the shelves was a new Barneys bag.

"I was so lonely today," he said with an embarrassed laugh, following my eyes. "I had to buy myself something. Two hundred dollars." He winced, holding up a plush wool sweater.

"I love you, Tom," I said, but halfway through the words, I doubted myself. I knew nothing of my ability to love. Tom looked to the floor and I saw how it would all happen—in my confusion, my sad selfishness, I would lose him. Alone, after everything with Stephen, a stranger, had proven to be meaningless, I would realize all I'd had.

"Maybe we just need to talk more. We never talk," I said. "We don't understand each other."

"We've been together for nearly three years. If we don't understand each other now"—he stopped for a breath that caught in his throat—"maybe it's just not working."

We held each other's eyes, and I was afraid if I looked away, he would be gone.

"I just moved all my stuff here. This is my home." He shielded his eyes with his hands, and I held him, his folded arms between us.

"How can I make you happy, Tom?"

"Just love me. Don't stop."

He hung his head as we walked to the bedroom hand in hand. He lay on the bed, and in the shadowy darkness, I lifted his back, like sad, heavy dough in my hands, and took off his sweater.

"I do love you, Tom," I whispered in his ear. I kissed his neck, the sore from his violin, and then his chest, rough with dense curls. I kissed down to his belly button, usually ticklish, but now he didn't move, didn't even begin to laugh. I unzipped his jeans and took out his cock, which was only just hard enough, and licked him up and down.

He touched my shoulders, and for a moment I hoped he wanted me to quit. Instead he pulled me up to him and kissed my lips, ran his hand up my thigh where Stephen had touched me just an hour before. I lay still to feel Tom's fingers. I was wet, wet from the whole evening, but I didn't feel anything.

"Is this right? Is this okay?"

"Yes." I closed my eyes, buried my face in his neck.

"I don't know what to do." He stopped touching me.

Part Three

14

On the A train to Brooklyn, I tried not to lose myself to anxiety and to study the Vivaldi score. Pam had recommended me for a gig she didn't want. She'd told me the part was easy, but still I dreaded the moments I knew I would mess up. Tom had left in the morning for Eastman, the music conservatory in Rochester, New York. Neither of us had been able to sleep the night before. Tom had watched television in the living room, and I had stayed in bed, startling awake all night.

"It's just a week," he said in the morning, his voice hoarse from lack of sleep. We hadn't slept apart for over a year. Neither of us mentioned that, in a hopeful mood, we had discussed taking this trip together. We went through the whole morning, coffee and breakfast and him packing, being courteous with each other and avoiding what was most important.

Finally, at the door, his violin over his shoulder, Tom kept his back to me and said, "I just need to do this alone. Is that terrible?"

I knew if I pleaded, told him I needed him, he would take me with him. But after what I had done with Stephen, I didn't feel I could ask anything of him and I wasn't sure if I wanted to.

Twenty minutes after he left, both my parents called, but I didn't pick up for either. Betty Blue chirped above their voices on the machine. Both had read a review of Tom's quartet in the *New York Times,* which I had forgotten to look for.

"I'm sorry," my father said wearily into the machine, "if I hurt you by coming to the concert. Your mother and I have had a painful time. I'm sure you and Tom have seen the wonderful review in the *Times*. Congratulations. Please call me to let me know you're okay. Your old dad is worried about you."

My mother read a part of the review. " 'Tom Bassi, the newest member of the group, played not only with technical brilliance, but with a freshness and energy that brought new life to the Prokofiev Quartet and to the music.' Couldn't do any better than that!" my mother squealed, and I found myself smiling at the machine, as excited and proud for Tom as I had been before the concert. I had lost the feeling so quickly. I was always like that—feeling love, then losing it.

Nostrand Avenue was farther out than I'd expected, and it was in Bedford-Stuyvesant, something Pam had either not known or not mentioned. The A train emptied by the time it passed Fort Greene. The only people on the train were two teenage boys with pimply faces and tattooed arms, and a man half-wrapped in a blanket, sleeping on one of the end seats. Shafts of light streaked across his swollen feet when the train went above ground at Nostrand Avenue. Outside, the platform was empty. Before me was what seemed like miles and miles of abandoned streets and boarded-up brownstones.

I stuffed my oboe in my knapsack, a conspicuously fine brown leather, and turned inward the glittery amethyst of my ring. The heels of my boots made a hollow, metallic ring on the steps down to the street. I was alone at the bottom of the stairs. Down the avenue, there were only burned-out houses, one after the other, and alleyways with cement, shoots of grass, and broken bottles. Ten feet ahead, two men in hooded jackets huddled together on the corner.

"Look at those titties, look at those titties," they chanted as I passed.

My hands were in fists in my pockets. My anger changed to shame as I remembered how I'd pressed up against Stephen, letting him feel my wetness. A huge abandoned brick building surrounded by a split-open fence took up the whole next block. The stone letters on the graffitied entrance read Public School 165. The empty schoolyard was littered with broken glass.

I could not find one street name that resembled a name on the conductor's directions. I knew Tom would have told me to turn back.

He had grown up in a similar neighborhood, and he would never have let me walk here alone. He didn't even know where I was now. Anything might happen to me, and our last words to each other would have been the disappointed words of a failing love.

Finally I found Avenue J and the white church. The paint was chipping off, the shutters hanging on their hinges. Alone in the small entrance, I could hear an out-of-tune version of the Vivaldi continuo part. The playing was coming from a large, echoing room; the sound hung all around me, but I couldn't tell which closed door it was coming from. I opened one door, which lead down a narrow, broken-down staircase. The next door opened into a room with a stopped-up toilet and a string hanging from the bare bulb.

"Are you our oboist?" A man peeked out of the third and last door. He was dark-skinned and round and soft-looking in corduroys and a burly wool sweater, the kind my father would wear. Under his arm, he clamped a score and conducting baton.

"You're Mr. Baxter." I grinned with relief and apologized for being late.

"We were wondering what happened." He looked at his watch, which was sleek and expensive and comforting to me.

I was the only white person in the church, and my whiteness seemed to glow all over me. A fiftyish woman in a blue-flowered dress stared at me from the audience of fold-up chairs. On the stage, the small chorus of junior high school kids were fooling around, slapping each other's legs. One boy, who looked Caribbean, pointed at me, and the girl next to him kicked his ankle. The gray-haired woman at the old upright piano shushed them, then looked around to see whom they were pointing at.

There was no orchestra. Only a violinist, one cellist, and one violist.

"I know you," the violist said as if he weren't glad at all to recognize me. He had enormous, thick-framed glasses and his legs were so long, he had to wrap them twice around the legs of his chair.

"From Juilliard," I said, worrying that he might have been one of those in the Merkin orchestra who had seen my humiliation. "You're Sylvester."

"Silver," he corrected, then mouthed to me, "This gig is the fucking pits."

"Sucks," I whispered through my teeth, though it was the only new gig I'd gotten in months. I put my reed in to soak in my film-container cup of water. It was an old reed, my audition reed. I hadn't been making reeds steadily since then.

"Who are you studying with now?" Silver asked, and I was sure he'd heard about what had happened, all of it, and how Mr. Barret had turned against me. I was glad to say Mr. de Laney, which impressed him.

"Why don't we rehearse the first chorus," Mr. Baxter said, licking his index finger before turning each page of his score. "I'll give you a measure for nothing. Ready?" He caught the eyes of each member of the chorus.

They all straightened and faced forward except one girl, big for her age in a bright pink top, who smacked her lips as if she couldn't care less.

"Ms. Easton," Mr. Baxter warned. "Measure for nothing." He conducted with precise, well-schooled hand strokes.

"Gloria! Gloria!" the chorus sang. Their voices quivered with false vibrato. Only one guy was covering the bass part, and with no one to follow, he kept losing his pitch.

"Jesus Christ," Silver muttered. The violinist shook his head at him, scolding. He was an older man with white hair and checked pants. His violin was a cheap student instrument with a tinlike sound. We sounded terrible together. Silver hacked through the harmony twice as loud as the violinist and I played the melody. No one followed Mr. Baxter's beats. I stuck with the old violinist, whom I felt bad for, and as I played, I thought of how I might recount the story of this gig later, and then I thought I wouldn't tell anyone about it at all.

"Let's rehearse the Sarabande. The oboe and soprano duet," Mr. Baxter said.

The girl in the pink top stepped forward. One of the boys shook his head at her wide behind, and another one whispered. She wiped her forehead, cleared her throat. In the audience, the blue-flowered-dressed woman fidgeted in her seat.

"Are you ready?" Mr. Baxter asked. All the other musicians relaxed back in their chairs, watching me.

"Ready," I said. Mr. Baxter raised his baton. In the small, high-ceilinged hall, my sound was sweet and resonant, and I thought maybe it was beautiful. I'd worked all my life for it. I let myself lilt and swing with the 6/8 dance. It always snuck up on me, my love of music. Just when I thought it was gone, I would feel it again.

The soprano caught her breath three times before Mr. Baxter made a huge swooping arm motion to signal her in. The girl's voice was shaking so much she couldn't hold the pitch or the rhythm. Her time was all over the place. I tried to help her and to keep the duet together by playing so strongly that she would have to follow my beat. But she was still too nervous to hit any of the high notes. One of her high G's cracked so much that, behind her, the boys, who had been covering their mouths, burst into laughter.

"Excuse me." Mr. Baxter beat his baton on the podium. "Mr. Regis and Mr. Brown," he said to the boys.

"Like a wolf," Mr. Regis hooted. "She sounds like a wolf."

The girl sobbed into her hands, and I wanted somehow to comfort her and take away her shame. I knew how long she would remember this day.

"You be quiet," the woman from the audience told the boys as she hiked up her dress to climb onto the stage. "You don't know anything. Just be quiet."

The girl collapsed against the woman's spongy chest, and I watched them hold each other tightly, bodies pressing. My mother had never held me like that. But then, I wouldn't have let her if she'd tried.

"Nice work, oboe. Beautiful tone," Mr. Baxter said. I stuck my reed into the center spot in my reed case, the spot I reserved for my best reeds. For a moment, I imagined Mr. de Laney and Mr. Barret together, discussing how I was the most musical student they had ever taught. "A true poet," Mr. Barret had once called me, though later, after Merkin, his judgments had only been cruel.

Mr. Baxter pulled me aside after I had packed up my oboe. "During the concert, just follow her." He told me the oboe wasn't needed for the other arias. "We'll see you next week for the concert." He patted my arm in a fatherly, respectful way, and I could not tell him that I would not be coming back.

Outside the church, the low sky was a deep blue above the blocks of crumbling brownstones. On the corner, one man was curled on the sidewalk while two others swayed over him, laughing and pointing at him. I returned to the church, hoping the rehearsal would soon stop and that someone would walk to the subway with me, but they played and played, carelessly and out of tune. A half an hour passed. My oboe tight in my hand, my quarter ready, I went back out into the near-black night. The receiver had been torn off the phone. Splayed green wires stuck out from the socket. Two blocks away was another phone, and I stood on the corner too long, debating whether to go to it.

All I wanted was to hear Tom's voice. I dialed home, hoping Tom was suddenly there, not in Rochester. But of course, no one answered, and so I tried my mother. But as I waited for her to pick up, I worried she would be angry at me for calling or that somehow calling her in sadness would bind me to her in a way I didn't want to be bound. I was almost relieved when she wasn't home.

I called Daphne and she said to come over to her apartment uptown in Inwood.

"Are you sure?" I said, knowing she wouldn't refuse me. I snuck along the pavement to the subway, my boot heels fast and quiet, and I made lists of all the things I needed to do to improve my life. I needed to get Tom back and to learn to love and appreciate what I had and make it work. Next Saturday, a little over a week from now, I had a lesson with Mr. de Laney. I would ask him my question. A question I hadn't yet formed completely, but I knew he would tell me the truth. Perhaps his answer would release me. He would tell me I would never be good enough. And for a moment, the thought of that made me enormously relieved.

The winding melismata of the Indian singer droned on Daphne's old turntable as I sat like an orphan in her bed in her terry cloth bathrobe, sipping chamomile tea.

"It's Meheru! Baba's sister." Daphne smiled at the photograph she held in both hands. Her legs in a perfect split, she was sorting through photos of India to show me. I had nearly forgotten how she looked when not jogging: her long, straight blond hair was flattened to her temples by a red, purple, and green scarf, which dangled down her back, and her eyes sparkled beneath her blue mascara, a color she had been wearing since she was a teenager.

My legs cozy under the covers, I studied the picture of Meheru and Daphne in a sari, alongside a dusty jeep and a rubbery-looking bush I'd never seen before.

"There are so many places I've never been," I said to Daphne. "I always forget how narrow my life is. Even today I was taken out of my own sheltered world."

"And you played well."

"Only because there was no pressure. I mean, I liked the conductor and I cared, I always care, but it wasn't an audition."

Daphne's fingers lay curved on the rim of the carton marked PHOTOS. "I used to always have these voices over my shoulder telling me where I should have been as opposed to where I was."

"Those voices." I nodded. I knew them well. "I can't get rid of them."

"You're torturing yourself."

"Why is Tom such a success?"

Daphne shook her head vaguely. It wasn't a question that would occupy her much longer.

The Indian singer finished his coiling song, and he was replaced by the merengue, floating in from Dykeman Street. Daphne grooved to the beat, each pulse sending a graceful, rhythmic wave through her hips and shoulders. When I was a teenager, I would watch her onstage, and I would long to have the freedom and ease she had with her body.

"Did your mother tell you she's started piano lessons again?" Daphne said.

"No." I wondered if my mother only told me the bad things. "Do you believe what she says about my father? Please tell me."

"I don't know." Daphne measured her words. "It must be somewhat true, don't you think?"

"You believe my father could sneak around and lie for ten years?" I meant the question to seem immediately ridiculous, but Daphne looked at me sympathetically with her clear eyes.

"I don't believe he could," I said. The horns of the merengue suddenly blasted from the street, and I took a long sip of the hot tea, which seemed to jump down my throat. Tom had not called, but

Stephen had left a message saying he was a composer from Manhattan School who had to speak to me immediately about an oboe part in one of his pieces. "Call me back. I need to know as soon as possible," he told me, but then he seemed reluctant to end his message. There was a long silence before he hung up.

"My feelings about Stephen are completely unstable and unclear," I announced. "I don't know how to know anything."

"Maybe you do really like him, I felt you did when you told me about him."

"He's from the South." I made a sour face. "I only like New Yorkers. He seems foreign to me. Can you imagine what my father would think? An unemployed composer from the South?"

"It's terrible being so ambivalent."

Later that night, Daphne brought up Tom with me again, but I was too snuggly and warm under the covers of the pullout couch to want to talk about him. Daphne sat by my side and asked me if I needed anything. The only thing I wanted was something I was ashamed of wanting: I wished she could hold me in bed or rub my back until I fell asleep.

"Are you feeling a little bit better?" She yawned. It was midnight and Daphne was tired. She kept widening her eyes to keep them open. "You know what I think about you and the oboe? I think it's all there inside of you. It's your life's work to allow what you have inside to come out."

I nodded, comforted by her hand on my hip under the covers.

"I don't think you should go to your lesson on Saturday expecting to get huge answers from de Laney. I don't think you should listen if he tries to give them to you."

She kissed my forehead and I tried not to feel any kind of ache when our evening was through.

Her living room was brighter than my room. Street lamps shone through her shadeless second-story windows, and three cars in a row screeched into parking spots below. I curled on my side, hugging the pillow close to me. Tom slept this way. He clenched the pillow like a body in his arms. And he had dreams all night that made him sweat and murmur, though he never remembered them.

But was I happy with him? The sliver of light beneath Daphne's door vanished, and suddenly the living room seemed alive with silver shadows and half-open closet doors. The police lock on her door kept seeming to move. I pressed my eyes shut, but was unable to sleep.

I had forgotten the pleasure of being alone in the apartment. I could leave my music and clothes and cigarettes all over the couch, and I didn't worry about what Tom would say. I smoked in bed and walked around naked, enjoying the feeling of the brisk morning air on my breasts and then the graininess of the couch against my skin. The apartment smelled only of me, me and Betty Blue, whom I chattered with constantly.

I spent hours looking through boxes of old letters and photographs and was surprised to see how happy my family had been once. In one photo, I was between my parents, swinging their hands. My father was smiling, his pipe dangling from his lips, and my mother laughed, her head thrown back, holding on tight to a black beret. They were twenty years younger, and their faces had a vividness and a clarity that they lacked now. My father's expression was not sad or baffled, and my mother's face was open, not bitter and dissatisfied.

I put the picture on the bureau next to my other happy picture of them. It didn't feel as if I was being nostalgic; I was reconciling myself to what had passed.

A week after the concert, five days after Tom had gone, my mother called to tell me what Daphne already knew: she had started taking piano lessons again.

"It was time to do something for myself," she said, cheerfully, for the first time in months. She told me she'd only had two lessons so far but already she could feel her technique coming back to her.

"Twenty years without practicing is nothing!" she said with a laugh. "But seriously, it's astonishing how much I remember. And it's giving me strength to play again. I'm reconnecting with a part of myself I thought I'd lost."

"You're feeling better." I exhaled, trying to feel relief.

She lowered her voice. "Sometimes I think I was much better than I ever thought I was."

I huddled over my table in my quiet kitchen. "I always knew you were good."

"When I play, I feel most like myself. Nothing seems more natural to me."

"I know." It was the same for me.

"When I moved to New York, I was so frightened. I got on that bus, my music in my lap, and I thought anything might happen to me when I got off. I feel now exactly the same as I felt then. My life has changed completely and I don't know how I'll come out."

"You'll be okay." I cradled the phone and waited for her to reassure me.

"I was so brave then. I had no one behind me. My father told me, as he always did, that I wasn't good enough. I don't know how I was so courageous then, coming to New York, and I don't know why I couldn't have kept on going. I could have pushed myself."

"But you didn't. And maybe that meant you couldn't. You did all you could do."

I worried this would hurt her, but she surprised me.

"Yes," she agreed easily, as if she had accepted this long ago. "I did as much as I could. I was a person who did not know how to bloom. But you do. You know how."

I grunted to be funny, but my mother didn't hear me.

"And I feel like I've given that to you. I've gone through struggle so that you would be less unhappy, less unsure." Her voice became juicy, secretive all of a sudden. "My piano teacher is taking me to hear Claude Frank next weekend."

"Is it a date?" I felt stupid, shocked.

"It's been so long I've forgotten how you tell. He's only thirty-five. What would he want with an old woman like me?" she said, but then laughed as if she did think he was interested.

"What's he like?" I tried to make my voice breezy as if I were talking to a friend, though the momentary comfort I'd felt with her was gone.

"What's he like? Hmm." She thought for a moment. "He's sensual." She laughed. "That's the most important thing. He likes sex, I can tell."

My face turned red, even across the city from her.

"The outer of my life is suddenly moving faster than the inner," she said. "Well, my inner will catch up."

I told myself I should feel happy that she was feeling better, that even if the guy was thirty-five, it was a good thing. I wouldn't have to worry so much. As long as she had someone else who cared. In a strange moment, though, I pictured my mother pressing up against

Tom, who was only a few years younger than her piano teacher. It was a horrifying, fascinating image that I had to forget immediately.

Arms hooked around my knees, I waited for Stephen on the stone steps of the Museum of Natural History. My hair was braided and I wore the colorful Peruvian jacket my mother had given me. It was her style more than mine, but in the heavy wool, my body felt like hers, small and delicate as I'd always wanted it to be. A class of nine-year-olds had been herded into the museum, but otherwise I was alone on the steps, and I felt bad for the unvisited museum. I imagined it was lonely and jealous of the Metropolitan, just across Central Park, whose steps were packed with tourists.

It was the first time Stephen and I had ever met someplace away from Manhattan School together, but I'd sworn to myself we would not even kiss today. I would not let myself sink further into confusion. Instead, I would just be open with him, open to feeling who he was and was not and what could or could not be between us. I would find an answer. Tom was still in Rochester, and Stephen and I had the whole afternoon, but he surprised me by being twenty minutes late. Coming down Central Park West in the wealthy-looking crowd, he seemed out of place in his old black overcoat with a frayed paperback sticking out of the pocket, and his hair combed back in a wave off his forehead, Louisiana style, he'd said.

"I used to come here all the time when I was a child." I smiled brightly into his blue eyes, which seemed to be studying me, too, assessing something. He didn't apologize for his lateness.

"Your hair looks nice like that." He gave me a quick smile, but then was distant again.

"What's this?" I pulled his book, *Naked Lunch,* out of his overcoat pocket, and he stiffened at my touch. An old woman and man, slowly climbing the steps, said something to each other about us and then nodded.

"What were they saying?" I asked Stephen nervously.

"I don't know." He dropped his head for a moment. "I *am* happy to see you." He looked back up at me. "I just didn't want to admit it."

"I'm happy to see you, too." Our words hung in the cold air between us, and then we both quickly turned away. Stephen's overcoat

made a soft swishing sound as we walked in silence to the ticket
counter. He donated a dollar, less than I would have, but I didn't want
to make him feel bad by giving more.

"Are you practicing again?" he asked as we climbed the marble
steps to the second floor.

"I make myself do a certain amount every day. But I feel like I'm
digging at the bottom of my endurance."

A mother dragged her child down the steps, and Stephen waited
to speak until they had passed.

"You know you're you, the same person, whether you play or
not."

"I've never done anything else. I started piano at six, went to
Juilliard Prep at ten, Performing Arts High School. I've never taken
a real academic class."

"But still, if you decided not to play, you would be no less than
you are now."

He was the first person who had said out loud that I might not
play anymore, and it was almost a relief to hear him say it. He'd spoken as if it was not so terrible, but I argued with him, as if with
myself.

"Maybe you haven't only been a musician, as I've only been."

"I lost my marriage for it. In a way."

"I'm nothing without music."

"You're wrong." He stopped, his foot up on one step. "You're so
much more."

The African-mammal section was a dim, cavernous room with
stuffed tigers, zebras, and rhinoceroses inside glass displays. Besides
the guard, no one else was in the room, no one to catch us together.
Our shoulders touching, we stood in front of an elephant with her
trunk raised above her head and her baby huddled by her back leg,
and we smiled together, pointing at the fake bugs in the grass. After
a moment or so, Stephen pressed my lower back, guiding me to the
next display, the rhinoceroses. We had a rhythm together: the touch
on the back, the quiet laughs, the few inches we stood apart, sensing
exactly when the other wanted to change displays. I didn't know if
Tom and I had ever been so in tune with each other. In front of the
deer, Stephen's hand slipped slightly down my back, his fingers graz-
ing my ass.

"Let's go," I said, just so I could feel his hand again. In front of the buffalo, I moved closer to him.

"I like the way you touch me," I said, then felt ashamed, as if I shouldn't have confessed, but Stephen took my hand suddenly and pulled me into his arms.

"I want you," he whispered, clutching my hair in his hands. There were footsteps behind me, though, and I couldn't help from breaking away. Another couple, young, but conservative, entered the room. They were holding hands without caring who might catch them.

Stephen folded his arms across the front of his overcoat and would not look at me.

"I'm sorry," I said.

"When will you stop pushing me away?"

"Soon." I laughed without meaning to.

He knotted his eyebrows, pretending to reread the description of the buffalo. "So who does your boyfriend think you're with right now?"

"No one. Or maybe a friend," I said, embarrassed for the lies Stephen must have imagined I'd told. He knew what it meant to be betrayed. He walked steadily a few feet ahead of me until we had wandered into the prehistoric-animal room. Kindergarten groups teemed around the skeletons.

"Now where are we?" Stephen glanced at me.

"Let's go back," I said, but his hands were shoved in his overcoat pockets, and he wouldn't move. It was the first time he had been angry with me, and I learned that his angers would be like this: silent and resentful. His face was fair and serious and reserved, so unlike Tom's, alive and silly so often. There was so much in me then—my parents' separation, Tom's being away, my lesson next weekend—that I could not pick out one clear emotion for Stephen.

Thirty kids, holding hands, thronged by us.

"I never really cared for anyone besides my wife," Stephen said without turning to me. "I came here to New York to start a new life. I'm risking something, too."

I stared at the twenty-five-foot dinosaur, his bones as shiny as toys.

"You need to make a decision," he told me.

I nodded, but didn't look at him. I felt him gathering himself and I knew he'd been planning on saying this all along.

"We shouldn't see each other again unless you do."

"You're giving me an ultimatum?" I asked, shocked by the part of me that enjoyed this, the drama and being wanted.

"If that's what you want to call it."

We held each other for a long time on the sidewalk outside the museum But still, after all, I could not feel one pure thing. It was simultaneous, this melting into him and the part of me that kept separate, wondering whether I more cared for him or needed him.

The night before my lesson I sat at my reed-making desk for five hours, unable to come up with a good reed. I had twenty pieces of gouged cane soaking in a bowl on one side of my desk and a beer on the other. My head hurt from concentrating too long without getting up or even turning on the overhead light. The voices in my head wouldn't stop telling me I would play terribly tomorrow. Tomorrow, I would ask Mr. de Laney my question, and he would give me my answer, my final answer. No, I would never be good enough, he would tell me, and I would be free. Free from this effort. Free to do what I wanted. I would find some way to like myself without being special, without being able to say to myself and to others, "I am a musician, an oboist." First, I would learn how to be nothing, and then I would be something else.

I spoke to Pam, who told me her second-round audition had only been all right.

"After all this, I'm sure I won't get it," she said. Maybe it was the frustration in her voice, lesser than mine but still similar, that made me blurt out what I'd longed to confess to her for so long.

"Sometimes I don't know if I can go on."

Silence widened between us.

"What are you talking about?" she asked finally.

"I don't know what takes more courage, to continue playing," I said carefully, "or to stop."

She didn't speak and so I continued, "Sometimes, though, I still love it so much."

"You have to be tougher. There's tragedy all the time. You have to learn to get through things. Or else you'll quit everything. The oboe is nothing, compared." She hissed in on her strong cigarette, then slowly exhaled. "My mother died. All of a sudden. Like that."

I could think of nothing to say in response except that I was sorry.

"You have to toughen yourself," she told me. "If you let rejection get to you so much, you'll never do anything."

I remembered all the times she, too, had lost series of auditions and sunk into doubt, though never as bad as mine. "How did you recover? How did you feel confident again?"

"I don't even want to think about those times." Pam laughed once and inhaled her smoke. "Never again."

"Do you think we'd still be friends if I no longer played?"

"What a question!" She laughed again at how silly it was. "Of course we would be."

As soon as she said that, I knew it wasn't true. I would not be able to stand her success if I no longer played, and she would not want to be around so much disappointment.

My cigarette burning on the edge of my desk, I tied up the soaked, ready cane onto a tube with yellow string, my good-luck color. Five of the pieces cracked right as I was tightening the knot, and I had to put more pieces in hot water to soak. I worked quickly with my knife, shaving off the shiny cusp of cane and then clipping off the tip. One reed looked too open, the other too closed. I scraped out the back of the open one to give it some lows and it sounded better. I took a long swig of beer, finishing one bottle, and then I brought another one back to my desk.

Nervous now, because the reed was the first nearly usable one I'd made all night, I drank down half the next beer and began thinning the tip to make the pitch more stable and even. It sounded like tin. I scraped on the heart to make the sound flow through easier to the back, the lows of the reed. But when I tried the reed again, it had collapsed and the sound was all over the place.

I smashed the reed up against the wall, then clamped my forehead with my fingers and let myself sit there for two minutes before starting another.

It was a five-minute walk from the Wynnewood station to Mr. de Laney's house. Out here, in the near country, branches were already bare except for a few clinging brown leaves. The morning frost glistened on the trimmed lawns, and I shivered in my suit jacket, my only one. I'd stayed up until 4:00 A.M., unsuccessfully attempting to make a good reed. My whole life, I had never let myself stop trying, had never gone easy on myself, although now I wished for an excuse. I wished I could say, if I'd only worked harder and denied myself more easy times. But I had always tried my best. There was no excuse.

The de Laneys' stately home looked as ordinary and unused as ever. Even the coils of the watering hose, wrapped on a peg inside the garden, seemed to be in the exact same formation as before. The Chrysler was alone in the driveway as usual; their trips, even to town, seemed few. There was no sign of what Mr. de Laney did with his time since retiring. Inside his home with the living room set and crystal, there were no books or paintings and nothing was out of place. Their home was completely different from what was familiar to me, but I felt a kind of safety entering it. The de Laneys had loved each other all of their lives, and before I rang their doorbell, I stood there for a moment trying to tuck away the fear that I would never have such a love with Tom or anyone else.

Mr. de Laney tapped open the door with his elegant rosewood cane.

"Hello there, Gala." His face was long and wrinkled, but still he towered, his fisherman's hat nearly touching the top of the entranceway. He wore a royal blue Polo cardigan and chinos. I felt girlish before him. He was the person I was going to ask my most urgent question.

With his cane, he pointed toward the studio. "Warm up for a few minutes," he said, curt as usual. "I'm getting some tea." On the way to the kitchen, he stroked the elegant handle of his cane with such care and sensuality that, for a moment, this seemed the reason for his greatness—his love of details, his love of the smallest texture of sound. But then I thought, anyone could love what he loved. I didn't know what had gone wrong with me, why my love had not been enough.

His studio smelled of the two boxes of fresh cane on the floor; they had just arrived from France. His knives were unsheathed on his reed-making desk. He must have started playing again. His old oboe, the one he had used for most of his time with the Philadelphia

Orchestra, was on the piano. He'd polished it; the silver was less dull and acid-worn, and the wood looked rich again. I touched the bell. It was soft and moist from wood oils. I wanted to ask Mr. de Laney if I could try his old oboe. I didn't want to ask him any other question.

I warmed up with long tones. Mr. de Laney thought the way most people warmed up, showing off with quick runs, was a waste of time; you couldn't feel out your reed or open up your sound that way.

I played a long tone on a middle D, the most covered, dark note on the oboe. I started softly, hearing Mr. de Laney's words: "The sound must start from nowhere, as if it began long before you started playing."

"Sounds good," came Mr. de Laney's gruff voice as he turned the corner into the studio. Holding the edge of his reed-making desk, he lowered himself down onto his chair and squinted at me above his black reading glasses. "You've got a good reed, huh?"

My reed had sounded good just then. It was the reed I'd made at 3:00 A.M., the one I had pushed myself to make.

"You took a little too much out of the heart. See." He held the reed up to the light and pointed to the heart. "That's why the sound is a little small, closed up."

"It's small?"

"I said it was a little small. Not very small. If you'd left more in the heart, the reed would be more sturdy. You're going too fast. Are you doing what I told you?"

"Yes," I lied. Last night, I'd made reeds frantically, the opposite of what he'd told me, which was to make reeds in stages, letting the cane settle after each cut.

"Well, it sounds better," he said, and then with a large sweeping motion, he surveyed the room as if preparing to say something important. About the audition, I thought, and why I didn't make it. I hoped he would answer my question before I needed the courage to ask it.

"So." He slapped his hands down on the knees of his chinos. "What are you going to play for me today?"

"Boston Pops audition is next month." I had copied the list of pieces I was supposed to play onto a scrappy sheet of paper. Stupidly, this morning, it hadn't crossed my mind that I should not give him something so sloppy. Mr. de Laney frowned at the frayed edges of the paper.

"It's all part of the same problem, Gala. Everything is so . . ." He waved his hands chaotically in the air. "Look at my desk." He opened and shut every one of his tiny wood drawers to show me the perfect order of his tools—knives lined up in size order, tiny, slippery plaques in a neat pile, fish skin and beeswax in little bags.

"If you keep all this ordered"—he lay his hands heavily on the desk and then pointed to his head—"you'll keep this ordered. It's all discipline."

As he looked down the excerpt list, I kept expecting him to say something, to tell me there was no way I could do it, no way I could make it.

"Well, let's hear some scales. E-flat major." He began conducting before I had a chance to say anything else. "Three, four . . ."

I started up, but Mr. de Laney interrupted me. "Yes, yes, but couldn't you remember to keep your fingers closer to the keys and less active?" On his own oboe—his old oboe—he imitated my fingers, flailing messily over the keys. "I'm exaggerating, of course. You know that."

I nodded, but it was embarrassing to think my fingers looked anywhere near his imitation. I played the scale again, keeping my fingers more relaxed and closer to the keys.

"Do you hear how much smoother that was, Gala?"

Mr. de Laney stood close to me, and I tried not to smell him— the dampish wool, the talcum powder. He smelled as if he'd just taken a bath. I didn't like to think of his body.

He reached across me to smooth down my music. His large hands were crinkled and knotted at the knuckles.

"Brahms Symphony. Let's hear it."

I knew I should talk to him now. If I played badly, I would lose my courage entirely.

"When you play this solo, you've got to hear it all in your head first. The legato. You should always do that anyway. You should be playing what you hear in your head. What you hear in your head should be exquisite. You should not be accepting what you play."

The Brahms, a slow, bittersweet solo, was something I had always played well, even at my last audition. I closed my eyes and listened to the strings, the violins pressing, urgent, straining, and then the pounding chords of the basses. They silenced and I began, my tone placid and bare, and then I played the phrase again, sweeter the second time. The third time through, I let my sound open, joyful for one moment and then tentative again.

Mr. de Laney nodded. "You know what? That was beautiful."

I took those words in, repeated them to myself.

Mr. de Laney tipped his fisherman's cap back off his head. "That was beautiful playing, Gala. Do you know that?"

I shrugged, shook my head.

"Can you do it again?"

I didn't know. I doubted it. I closed my eyes and felt how tired I was. I played and the music grew and then bloomed again, even more sweetly than before. Better than the first time. Better than the audition.

Mr. de Laney had his hat in his lap and he leaned back in his chair, staring at me. I had played as beautifully as I always knew I could, underneath it all. I fingered my music on my stand, pretended to be choosing what to play next. I wanted to talk to him now. I looked out the window at his patio, the ordinary white chairs and table, the raked pile of brown leaves.

"Let's hear *Tombeau.* We need to work on that. I don't want you to have trouble with that again."

I tried to gather all of my nerve. On his desk were three reeds he must just recently have made. It had been a year since his heart attack. I'd never heard him really play, in person.

"Could I hear you play it first?"

"Me?" He pointed to himself with a boyishness that made me smile.

As his reeds soaked, he readied his old oboe. I imagined he'd prepared to play thousands of times and that this time meant nothing compared to those other times; still, he checked and rechecked both octave keys for water, tested and retested two reeds. He would never let himself sound any worse than his best.

"I've been practicing a little bit lately. Getting these back in shape." He wiggled his fingers in the air like a crazy magician and I laughed.

He did not warm up except to test a single low-D attack to feel his reed's responsiveness. He looked blankly across the room and then took a huge breath as if to attack his oboe, so small in his hands. When he played *Tombeau,* it was light like a child's game—the turns like ringing bells—but also twirling and elegant. When I played *Tombeau,* there was no music, no lightness. I could only hope I got to the end without any glitches.

"That's how it goes." He dropped his oboe to his side when he was finished, and I thought he looked a little sad. "My last recording of *Tombeau* wasn't very good." He shook his head and I waited for him to say more. I wanted to hear him play again. I didn't want to ask him my question. I wanted just to listen to him and to be his student forever.

"Could you play Mozart for me?"

"Slow movement?" he said as if he knew me and what I loved exactly. He was a tall man with a creased, regular face, and his starched, pressed clothes showed nothing out of the ordinary, except that he was meticulous. I could never see in him any signs of genius or what made him—with his attacklike breaths—able to play the most delicate Mozart I had ever heard in my life.

"That's it," he said, suddenly stopping midway through. He massaged his chest as if he were feeling for pain there. I raised my eyebrows, asking him if he was okay.

"Fine, fine." He dismissed my concern, then sat down easily on his desk chair, swinging one leg over the other. "Let's hear some *Tombeau.* And then *La Scala.*"

I cleared my throat. "Mr. de Laney," I said, but the words didn't really come out.

"This tempo first." He looped his wrist gracefully to the beat.

"Mr. de Laney. I wanted to talk to you." I was smiling suddenly, embarrassed.

"About?" he said, but then he knew. He tipped his cap forward on his head and leaned back in his chair, preparing himself.

"I was just wondering . . . I just feel it's so difficult." I mustered my courage. "Will I ever get something?"

Mr. de Laney's face strained. I waited.

"Gala, what do you mean by 'get something'?"

I knew what his answer was. I stared at the clean, starched knees of his chinos.

"That's a vague question. It depends on what you mean." Looking away, he fingered the edge of the table, his thumb anxiously working back and forth, but his voice was gruff and impersonal. "If you mean, will you ever play first oboe with an orchestra like New York City Ballet or Boston Pops, I would have to say no."

He did not look up at me.

"If you mean, will you ever win other auditions with smaller orchestras, I would have to say that I cannot answer that."

Not even that.

He slapped his hands down on his knees, leaned forward in his chair. "You have to continue working hard. It's all ninety percent hard work. And then who can say? In a year from now, your playing could improve one hundred percent."

I wanted to ask him if I had improved these last few months, but I couldn't speak.

"You have something special, Gala. When you play like you did ten minutes ago, it is as beautiful as I could imagine. I haven't heard anyone who plays with more soul than you." He took a breath. "Other times, your playing is all over the place. Your technique isn't solid enough. I took you as a student because I wanted you to be able to play as I know you can."

I fiddled with my music for *Tombeau*.

"Your playing is terribly inconsistent."

"Mr. de Laney, have I improved?"

"Have you improved? Gala, I want you to improve. I want you to improve. Sometimes, I think you have and sometimes I'm not sure what's going wrong. Maybe it was all those years with Mr. Barret. He was rough on you, wasn't he?"

"I should have left him sooner." It seemed so clear now.

"Give yourself another year."

I nodded.

"How old are you? Twenty-six," he remembered, and then he was doubtful again. Twenty-six was way too old to have technical problems. "Give yourself another year. We'll work together for another year."

I nodded.

"It's up to you."

15

The last week of November, Tom's quartet went into the studio early every morning to record the Bartók Quartets. Dreamy and thick with sleep, I would lie in bed, listening to him warm up. He no longer rushed through scales or crashed through openings of flashy concertos; now, he warmed up as Mr. de Laney urged me to do. He played long, meditative tones, first with, then without vibrato to perfect his naked sound. The microphones at the studio missed nothing. The slightest flaw was exaggerated in recording.

Some mornings, as I was lying in bed, listening as Tom's meticulous scales filled the apartment, I tried to imagine waking up without him and to measure how great the loss would be. I thought about how months and years of unhappiness might pile up while I kept promising myself our relationship would get better.

Tom spent twelve hours a day in the studio with the Quartet, and he was far slower than the others. He needed five or six takes before he got passages right. When he came home at night, he was exhausted and wired and needed wine to sleep.

"I've never tried to play so perfectly in my life," he said. "And they could still fire me."

He told me about all the passages he'd done well the first and second takes and about the ones he'd had to do over so many times he could feel the Quartet getting impatient with him.

"What do you think they think of me? Do you think they'll fire me?" he asked over and over, more anxious than I'd ever seen him. I tried to reassure him and tell him I was sure they understood—this was his first time recording.

Both unable to sleep, we stayed up until two or three every night. We ate late with our plates on our blanketed laps, and then we lay under the covers with the lights out, watching reruns of *Saturday Night Live* on Comedy Central. Betty Blue chirped wildly and without pause every time the studio audience laughed.

"Our baby." I squeezed Tom's hand under the covers.

"She has a sense of humor. She's like me," he said, though lately he was always worried.

Stephen's ultimatum two weeks before was for the best, I realized. I needed to focus only on Tom and what could or could not be mended between us. We spent half of Thanksgiving Day with his mother and cousins and then the other half with my mother. His mother did not see how hard we were trying, how careful we were together. All she wanted, she kept saying, was to see us really start a life together: get married, have kids.

"That's the whole thing. The big caboodle," she told us. "You find someone. You make a life. That's it. I love this girl. Even though she gets a little moody sometimes." She gave me a look, both loving and threatening, reminding me of how I'd walked out of Tom's concert night.

Tom astonished his relatives with the technically impossible Paganini Concerto. He slopped over the most difficult parts, but no one cared and I kept my envy at bay. His mother gave me one of her noisy, wet good-bye kisses, and Tom and I cuddled all the way in the cab from the Bronx to my mother's house, just as we had nearly three years ago, the first time he had brought me home. He told me all the rough stories of his childhood on the streets, and they impressed me and made me laugh all over again. I would do as my father said: I would accept Tom and love him as he was. I would make my life with him, I thought as we planned where we might move now that Tom had money. We both wanted an elegant prewar building on Riverside Park or a brownstone in the West Village.

"That was where my parents lived. On Bank Street," I said, and all of a sudden, it seemed that I might relive my parents' lives, the magic they'd had in the beginning, only I'd make it right, I'd make it continue.

My mother had cooked a whole turkey, three kinds of vegetables, and a huge pan of sweet potato pie just for Tom and me. Even though it was only the three of us, she was dressed up in her flowing purple skirt and Navajo jewelry. It was the first holiday we'd celebrated without my father, and it was the first time I'd been in the apartment since she had fallen apart. The track lighting was dimmed over the table, and a women's chorus chanted softly on the turntable. Before we ate, my mother made us all hold hands as she read a poem from her women's poetry book. The words were bitter, assailing God for all the earth's suffering.

"And we thank God for all the homeless people," my mother read in a strangely thunderous voice from the head of the table, her bracelets jangling on her wrist. "And for all the lonely motherless men with no place to lay their heads at night and no place called home . . ." Her voice rose and fell theatrically and then she wiped the tears from her eyes. The poem was two pages long, and Tom stared at her with a smile frozen on his face. I could hardly look at her. If my father had been here, he would have interrupted her and made a joke about the poem. Either she would have gotten upset and there would have been a fight or else she might have laughed with him and with the whole table of guests. So many of their old friends were his alone now. They invited him and Marissa, not her, over for dinner, and they hardly ever called to ask how she was.

"Well." My mother covered her mouth when she'd finished reading. "I'm sorry I read that." She looked back and forth from Tom to me. "It wasn't so cheerful, was it?"

"It was good, Mom. A very good poem." My impatience was all over my face. My mother sucked in her breath, and I excused myself to get the wine, leaving my mother and Tom alone together. When I returned to the table five minutes later, my mother was praising Tom for his concert and all his good reviews.

"It all happened so quickly! It's just a miracle!" she said brightly, clasping her hands beneath her chin. "I'm so proud of you!" She asked him all about the Quartet, and I couldn't help but wish that it were me and not Tom who'd made her proud and made her laugh again, even effortlessly.

Our arms weighted with leftovers, I said to Tom in the elevator, "You're so lucky. I wish I had your success. Then my mother would be happy."

"She's not so bad. She laughed the whole night. That poem was wild though."

"You think I'm too conscious of her sadness?" I stared into Tom's eyes, but they darted away from me.

"I don't know." He laughed out loud, looking up at the descending numbers above the elevator door. "You pick at everything. You never leave anything alone."

The elevator squeaked, passing each floor. We were halfway down, on five. Tom stood in front of the door, and I was in the corner. I watched the back of his leather jacket and his red cashmere scarf tossed over his shoulder.

"I'd just like to be able to discuss things with you," I said.

Tom shook his head, his curls swishing on the leather, and I knew that he was rolling his eyes, defensive already, though I had not meant to accuse him; I had only wanted to speak openly.

"Maybe I'm stupid," he said. "Maybe I'm an idiot compared to you. I can't talk, can't think, can't do anything but watch TV. Is that what you think?"

I huffed to show I wouldn't even answer such a question. During the cab ride home we didn't speak, didn't cuddle as we had only hours before, and then over the next several days, our heaviness returned. We didn't make love and we became careful around each other again. I tried to do the wifely things that used to please him. I bought fresh flowers for the windowsills and made dinner every night.

"Aren't you excited?" I'd say, my voice bright like my mother's, as I opened the oven to show him his favorite dishes: pizza, portabello mushrooms with pine nuts, and lasagna.

"You think I don't appreciate you enough. I don't give you what you want," he'd say, and then he'd fall against me in that sad way of his. I'd finish cooking while he collapsed on the couch, exhausted. If I ever stepped outside of myself and thought of him and how strained and overworked he was, I relaxed and was able to give him my sympathy and my love. Usually, though, I'd run on about all the ways we should improve our home, our apartment, and if he didn't respond, I'd reproach him, "This used to mean so much to you."

"I'm tired," he'd say. "Cynthia was furious at me today. It took me seven takes to get this one measure. I never realized how bad I was."

He'd never put himself down like this before. He'd become like me with his worry, but that didn't make me more sympathetic with him. I didn't listen to him, didn't register his concern, not even when he told me he'd heard Cynthia mention something about another violinist they might have chosen.

"Didn't you hear what I just said?" he demanded, and then in the bedroom, he called an old friend from the Bronx. "Hey, man, it's been tough," he said, slipping into the rougher, deeper, easier tone he used with his old friends. Even through the shut door, I could hear him laughing more with his friend than he had in months with me. My days were slipping by shamefully.

Once when Tom called between takes at the studio, he told me, "Just start practicing again. Stop pitying yourself so much."

I held back my rage at both myself and him. "The problem is"— I steadied my voice—"is that I can't seem to make myself play anymore."

A Bartók quartet suddenly blasted in the background and Tom was distracted, pulling the phone across the studio.

"I can't make myself anymore," I repeated louder and with less true feeling. The Bartók stopped abruptly, in the middle of a viola trill. "What do you think? Do you think I'm good enough?"

It was an impossible question: there were too many factors, too vague and too difficult to predict, and Tom had witnessed so many of my defeats. Still, his silence made the tears stream down my cheeks.

"What do I know about the oboe? You sound great to me," he said finally. "Just make the tape for Oakland. It's not so bad."

"I feel like it's been taken away from me. Like someone came and beat my will from me."

Tom sort of laughed as if I'd told a joke.

"We need so much from each other, don't we, Tom?"

"What do you mean by that?" he said, defending himself already.

"We need so much but we're both so knotted up we can't stop fighting."

"And whose fault is that?" Tom said, still arguing with me. When we hung up the phone, I began my measuring again: how great the loss would be and what I would do if I were truly brave.

I ran fast and long that day in the cold, my breath freezing ahead of me. The Hudson was gray and wavy, blending with the sky, and the New Jersey skyline looked faraway and make-believe. I pushed myself to run twice to the boat basin, an eight-mile run, and I told myself that if I wanted to, I could do anything. I could be alone. I could give up music. I could start all over again. Alone or with Stephen. I fantasized about a quiet life in his small, intimate studio with the books, the music, and the teas. He would support me completely as I searched for a new devotion, and I convinced myself that his touch, so kind, would free me to feel all I had been afraid of before.

On my way home, my mind buzzed with all the different subjects I might study: philosophy, literature, psychology, anything. I hadn't taken a real academic class since Performing Arts, but I assured myself I could learn to love and dedicate myself to something else, even if my mother couldn't.

When I reached my block, I was so excited to study, to find something new, that I turned around and ran full speed, dodging baby carriages and students with knapsacks, downtown to Columbia to pick up a course bulletin. I stopped to catch my breath before the iron gates at the entrance of the university, where three months ago I'd caught my father with Marissa. Beside me two blond girls in jeans and clunky shoes were smoking and gossiping about a professor they didn't like and then about a party this weekend. A college life I'd never known.

I clung to the gates and hung my head, still out of breath. All of a sudden, I felt exhausted. The effort of finding the adult studies office and the fear of bumping into my father seemed enormous. I turned back home.

16

At Tanglewood Music Festival one summer when I was eighteen, there was an oboist who had quit and then started playing again. She was in her thirties, older than the rest of us, but no better than we were. In fact, we dismissed her completely from our discussions of who would get somewhere and who would not; we didn't know why she was even trying. Once, while the conductor rehearsed the first violins, I asked her how long she had stopped playing. Eight years, she told me, scraping on her reed, pushing up the rim of her ordinary glasses. Her brownish hair framed her even-featured face, ordinary, too, and tired looking.

Then, eight years of adulthood seemed an unfathomable length of time to me, and it included years of disappointments and second-guessing that frightened me to consider. By the time I was thirty, I expected to have a good job in an orchestra, to be somewhere. I asked her what made her quit and what made her play again.

"I thought I could live without it and then I realized I couldn't," she answered. Of course, there was much more than she was telling me, but I believed her when she said she'd discovered she couldn't live without it. And I wondered whether it was true for me, whether I couldn't live without it, or whether without it, I would be the same person, only better, more confident, not trying to please others anymore.

The conductor rehearsed the violins again from the beginning of the section and I asked her, "But how did you start playing again? How did you get the courage? After eight years?"

"No decision is final. Nothing in life is. Except one thing." She crowed on her reed to end the conversation. All my life, I'd pushed and pushed myself to work hard and stay ahead of the failure that always seemed about to overtake me. I was too afraid to stop, for even one moment, to see if I was happy.

hursday, a week after Thanksgiving, Pam was supposed to visit me at noon after her audition, but by two, she had not even called. We had the whole afternoon planned: first a manicure—she had finally convinced me to get my first one—and then the West End for afternoon drinks. We hadn't really talked in so long—maybe my jealousy was to blame—but finally we'd have all day. She'd tell me about her audition—almost all of me wanted her to do well—and I'd tell her about Stephen and my conversation with de Laney. I would be comforted because our history together was a history of boosting each other after small disappointments, and maybe my recent ones wouldn't seem so big, so irrevocable, after speaking to her.

"We need to talk. We have men, but we need friends," she'd said over the phone yesterday, but when the phone finally rang, it was George, my piano student, calling to tell me that he had decided not to take lessons anymore. He said he had no talent and wasn't getting anywhere.

"That's not true, George. You improved a lot."

"I liked the lessons, but I just wasn't getting any good."

I worried that all along I hadn't been supportive enough. "You are good," I encouraged him, but he'd already made his decision.

He needed more time for his studies anyway, he said. "I work all day at the post office, then go to school at night. It's too much."

As soon as we hung up, the phone rang again. I picked up immediately, hoping it would be Pam.

"Gala?" a woman said. I knew her papery, thin voice immediately. It was Marissa. Like every other woman I'd ever seen my father flirt with, every detail—her voice, her clothes, her bony, fashionable body—was permanent in my memory.

I said her name.

"You recognized my voice. Good." Marissa laughed confidently. She asked me how I was and I said fine in a blunt, flat tone. I would never tell her anything about myself. I would never give anything away. I immediately asked her about herself. She was organizing some exhibit of twentieth-century South American painters in a gallery on Madison Avenue. While she spoke, I ridiculed her richness, her sophistication, and her smugness twenty times to myself. My father had exchanged one woman a class above him for another of an even higher class, I thought nastily to myself.

"Your father and I would like to know if you and your boyfriend want to come for Christmas at our house. Jason would be there, of course, and your father and I think it would be nice, the five of us. You haven't seen his new home yet."

I thanked her and told her that I was spending Christmas with my mother.

"What about Christmas Eve? It would mean a lot to both your father and me," she said as if she were not the woman who had contributed, so directly, to my mother's misery. "We were thinking of an early dinner. Just Jason, you, your boyfriend, your father, and I. I know Jason enjoyed meeting you very much."

It was just like my father to have her call so I couldn't be rude and say no. Even if I wanted to go, I wouldn't. I was too loyal to my mother.

"I'll have to think about it," I said to Marissa, and five minutes after I hung up with her, my father was leaving a message to me about how I'd hurt her feelings and how I should call her to apologize.

"My feelings are hurt, too," my father said.

I picked up the phone. "I am not spending Christmas with you and Marissa. Since when do you celebrate Christmas anyway?"

"Don't shut me out of your life. Your mother plays a powerful victim. She did bad things, too. I never met a more powerful victim than your mother. I am not a bad man. You have to know, I tried. I tried my best. If the truth is that Marissa and I are old friends and that once or twice or three times over the years"—he paused—"we saw each other in a different way, is that so terrible?" He waited for my answer, and when I gave none, he went on, "Your mother and I were very unhappy together. We kept trying and trying again, but in the end all we did was make each other miserable."

I stuck with my anger. "If I don't want to come, I don't have to."

"You won't even think about it?" he asked in his baby's voice, which I realized was like my own.

"You don't know half of what's happened." I waited for him to ask me what I meant so I could tell him about my mother's despair.

"You can think about it tonight and call us back," my father said, deaf to me.

"There's nothing to think about." I hung up on my father and then rushed out of the apartment.

In Riverside Park, Grant's Tomb looked stark against the cold sky. Bare branches rustled against the stone tomb. I tried Pam once again, but she still wasn't home. I made myself walk past Manhattan School without even checking down the block for Stephen, but then at 116th, I turned back. There were five floors of practice rooms. I started from the top and worked my way down. I opened every door, received glares from numerous pianists and violinists, except for one tuba player who raised his eyebrows at me. I imagined that when I saw Stephen, we would rush into each other's arms. *I love you,* he would say, and I would give myself over. My decision would be made. Finally. With no going back. I would trust him and we would enter that warm, tender place together where everything was safe and my heart was no longer small and needy.

I went through all the floors, the fifth through second, but did not find him. The school orchestra was rehearsing the second move-ment of Tchaikovsky's Fifth in the auditorium, and I slipped in qui-etly through the doors to the dark hall. The stage was white with streaming lights, and the cellists and violists strained with feeling even though they were way out of tune.

The first oboist was a tomboyish girl in overalls. Her tone was flat and hard and she did not sing as she played her solo, but I closed my eyes and remembered the sweetness of playing this piece for the first time. The French horn and oboe passed the melody back and forth, interrupting each other as if neither could resist it. I had loved playing this solo with the pulsing of the violins beneath me. I had loved it all so much.

The conductor stopped the orchestra to rehearse the brass, and I was so shaky on my feet that as I left through the lobby, I leaned against a couch for support.

The silver sun glared at me. I shielded my eyes and then started across the street to call Pam once more.

I knew it was Stephen immediately, as soon as I felt his hand press my lower back.

"It's you!" He smiled, his round cheeks fanning open, and he introduced his friend Kent, who was as tall as he was and wearing the same worn blazer. Kent's face was plumpish and kind.

"Very pleased to meet you." Kent nodded at me affably, looking closely, and I knew I had been talked about. I was glad I had on my black leather jacket and red scarf, which brought out my lips and eyes.

"Steve and I received the same grant," Kent said. "We're both transplanted Southerners. Still ill at ease."

"Are you from Mississippi, too?"

"Baton Rouge, Louisiana," Kent filled in. "A city for Louisiana."

"Not like New York," Stephen said. He had been studying my face, looking for signs. It had been three weeks since his ultimatum.

"Nothing is, correct?" Kent elbowed him. "You'd think a Southern boy like him wouldn't like it here so much."

It was the first time I'd ever seen Stephen with a friend, and it made him seem part of a group: broke Southern composers in New York. Intellectuals. I could be friends with Kent, I thought. I could form a new life with Stephen. He and Kent opened their briefcases, both worn leather, and exchanged music.

"I know when I give my music to Steve," Kent said to me, "that he'll spend all night listening. He's a good friend. A good listener."

"Okay, okay . . ." Stephen waved him off. Alone, Stephen and I were suddenly shy together again.

"I saw a picture of your boyfriend in *Opus Magazine,*" he said slowly. "Tom Bassi. That's him, isn't it?"

"Right." I laughed, wiping my mouth.

"He must be good. Really good." Stephen's fingers, dry from the cold, tightened around his old umbrella. "You didn't tell me he was famous."

"Is he?" The word sounded so strange applied to Tom, whom I saw mostly half-naked, dressed only in an old T-shirt every day. "I guess he's become that way."

"It gave me a picture of your life without me. It made me think you'd never come find me." Stephen looked back down at his gripping hand. "I have another present for you. I've been carrying it around. In case."

"You've given me so much already," I said, but he held the gift in a brown paper bag steady between us. I hesitated, just as I had without knowing why that day on the stairwell, three months before, when he'd made his first offering. I looked into his blue eyes, which seemed to have known me so well right from that very first moment, and I took his gift, a CD of Robert Johnson, a Delta blues player. Stephen pointed to the songs he liked, touching all parts of my fingers, knuckles, tips, and wrist.

"It's a whole side of me you don't know," Stephen said as we walked on the cobblestone between the aisle of jagged trees. In the stretch of park beside me, a group of girls, nine or ten years old, in hooded down coats, were playing soccer. They giggled, bunching around the ball, even though the gym teacher kept shouting at them to spread out.

"So what are you upset about?" Stephen said. "There were tears in your eyes when I first saw you today."

I lifted my face to the wind so that I would speak and feel as empty and emotionless as it was, cutting my cheeks.

"A student of mine, George, just quit today. He said he didn't think he would ever be able to play as well as he wanted. And he was right."

"But that's not true for you. I know it."

"My playing is inconsistent. My technique isn't great. I mess up in performance. And I can't seem to change myself no matter how hard I try. And I am trying."

"Is your mother still so unhappy?" Stephen asked after a moment.

"She has a boyfriend."

"What's he like?"

"He's thirty-five."

Stephen widened his eyes to show me he understood how uneasy I might feel over that.

We rested our elbows on the stone wall and listened to the wind, gathering up the crumpled leaves. Down the hill through the trees was the West Side Highway and then the Hudson River, a pale blue strip winding far into the distance. Stephen's blazer tickled my wrist, and I yearned, with a deliciousness I'd forgotten, for him to touch me.

"What do you want in life?" I asked.

"What do I want?" He faced the river and not me. "I want a house by the ocean. I want to wake up with the sound of the waves. I want to have a piano, some books, and some music. But not too many things."

I imagined the life he was describing, and I thought I could want it, too. I thought I would want to be with him anywhere, anywhere that I could talk to him just as we were talking now.

"Doesn't it bother you being alone so much?" I asked.

"I'm content." He traced a twig over the ruddy stone wall.

"But you're alone a lot." I wanted to know what it was exactly that he wanted from me, but he only shrugged, letting the twig fall from his fingers. The wind whipped through the bare trees, then a silence settled around us. Two joggers, a man and a woman, in matching fuchsia Lycra, jogged toward us.

"You came to find me today," he said finally. "Does that mean you've made a decision?"

I held my breath, and when I spoke, I hoped I was sure and that saying the words out loud would keep me that way. "I want to be with you. At least I want to try."

"I think I could love you," Stephen whispered, or at least I thought that was what he said. The wind was blowing again and he was facing the other direction.

"Stephen?" I called his name.

"Stay with me," he whispered. His lips touched mine and then he whispered it again. "Please."

"I remember this." I stood in the doorway to Stephen's tiny studio, taking it in again: the upright piano with his worn music on it, the cabinets containing the tea and the health food, his old editions piled in the milk carton, and the tidy bed with the extra blanket folded on the bottom.

The box of his ex-wife's watercolors was either gone or hidden.

I sat on the piano bench as I had before, but this time Stephen sat down right beside me.

"Are you nervous?" He stroked my hair.

"No." I shook my hanging head. "Maybe a little."

"We can just talk. We don't have to do anything else."

I made a sound, like a laugh, and slumped on the bench. Just now, Tom was at the studio, struggling to find his place with the Quartet.

"I could make you something to eat," Stephen offered, and I hung around the kitchen alcove as he cut up celery for a tuna salad. He minced the onion into perfect slivers. He had taken off his blazer and shoes. His socks had holes, and I had the urge to hug him again.

We ate side by side on the piano bench. "There are many things that need to be improved," Stephen said. "I need a better place."

"You do. Definitely," I said, and we talked, as I had once talked with Tom, about the best places to live in the city, hinting, but not saying it out loud, that we would be together. Shadows leaned across the room as the afternoon sun slipped away. I imagined making the trip every night from my house to Stephen's and how we would be together in this quiet room, which did feel intimate and safe to me. My life with Tom was much busier and brighter and people-filled. Happier from the outside maybe, though I wasn't happy.

"Will you come to my performance at Town Hall next week?"

"Of course." I nodded. There was a leap in every promise I made. I would have to tell Tom by then. "Play me some Delta blues."

He played a few chords and then stopped. "I can't do it justice anymore." His shoulder brushed mine as he smoothed his hands up and down the knees of his jeans. At any moment, he might slide his hand over onto my thigh. I wanted to know more about Stephen's life, this life I might leave mine for.

"Do you have many close friends in New York?" I spoke into my lap, my hands clasped tight.

"Not really. Except Kent. My closest friends are still back home."

I waited for him to say more.

"Do you miss being married?" I asked.

"I miss being married more than I actually miss my wife. If I'm honest with myself."

"I thought you said you were happy to be alone."

"I didn't say 'happy,' I said 'content.' "

I waited again. "I want to know more about you."

"I think the things you want to know," he said slowly, "only us spending more time together could tell you."

"I want to know everything."

"You want to know whether you'll be able to rely on me when you leave Tom?"

I shrugged. It was strange to hear him say Tom's name, as if there were a betrayal even in having given Tom's name to him. Of course, Stephen couldn't be concerned about that. Tom's feelings were my responsibility, and I had been a traitor to him for weeks. I looked down at Stephen's and my dangling feet, his hiking boots with mud on them and my lace-up boots that had once looked expensive and stylish.

"You can rely on me," he said slowly. "Nothing can ever be for sure, but as much as I can say now, you can rely on me."

He put his arm around me and I felt the coolness of his watch against my neck and then his fingers lightly caressing my neck.

"No one has ever been as kind to me as you," I whispered, and I tried not to be afraid as his hand cupped my cheek. I had come here for this, had wanted for weeks to feel exactly this: his hand on my lower back, guiding me to the bed. I wanted to feel everything I thought I'd missed.

I moved onto his lap and wrapped my legs around his waist, and I ground my hips deep into his until I felt his cock harden in his jeans. I arched my back so that my breasts were large in front of him. There was no shame in this. There wasn't.

"I want to be with you." He buried his face between my breasts, and he began pulling up my shirt. I got this fear about the scars I'd carved in my chest. I held his hands, prevented him from taking off my shirt until he'd turned out the light. And then we were in darkness, and Stephen was large and shadowy, faceless, as he negotiated me, pulling off my shirt.

"Where are you?" I tried to pull him close.

"Let me make you happy." In the darkness, he played with my breasts.

"Please come here."

He came down on top of me. I closed my eyes and felt his hands all over me, my stomach, thighs, between my legs. I gritted my teeth so I would feel nothing. He pulled off my panty hose and I lay naked before him. My eyes were closed, but I could feel the coolness of the room and his eyes all over me.

"Look at you," he whispered, and he placed his finger on my nipple. I jumped, afraid he would hurt me, but I did not open my eyes. I would give myself over, let anything happen. Tears filled the cavity behind my eyes, but I swallowed them back, letting none escape. Sex had always been like this for me—with this bottomless despair. It was no different with Stephen.

"Let me massage you," he said, and I kept my eyes closed as his hands came toward me. But then he was gently caressing my cheeks. I tried to breathe in and out, in and out, to relax.

"Why are you so afraid?" he whispered, stroking my hair.

"I don't know." I had thought his tenderness would change me.

"We don't have to do anything you're not ready for."

"I want to." I wanted to please him, to obliterate myself. Still, though, he sat up, considering me. I was too ashamed of all my fears.

"Come here." I pulled him toward me. He resisted for a moment, but then I pressed my body against his and something in him gave way. He undressed himself, too, laying his clothes quietly on the floor. I opened my eyes and saw his chest, thick and fair with blond tufts of hair, and his cock sticking up toward me.

"I'm on the pill," I blurted out, then closed my eyes again as he spread my legs and began caressing me with his fingers. I wanted to tell him not to bother. Nothing would happen that way. I pulled him down, gliding his cock inside me. His movements were unfamiliar; I couldn't catch their rhythm. I had forgotten what it was like to sleep with someone for the first time. He stopped moving and concentrated on my neck, my shoulders, kissing my breasts, but I was distracted, worrying too much about whether I would feel something or not, and also thinking of Tom, whom I had loved and was now betraying.

I exaggerated my pleasure with Stephen as I had done with Tom and many others. His body lurched in and out of mine, and after he came, he lay heavily on top of me.

"Are you okay?" he whispered.

"Great," I whispered back, and stroked his hair so he would not raise his head and see my tears.

Home, I wrapped myself in my old terry cloth bathrobe, hiding my body from myself as the water filled my bathtub. In the next room, messages collected on my machine. First Pam apologized for not having called earlier. The audition had gone well, she said, and then she'd bumped into Elaine Douvas, who was one of the judges.

"Of course, Elaine couldn't really tell me how she thought I'd played . . . but she sort of hinted that I'd done well enough to get into the finals." Pam paused, then hearing her words as I might hear them, she added, "She didn't say anything definite, of course."

As soon as she hung up, Tom called to tell me the address of the studio in SoHo and that afterward he would take me out to a great Italian restaurant right nearby.

"I can't wait for you to come. I can't wait for you to hear me in the studio." He asked me how Betty Blue was. She had been puffed up with her eyes closed since yesterday morning. Tom had woken up three times in the middle of the night to check her.

"I wish you would have called me today to tell me about her," he said into the machine. "I worried all day." Before hanging up, he gave me a list of things I should do for her to make sure she was okay, and I didn't know how anybody ever left anyone they had once loved.

I dressed without noticing what I wore, and I lost my way looking for the studio on the unlit streets in the outskirts of SoHo. The cold numbed my fingers so much that I couldn't straighten the crumpled address enough to read it. I imagined my father, sneaking around these streets with Marissa to Hannah's gallery, stopping to kiss her beside an old arching entranceway and a garbage can. I wondered if he'd thought of my mother as they embraced and what he told my mother when he got home, and I asked myself if it was all more forgivable to me now after what I had done with Stephen.

The entrance was not at all as glamorous as I expected from a famous studio; the metal door was bolted five times, and the buzzer was marked with a taped-on slip of paper saying, "AMI Studios." I was buzzed through the door and then I followed a carpeted hallway leading to Studios One and Two. Studio One had a brown leather semicircular couch facing panels of sleek recording equipment. I did not see Tom at first. Two members of the Quartet, Andrew, the cellist, and Cynthia, the violist, were negotiating something behind the panels with a long-haired guy in a Led Zeppelin shirt who must have been the engineer's assistant. The three of them faced a window into a soundproof room where Tom was by himself behind the thick glass. Headphones on, hair flattened, he looked grim. He plucked vaguely at one of his strings.

I waited in the entrance behind Andrew, Cynthia, and the engineer, who were annoyed, discussing how many takes Tom had needed to nail a certain passage, and I watched Tom alone behind the glass where he could hear nothing now, except what the engineer allowed through the speakers and the small, disconnected sounds of his violin strings. I ached with sympathy for him and I thought first how much I still loved him, and then in the next moment, I told myself that I did not know how to love at all.

"Do those four bars again. From letter G," the engineer in the Led Zeppelin shirt said into a microphone, and then he flipped a red switch on the panel. I heard nothing; the rest of the quartet parts must have been coming through Tom's headphones. But Tom's sound boomed through the speakers above the panels. He hit a high G way out of tune.

"Jesus." Tom covered his forehead with his hand.

"No good." Cynthia's face soured.

"I'm sorry." Tom shielded his eyes, shook his head. His hair stayed pinned against his ears by the headphones.

Cynthia flicked off a switch to the microphone in Tom's room. "What's going on with him today?"

"It's no big deal," Andrew said. "He'll be fine."

"This is the tenth take of this."

One more time, Tom mouthed, holding up one finger, then said into the microphone, "I'll get it this time, I promise."

"Relax, Tom. Take it easy. No big deal," Andrew said to Tom, and then to Cynthia, "Take a chill."

"Letter G again," the long-haired engineer said.

I squeezed my eyes shut, blaming myself. Somewhere, somehow, he must have known what I had done today. Please, I prayed, and the next time he played the four bars perfectly. Cynthia and Andrew let out long sighs and relaxed.

* * *

"I can't believe you came in just at that moment. That was terrible." Tom banged his head back against the metal of the elevator, and I rubbed his shoulder, trying to convince him that everything was okay. He had gotten it right in the end.

"There's something wrong with me," he said. "I don't know what it is. Something awful."

Outside, the cold of the night was startling and we braced ourselves, slumping into our coats. Tom shuffled along the broken-up sidewalk, his violin clasped tight.

"My father's in the hospital again," he said. "The doctor says if he doesn't stop drinking, he's going to be dead in five years."

"That's terrible."

"His girlfriend wouldn't even let me speak to him. I've never been so unhappy. Since I started this whole thing. Never. The Quartet was talking about that tour next summer and I had the feeling they weren't sure if they were going to keep me or fire me by then."

The Quartet was planning to go to Italy where all of Tom's father's relatives lived. Tom had never met them before. I told him over and over I was sure they were not going to fire him and that he would meet his family. Tom never used to berate himself like this before he won the audition, before I started accusing him of not giving things he was unable to give. Before I started betraying him with Stephen.

"You're so supportive," he said. "I don't deserve you."

"It's me who doesn't deserve you." I pulled him close to me, but his body already felt so separate from mine, as if I had already lost him. Still, I breathed into his ear, "It's okay, Tom. It's okay. Everything will be all right."

That night I babied Tom. He lay in bed, watching television, and I made him buttery garlic bread, his favorite, and split-pea soup, so thick his spoon could stand up in it.

"I'll take care of you." I stroked his forehead as if he had a fever. "Don't worry. I will." I tried not to feel that I was resigning myself.

The next day when Tom was back at the studio, I called Stephen and told him I did not want to see him again. I didn't even want to be friends.

"You mean you don't want to be with me anymore?" he said finally, as if my words had made no sense to him. His voice seemed no different over the phone. It was slow and kind and just as close to my heart.

"I made a mistake. A big mistake. I'm sorry."

"You ran away so quickly yesterday," he said, then lowered his voice. "Were you afraid?"

"What are you talking about?" I snapped to keep up my resolve and to ruin everything between us.

"I felt it then, you know. Like you had vanished on me . . ." He didn't finish, but I knew he had sensed my fears. He had understood me better than anyone else ever had. With him, I thought, I might change myself. But I could not waver again. Instead, I humphed with disgust.

"It's not going to work, Stephen. Let's just forget it."

"Are you sure? Are you sure you're doing the right thing?"

I reached for a cigarette on the coffee table, flicked the lighter three times, and snapped at him again. "Of course, I'm sure, I'm very happy right now. I've never been happier."

"I guess you know what's best for yourself," he said, obviously implying that I didn't know, and I sucked on my cigarette trying to block out his words. A part of me was sure that Stephen was my chance and that I should have left Tom when I had some courage.

"Since you don't want to see me again," Stephen said, "I might as well tell you what I was going to tell you, since it doesn't matter anyway." I held my breath, knowing I should get off the phone before he told me anything. "I think, I think we could be perfect together."

I smoked my cigarette quickly. "I have to get off the phone." As I hung up, I was certain I had ended anything that might ever have happened between us.

18

*M*y mother was happiest in Woodstock, near Bearsville, her birthplace, in the house we used to rent on Overlook Mountain. She did not get those headaches or spells of grief that kept her in bed for days, the cloth over her eyes. She liked to do the things she'd done as a girl, and in all these activities—hiking, walking, swimming—she was sturdy, reliable, unlike the mother I knew.

"See that, see that, look at your mother," my father would huff, his bike swerving beneath him, as my mother pushed up the hill far ahead of us. "Pretty amazing, isn't she?"

My mother would show off, riding with no hands, shouting back to us, "I used to do this all the time when I was a kid."

My father would make some joke about the street corners he used to hang out on, the hours he spent working in the candy store. "While you were riding through mountains," he shouted, "I was making a penny on egg creams. How's that for guilt?" He turned to me, swerving, and said, "Is there anything better than this?"

I groaned, not wanting to admit how content I did feel then, just the three of us, my mother indomitable in the lead, exactly where she liked to be. She was exhilarated at the top of the mountain. Standing by her bike, waiting for us, she raised her arms to the sky and cheered, "Made it again. Look at me, everyone. I made it again."

But as if they could not stand their good times to last any longer than necessary, my parents inevitably fought during the car ride home. My mother was nervous in cars, and my father was a sloppy, absentminded driver who slipped in and out of lanes. The drives might begin with my mother in the passenger seat covering her mouth every time my father veered into the wrong lane, but by the middle of the trip, she would be gripping the dashboard, criticizing his every move. By the time we reached the Palisades Parkway, my father would have slammed on the breaks, pulled off the road.

"Quiet," he'd hiss, cutting the air with his hand

"You never consider my feelings. Never. I can't take it anymore. This is it," she'd cry, threatening him in that way he despised and that pushed him away even further. But he never made the effort to drive any more carefully, and if my mother insisted on driving too often, he felt controlled and punished, banned to the passenger's seat. He might not speak to her the whole way home.

Through twenty-eight years of marriage, no compromises were ever reached—over any issue. My father's dismissal of my mother and his attention to other women never ceased; my mother persisted with her jabs, her complaints, and her lists of disappointments.

"I need someone who recognizes me. I need someone who can really be with me," my mother would tell me. But I didn't know if she could really be with anyone. And I did not know if I could either.

"I can't stay for long," my mother said as soon as she walked into my apartment a few days after I ended everything with Stephen. She hadn't been to my home in over a year. We lingered in the short front hall, not knowing what to do with each other. Age had sharpened, bittered her features. She was fifty-six, more than thirty-five years older than the girl who had ridden the bus to New York City, the girl whom my father had first fallen in love with.

I tried to feel adult with my mother in my apartment, which was cleaner and more thoughtfully arranged since Tom had moved in. We had flowers and plants on the windowsills, Tom's Naguchi lamp and his collages framed on the shelf near Betty Blue.

"And look at you!" My mother smiled up close to her cage. "Aren't you pretty?"

Betty Blue, who was feeling much better and only needed a small bit of attention to feel happy, began chirping, her beak all the way open, pink tongue curled.

"Your father hated animals," my mother said, still up close to the cage. Her purple canvas bag was clamped under her arm, and she fiddled with the color photo of Swami Muktananda that hung from her necklace. "Remember how Ethel used to pee on all the carpets and what rages your father used to have? Remember?"

"Sort of," I said to avoid hearing anything about it. I wanted to be free. I wanted to be relieved of her and the fear that she would hurt herself again. She seemed to be feeling a little better, though. She was taking her yoga classes, volunteering at NOW, sending out résumés for social work positions, though she wasn't sure she really wanted that kind of job. She'd gone out a few more times with her piano teacher. For some reason, I'd bragged about his age to Tom and Pam even though I found it alarming.

On the couch, she sat cross-legged in her white drawstring yoga pants, her thin wrists balanced on her knees, and I asked her how the piano teacher was, though a part of me didn't want to know.

"Oh, Carlton! What shall I say?" She laughed almost gaily. "Perhaps I'm just chasing after my youth. Youth!" She raised her hands to the sky, praying for it again, and by accident, she spilled some tea on her lap. I jumped for paper towels.

"He's quite intense," she said. "He's the kind of moody genius I would have fallen in love with at twenty. You know, cynical, underfed, depressed . . ."

I smiled, trying to be easy with her.

"I'm like his mommy. I cook dinner for him. Give him carrots while he watches TV. It's nice though, to have someone pay some sexual attention to me. You know your father never did."

I sipped my tea. The steam rising in my face made me dizzy.

"Your father ignored me half the time."

"Mom, I don't want to hear this," I grumbled into my cup.

"You don't know what it feels like to be rejected night after night."

"Please." I gritted my teeth.

"Your father rejected me so much I'd forgotten what it is to be touched."

"I can't hear this, Mom. It's too much."

"I'm telling you the truth," my mother said, but she was stung by my words. I let there be silence between us and I did not apologize.

"Where's Tom?" my mother finally said, looking around, suddenly noticing he was missing. I explained the CDs he was making for Columbia Records.

"And how do you feel about all this?" She squinted at me, and though perhaps what I lacked and needed most in this world was love from my mother, with her studying me so closely, I could only shrug her off and answer, "I don't really care."

"You're not jealous?"

"No."

"Being a woman is terrible," she said and I agreed. "We should have both been born men. At least, Tom's nice. That's the most important thing. You can't expect someone to change this. This only you can fix." She pointed to her heart, which we both knew was the same as mine. "Have you sent your tape to Boston Pops?"

I flashed through all possible answers in my head, but decided to tell her the truth. "I've decided to audition for Oakland instead."

"Bad choice. You're doing it again." She waved her finger at me and laughed. "You're being like me."

I took a sip of hot tea. "I'm being realistic."

"How do you know what's realistic? You've always undermined yourself. You've never tried your best."

I stared at the cigarette burn on the carpet beneath the coffee table.

"I always tried my best," I said to the burn. "It's true."

"Well, I don't believe that for a moment. Remember that Christmas concert at Juilliard?"

"I don't want to talk about this."

"I pushed you to play. I kept telling you you had to do it, no question about it, you couldn't go through life saying 'I can't,' and everyone, including Mr. Timm, thought you played beautifully." She nodded at me, waiting for me to agree with her. I would not. "Wait till you're a mother, and then you'll see. It's not so easy. No one tells you how to do it. No one makes you a perfect person first. You do what you can."

I thought I knew already how terrible motherhood could be and I tried not to listen to her.

"I was always angry at my mother," she told me. "She was cold. She never gave me enough love. She never held me. Never. Not once.

Can you imagine that? I was alone. Then and now. No one thinks about me in the middle of the day."

She wanted my reassurance; I was cruel and refused to give it to her.

"For years I blamed her. For that, and for her inability to even recognize how my father was abusing me." My mother's face screwed up awfully. "And then, you know what?" She clapped her hands together. "I realized that she did the best she could with what she had. She loved me. She did. And I realized I had to accept her. Gain sympathy. That's the highest human quality: sympathy."

Sympathy, sympathy, I made the word ugly in my mind, mocking her to myself. I, too, had needed a mother who would love me and give me a safe, confident feeling in this world.

"I know I must have scared you that day, Gala."

It was the first time she had acknowledged how I might have felt.

"I'm sorry," she said.

I felt the tears breaking in me. I clenched my teeth.

"I'm okay now." She nodded. "I mean, I will always be me. I will always have to struggle with myself." She waited for me to say something encouraging. "I love you. Whether you feel it or not. I've always loved you."

I nodded, said nothing, and kept myself separate from her.

"I did my best. You'll know that someday. You were such a sad, angry child. I don't understand it."

Because I decided that my mother was right—I had never tried my best—I told Pam I would play Prokofiev's Fifth with her for a Christmas concert with the Westchester Philharmonic, a good orchestra in which she played first oboe. The second oboist would return from out of town for the next concert, but Pam said she had a feeling the second oboist might soon move away permanently. Maybe if the conductor liked me, I could take over the gig. I had not played in over two weeks, the longest time I had ever not played, and my fingers felt enormous and cloddish. I could not get them to learn the fast turn in the last-movement oboe duet. I did my usual, playing it ten times at each metronome speed, but I only made it up to tempo twice.

I feared horrible things: the conductor making me play it alone in front of everyone, disgracing me, and then Pam, so scornful, she would hardly look at me. And I would leave the rehearsal, never wanting to play again.

What would my mother say? I thought, like the child I was around her. My quitting would be angry, like a suicide note back to her.

I remembered that Christmas piano concert, the one my mother had refused to let me drop out of. "The more you do it," she said, "the tougher you'll be." And I had ended up being loved at that concert. I was an anomaly, an eleven-year-old girl who could pour a heart's fill of loneliness and longing into Chopin.

It was almost like my trick, first on the piano and then on the oboe. I could make an audience cry with how much sadness I could pour through my reed. Playing, I could turn it on and off exactly when I wanted to.

"I'm nervous about tomorrow," I said to Tom the night before the rehearsal. I was stirring spaghetti sauce, watching it bubble in the pan. It made him happy if I cooked dinner for him after his days at the studio, which never went well.

"What's there to be nervous about?" he said from the couch. "It's not like they're wasting two thousand dollars a day on the best studio in New York every time you make a mistake. It's just a rehearsal."

I held myself back from again accusing him of not understanding. "Have you ever thought of what life would be like without music?"

"No." He flicked the channels on the remote control.

"Just 'no'?"

"What else am I going to be? A gangster?" He smiled at something on television, *The Simpsons,* it sounded like. I wanted him to ask me more about what I was feeling. I was sure he must have known that, except that he was tired and grumpy from ten grueling hours at the studio and he wanted to prove he didn't have to talk just because I wanted to. I stared into the simmering sauce and I remembered how easy it had been to talk to Stephen about the very same things. I could not be with someone I could not talk to.

"You don't listen to me, Tom."

"Jesus." He sighed despairingly, and he covered his face with his hands. "You're always angry at me. Everything I do is wrong," he said into the darkness of his palms. "How could I have responded differently? How could I have made you happy?"

"Show me that you're interested. Ask me questions."

"So if I follow your orders and ask you a series of questions, any questions, you'll think that I'm listening to you and you won't get angry at me?"

I tried to suffocate my need to speak my mind, to squash my own voice once again.

"I'm sick of following orders," Tom said.

"I need to be able to discuss things with you. It's something I have to have." I faced him. "I can't live without it."

"I'm so tired right now, Gala. Every time I go into the studio, I do something wrong, and then I come home and you tell me what's wrong with me."

He went into the bedroom, shut the door. I waited for the lights to go on, expected to hear the television or the radio, but instead the room remained silent. I could still have salvaged the evening somehow, as I had done so many times, but I thought it took more strength to just stand there, stirring the sauce, knocking the pretty flowers of broccoli against the peas.

Half an hour before the rehearsal, only a few wind players were on the stage warming up in the center of the hundred music stands and empty folding chairs. I looked around for Stephen as I always did now, hoping for some flukish reason he might suddenly appear. I imagined his slow, Southern voice, telling me how we could be perfect together, and how I would argue, "There's no such thing as perfect, everything's the same. It's this." I would point to my heart, as my mother had. "It's this that needs to be fixed." Of course, he would not listen to me. He would take me in his arms and my fears would give way, and suddenly, perfectly, I would know love as it should be, in all ways kind.

Pam had not yet arrived and I felt self-conscious alone, walking down the dim velvet rows of seats to the stage. John, an oboist who had witnessed Merkin Hall, was playing English horn. I'd bumped into him once or twice since Merkin and he'd never mentioned anything, but I was sure whenever he saw my face, all he thought of was my ugly playing. On the stage, he was stretching across the two oboe chairs to talk to the first flutist, Oscar, from Juilliard and from Spain, who did not stop playing to listen to him. Oscar was fluttering through the flute version of the Mozart Concerto twice as fast as any oboist would attempt to play it. He double-tongued through the arpeggios, which most oboists clunked through.

"Hi." I broke up their conversation, my face red as if the humiliation had happened yesterday.

"What's up, Gala," John said. He was awkward himself with his freckles and long, skinny fingers, which flattened out, double-jointed, over his English horn.

On the stand, my part was open to the solo duet I'd been unable to learn at home. John asked me if I had been getting good gigs lately, and I shrugged and said vaguely, "Pretty good."

Behind me, the bassoonists were taking turns playing the opening of *The Rite of Spring.* One of them imitated the European style, making his sound bright and wobbly with vibrato. I didn't want to warm up with so few people there. When the clarinetist played loudly in his high register, I started to play, too. My fingers were clumsy, and my lips felt huge and insensitive. My low notes jerked out and I saw that John had stopped playing and was listening to me.

"I'm out of shape." I gave a small laugh and was too self-conscious to practice the hard solo.

"There's Pam." I pointed to the front of the auditorium to divert attention from myself. Oscar and John both stopped playing, sat back in their chairs, waving too eagerly. She crinkled up her nose, waved back, her breasts loose under her sweater, her narrow hips swaying in her leather pants. When we were close and spent every afternoon together, she used to take baths in front of me, soaping herself everywhere. She handled her breasts as if they were ordinary, functional, and not especially delicate parts of herself.

Pam plopped her music bag down in front of our stands.

"What a mess." She rolled her eyes and blew away a blond wisp. "Somebody pulled the emergency break on the 1 train. Hey, babe. It's been so long since we've played together." She gave me her cheek to kiss, and it was smooth and cool from being outside. Her leather pants squeaked on the metal folding chair. "Gala and I used to have every rehearsal and every concert together," she said to Oscar. "We even practiced together. I want to try to get Gala in here permanently."

"You'll have to kill off Lucy," John said. "You can put cyanide in her reed water."

John and Pam had both played the semifinals of the audition and both thought they'd done badly. Pam said her reed had been too harsh; John said his had been too stiff and his articulation on *La Scala* had come out fuzzy.

"Now, it's up to fate," Pam said.

"Fate named Elaine Douvas," John said. "But you've got her in the bag."

"I wish," Pam said, but I could tell she believed it was true. In a moment, I tallied up our lives and their respective hardships, and hers seemed to easily outweigh mine. There seemed no reason why she should be someone so much more full of herself than I, why she seemed to get through life safely, protected, without this endless self-doubt. At Juilliard, we had established between us a balance of strengths and weaknesses, false or true; I was the more soulful player, the more musically thoughtful. I had taught her reeds, but she had greater finger technique, greater command, greater experience. I had to practice hours to learn a part that she could simply go over half an hour before a rehearsal, and even then, my playing was so much shakier, so much more liable to fall apart.

We used to support each other and bad-mouth anyone who put the other one down.

"We're different players," we would tell each other. "Different but equal."

We could have said anything we wanted. Nothing was true. Our sounds lasted for moments. Who could ever decide completely and finally that one of us had it and the other one didn't?

The orchestra was almost full by now. Of course, the strings were playing concertos for each other instead of practicing the orchestra music. And behind me the brass players were blasting the *Night on Bald Mountain* solo as loud as they could. I closed my eyes and listened. There was nothing better in life, I thought. Nothing more close to the heart, the root, the noise, the everything of life, than this beautiful, disorganized sound.

"So how are you doing since your lesson?" Pam asked me, but then a preppy-looking guy in his forties with short brown hair jogged onto the podium. The orchestra became so silent that the sound of him flipping the pages of his score seemed loud. He nodded to Evgeny, the concertmaster, from Juilliard, to take Pam's tuning A.

The whole string section turned to look at Pam and I felt nervous for her. I hated giving that A, that first note of the day, with everyone silent and listening. It always blipped or burbled or wobbled in pitch.

Pam sat up straight and did not hesitate. When Evgeny, a Russian with white skin and hair, jerked his bow in her direction, she played her A, fat and strong and exactly in tune. Evgeny motioned with his chin for the A for the winds. I caught his eye and was sure he raised his eyebrows just slightly at me.

"First movement, Prokofiev," the conductor said, and I relaxed a little. If we didn't do the last movement, everything would be fine.

"Half a measure for nothing," the conductor said. His beats were chaotic and too big—his elbow rose all the way up to his head for "one"—but still, Oscar and the bassoonist played perfectly together. Their blended sound was not that of a flute and a bassoon, but of a different instrument, a perfect combination of both: deep and solid and ephemeral.

Pam bobbed her head, her reed balanced on her lower lip, marking the beats until her solo. Her sound was sturdy and commanding. It was clear why she had been moved into the semifinals; she was good, very good, and much better than I.

The strings began the heavy Slavic theme. As I played, I lost myself, drowned in the lush, massive sound of the full orchestra building together, and then the music twisted suddenly again and fell back with the dark dissonance of the bass.

"Last movement," the conductor said, and I felt my heart beating fast as if I'd already made a mistake.

"Here we go." Pam rolled her eyes again. "I spent two hours on that solo last night."

The conductor raised his arms for the upbeat, then cued in the French horns. One horn cracked the first note, but she recovered immediately, did not let her mistake ruin the rest of the solo. The flute and bassoon played the restatement of the first-movement theme in a solo duet that Pam and the bassoonist had to mimic and answer. Pam did it perfectly—perfectly blended, perfectly in tune with the bassoon.

All the winds applauded her, shuffling their feet on the floor of the stage.

The allegro section was much faster than I had practiced it.

"Almost there," Pam whispered at me, and we counted measures on the edge of our seats. I tried to feel as brave as I felt before entrances with the New Amsterdam Orchestra. The clarinetist's fingers were fast and easy over his solo. Five measures to go, four measures, three measures. My fingers felt watery and trembling. That same old feeling. I couldn't stop it. My fingers kept shaking. I began a little behind Pam. I lost control over the turn. I tried to catch up, speeding up on the staccato notes.

"Hey, hey, oboes." The conductor stopped the orchestra. The first violins swiveled around to stare at us. Pam sat up tall, but a blush rose up her neck. Evgeny pointed at us and whispered something to his stand partner.

"Let's try that again," the conductor said. "Letter B. Five measures before the solo."

I spoke to myself. It's okay, it's okay, just one moment out of many. One moment. You can do it. But my fingers were shaking so badly that I fumbled through the turn and got a full beat behind Pam.

"What's going on?" the conductor asked.

"You were behind, Gala," Pam whispered through her teeth.

"Let's hear the two oboes alone," the conductor said, and I thought, no, I couldn't do it. I just couldn't. The strings rested their bows in their laps, watched Pam and me.

"Just stay with me. Don't get behind," Pam hissed at me. "Play softly."

The conductor raised his baton and I concentrated hard to send him a message: Don't make us do it, please. It was silent as he beat three counts, and then when we came in, I messed up worse than before. I lost control so badly I didn't even make it to the staccato notes. But Pam continued playing, and she played the solo alone perfectly. The whole orchestra was staring at me, John was staring at me, Oscar, Evgeny, everyone stared at me, except Pam, who sat up straight, fixed on the conductor.

"Second oboe," the conductor said. "Have you looked at this part?"

I opened my mouth but no words came out. Beside me, John was looking down.

The conductor gave me a look that made me and everyone else know I was fired.

"Letter C," he said, and started the orchestra again after the place where my solo was supposed to be. I played through the rest of the piece, but I wasn't there. I didn't exist. I felt glazed, whipped into a little box. And the sound continued around me, the flutes, the clarinets, the violins.

It was what I knew best—this deep, sexual shame—as I lay in bed on my stomach, breasts pressed flat on the mattress, fists pressing into my cheeks so that it hurt. I had the covers up over my head, my eyes squeezed shut. I'd packed up quickly, stuffing my reed-making knives into the side of my case, and Pam was silent beside me. I kept hoping something would happen, anything—maybe all the lights could suddenly fall from the ceiling, knocking over all the rows of music stands and chairs—and Pam and I would laugh together again and the rehearsal would be completely obliterated from time and memory. But Pam said nothing to me, and I rushed off the stage, letting my new oboe rattle in its case.

Tom called from the studio. I reached for the phone beside the bed, held it under the covers. I told him what had happened.

"I was humiliated." I began shivering.

"You want to know what you should've said? You should have told the conductor, 'I got the part this morning. Big deal. I'll know it by the concert.' " Tom made his voice smug and indifferent. "You shouldn't have let him intimidate you like that."

I shivered. "I don't know."

Tom sighed. He didn't know what to say to me anymore. "Why do you let people intimidate you? That's your problem. 'Fuck you,' you should have said."

"If I could be someone else, I would. I want to kill myself."

"Gala . . ." Tom laughed uncomfortably. "What's wrong with you?"

A few measures of the Bartók blared suddenly and then stopped on his end of the wire. I heard Andrew and the engineer arguing about something.

"I like that section," Tom shouted away from the phone.

"I feel so lonely," I said, but Andrew was talking to Tom and it took Tom a second to come back to the phone.

"Hello," Tom said, "sorry about that."

"We're so far apart, I can't stand it anymore."

A sudden, sweet, lighthearted violin run interrupted us, mocking my words. It had all come down to this moment, over the phone. "It's too much," I said. "I can't do it anymore. Nothing's changing. Do you hear me?"

"I'm coming home," Tom said finally, though Andrew was shouting at him. "I'll be there in an hour. Don't go anywhere." He hung up the phone.

I poured myself a glass of wine and sat on the edge of the bed facing the mirror. In the shadowy dark, my white, folding stomach, hanging breasts, spread thighs, looked like any woman's body. I knew if I wanted to, I could make everything right between Tom and me. I could beg for his comfort after the humiliation of my day and I could plead for him to give me another chance. We would lie in bed with our backs to each other, unable to sleep all night, but then it would be a new day. Tom would rise early to warm up for the studio, and I would make coffee, sit on the couch while he played for me all the parts he worried he'd mess up. I would have lost whatever courage I had tonight; I would never leave him.

This was how life could slip away.

I drank two more glasses of wine. There was a noise in the front hall and I jumped, worrying it was Tom. I wasn't ready yet to see him. I needed to make my decision tonight. I poured myself another glass of wine and glanced at the clock. It was ten. Tom would be home any minute. I was already drunk when I left my apartment in my high heels and tight red sweater, the one Stephen had liked.

I walked down Broadway toward Stephen's house. I told myself I didn't know what I was doing, that I was in a daze. But really, I felt dizzyingly alert, walking up the wide, dark streets, the wind whipping back my hair, rushing into my open mouth. I remembered how Stephen had touched me. He did it so curiously, so gently, testing my reaction to everything he did. He had noticed my fears.

Stephen lived on Morningside Park where I shouldn't have been walking alone. I wanted another drink but the West End was packed with Columbia students, sitting at tables with bowls of popcorn and beer. I changed my mind and left. I walked four blocks down Broadway, past men with red, wind-stung eyes in hooded down coats selling rows of Christmas trees on the sidewalk. Those trees always made me sad, tied up on the street. The Marlin Bar was near empty with just a few men leaning over their drinks at the bar. I caught a look at myself in the entranceway mirror. From lying in bed, my frizzy hair was disheveled, and I had a black mark under my eye where my mascara had smudged.

I moved up to the bar next to a man with long, oily black hair, sideburns, and inky eyes.

"Vodka straight," I told the bartender, and the man raised his hand and grinned at me. On the bar, our arms almost touched. The bartender reached under the bar and poured a shot of vodka into a small glass.

"Hey." The man swiveled a little on his chair, his arm touching mine.

The jukebox was playing Janis Joplin, singing "Bobby McGee" with the cracks in her voice you could almost see. I stirred my vodka and braced myself for the awful taste.

"A pretty girl like you isn't used to it yet," the man said.

I held my breath and drank down the whole glass. "Another shot," I told the bartender.

"Whoa," the man breathed at me.

I took the next glass, drank down half.

"Whoa. What's happening?" He shifted on his seat. His leg rubbed against mine. I felt ashamed in front of the bartender, an Irish man with gray hair and a corduroy shirt, and I turned slightly away from the man. His sideburns ran nearly to his mouth.

"Are you a Columbia student or what?" he asked me.

"No." I looked into his black eyes.

"Barnard?"

"Yes."

"What do you study? Books? Literature?"

"I study physics. I'm a physicist." I laughed. I felt swarming and lush and bitter inside.

"A physicist?" He moved up closer to me, the whole length of his leg touching mine. "My last girlfriend was a scientist, but she left me. All of a sudden." He flicked his wrist in the air.

The bartender asked me if I wanted another drink.

"Just one more."

"What does a physicist do?" The man moved his leg back and forth against me. His touch and the vodka flowed warmly through my legs. I thought of Tom, kissing me in his apartment in Chelsea and how I felt new and tingling and alive with myself as the streetlights flashed on and off and on and off and Tom lowered me to the floor. I let him do whatever he wanted with me, and sometimes it hurt and sometimes it did not, but when I tried to stop the part that hurt, he no longer wanted me. He felt criticized and judged, he said, and I understood that, but for the first time I thought with rage and pain about the despair I'd felt those nights when he came down over me, covering my eyes until I was no longer there.

"I'll buy the next round." The man grinned at me, and I moved away from him.

"I've had enough." I finished the last of my vodka and left twenty dollars, way more than the bill, on the bar.

I headed toward Manhattan Avenue to Stephen's. The cold dizzied me, but I decided if he wasn't home, I would still wait for him on the street corner. When he came, he would embrace me. "Thank you, thank you," we would murmur.

Four big men gathered on the corner of his block, smoking crack. The night was black through the windows of the burned-out buildings, and the single streetlight gleamed in a broken window. The glass door of the building I'd thought was Stephen's had been shattered, and the one right next to it had the same peeling green wallpaper as in Stephen's hall. I couldn't tell which building was his. I felt suddenly very drunk. I teetered on my high heels and then leaned up against the wood of the smashed door. One of the men smoking crack followed me with his eyes, measuring how much money I had.

A decently dressed woman with two narrow-nosed Doberman pinschers crossed the street.

"What time is it?" My words were slurred and sloppy.

"The time?" She studied me closely and I realized how I must have looked: I looked like a person in trouble.

"It's midnight."

"Thank you." I stumbled toward her. She pulled on the dogs' leashes and moved away from me quickly. I swallowed hard, gripping the window ledge, worried I was going to be sick.

I saw Stephen from a block away. In the darkness, he was featureless, but I knew it was him because of the umbrella, which he tapped ahead of him on the pavement. He was walking with a woman. They were not touching each other but they were leaning close together, intimately.

"Yeah, right," he said in a sarcastic but affectionate tone, and she laughed, a musical, sweet, feminine-type laugh. Horrified, I could not take my eyes off them.

Twenty feet away from me, Stephen suddenly stopped, shielded his eyes with his hands, perhaps searching into the darkness. I was half-hidden in the shadows of a stoop, but I did not wait around to tell whether he had seen me. I ran in my high heels and he did not call after me.

From the corner, I could see the lights were on in my apartment. Tom was home. Courage, I told myself. I knew I had it. Climbing the four flights up, I tried to feel the strength in my legs and the firmness of my stride and to feel a joy and comfort in this body, which was mine, walking up the stairs. I would not hurt myself as I had threatened Tom over the phone, as my mother had done. I would be okay. I would be alone, but I would be okay.

"Where were you? Jesus Christ." Tom wiped his hand down his face. "I was so worried. I thought you were dead. I thought you had done something to yourself. . . . Jesus." He stared at me, taking me in, the high heels, the short skirt, the messy hair and smeared lipstick. "You were with someone else tonight, weren't you?"

"No," I said, but I looked straight at him, denying nothing.

"You fucked someone else." Tom grabbed my shoulders. "You betrayed me," he shouted, picking up the empty beer bottle on the table and throwing it against the kitchen wall. Tiny green shards of glass splattered onto the floor. Above my head in her cage, Betty Blue chirped wildly. I kept telling myself this was a moment that would change my life, but I couldn't focus on it, couldn't look straight at Tom, and he left the room, slamming the bedroom door shut behind him. For a moment, there was silence inside the room, and I thought if I were to go to Tom now, if I were to deny everything, I might still be able to save us.

Instead, I rocked myself on the couch as I heard the sounds of something being pulled out from the closet and then drawers opened quickly. Tom was talking on the phone, his voice low, monotonous, then frantic for a moment. I knew I would only have to get through a few more minutes. I would hold my breath, hold myself tight inside, until he was gone.

"I'm leaving." Tom clutched suitcases in both hands.

"Okay," I said so softly my voice barely formed above a whisper. "I want you to go." My tone was sure. I felt my own will, beating in me. I said it again, louder. "I can't go on anymore. It's the truth. It's over."

He let out something like a sob, one short cry. His curls rustled against the back of his leather jacket as he adjusted and readjusted his violin-case shoulder strap, the brown leather one I had bought him. He waited another moment for me to call him back, and then without another word, he disappeared into the short hallway to the door.

I dreamed of bodies. Of men white like statues, but rubbery and cold to the touch. I was surrounded by rocks, below and above me. The concertmaster, Evgeny, who had witnessed my shame, was on top of me, his hips pushing against mine. And then he changed to Wendel, my old boyfriend, and I was on my knees, sucking his cock, his face contorting with a mixture of pleasure and taunting and pain.

I woke up, coming. When I opened my eyes to the darkness, my body was covered with sweat, and I was still breathing hard. I looked to the pillow beside me and saw that Tom was gone and that I was alone, completely alone. I let myself cry. My tears, my body choking, the sounds of only myself filled the room. I listened to myself crying as if I were above and beyond myself, as if I were watching and listening to another woman crying in her bed in the middle of the night, as if this couldn't possibly be me.

Later, with my blanket and pillow, I went into the living room, turned on the television. I had grown familiar with late-night television. I watched a nature program, a show about chimpanzees. In this show, a young, bearded man explained how he had gotten his chimpanzee to communicate with sign language. He and his chimpanzee, Zola, made complicated hand gestures back and forth. The palms of her hands looked tender and soft. Her fingers were small and even. The man gestured at her wildly, then she had to retrieve objects, such as a banana, a tire, and a sneaker. As a reward, the man hugged Zola and she clapped her hands together like a monkey.

19

Robin and her mother, Florence, stood above me as I searched between the octave keys for cracks in the wood. The only remnant of a scar were the two pins where the wood had been repaired.

"So we shouldn't buy it then?" Florence said.

"Most oboes have cracked at some point." My voice felt hoarse and too vibrant in my throat. I hadn't spoken to anyone since Tom left last night. Florence leaned over my shoulder. She smelled of the lilac soap my mother used. I was careful not to look at her.

"It doesn't mean that the sound has been hurt. Not necessarily," I said, not explaining myself well.

"It costs fifteen hundred dollars. Fifteen hundred," Robin repeated, liking the sound of all that money. She was nearly a teenager, dressed in black leggings, lace-up boots, and an oversize sweater. Her skinniness now made her look lanky and long-limbed, and I didn't know how mothers ever let their children go out so unprotected in the world.

Robin wedged the upper and lower joint of the oboe between her stomach and hand and pushed them together.

"Watch out," I told her. "Don't press on the keys."

"I wasn't." She rolled her eyes and dunked her reed into the Dixie cup on the teetering iron music stand. Her mother and I watched from the couch, her knee almost touching mine.

Robin took a huge, shallow breath from her chest, the kind I always told her not to take, but still the new oboe transformed her playing. Her sound was thin but focused, not wobbly or quacking as it had been before. The notes came out evenly in both pitch and volume.

"It's so much easier," Robin said. "I can't believe how much I was suffering before."

Robin and her mother hovered over my shoulders as I examined the oboe for the smoothness of the mechanism and how well the pads sealed the holes. When I played a long tone scale on the oboe, my sound had layers of depth and overtones; the thinness was Robin's problem.

"You can grow with this oboe," I said. "It's a good instrument."

Florence told Robin she wanted to talk to me, alone.

"Mom . . ." Robin blushed, but I could tell they had planned for this private talk, and I knew what it would be about. At every new step—the buying of a new instrument, the auditioning for Performing Arts, Juilliard Prep, and then Juilliard College—my parents had asked my teachers, did I have it? Should I be sacrificing more and more, giving up my options? Would I ever be good enough? The answer was always yes. As much as anyone could say, yes.

Florence sat beside me, her hands between the knees of her wool, pleated pants. She had stringy brown hair and sunken, nervous eyes.

"What do you think? Should we be investing like this?"

I evaded her real question, spoke again about comparative prices.

"But Gala . . ." Florence pushed aside her hair and tried to meet my eyes. "Do you think Robin has a special feeling for music? She said you told her that before."

I spoke to my feet. "She's very musical. She plays with a lot of feeling." I knew what a slim thing that was to build a life on, to base anything on. I thought of amending myself, explaining how difficult it all was, but that seemed premature and silly. A life of devotion to music, to anything, was the only life I'd known, and it was probably a better life than most.

"I think," I said, "it's important for her to have an instrument that will inspire her. She needs to sound good to herself or else she won't play."

Five minutes later, her mother was writing me a check for the lesson. It felt dirty in my hands as if I didn't deserve it.

"You've been a wonderful help to Robin. A wonderful teacher. In all ways."

I turned to the door, afraid I would cry.

"Are you all right today, Gala?"

"Fine," I said in a normal voice, and then I smiled at her and at Robin, who had put on lipstick in the other room.

"I'm going to throw my old oboe out the window," Robin said. "Maybe I'll burn it."

"Thank you so much," her mother said, shutting the door.

Outside, I was alone again as the dusky sky deepened above the row of brownstones. I leaned against a cold iron gate, lit a cigarette, and watched my breath, frozen and white, continuing in the air after the smoke left off. I was afraid to go home, to open the door alone to darkness, and so I walked slowly from Seventy-sixth Street up West End, quiet with vast, old buildings. No one spoke to me. Christmas decorations, wreaths, and lights hung inside windows, and I tried to forget how Tom and I had been planning on celebrating our first Christmas together this year. At Eighty-eighth Street, I looked up into my mother's apartment and saw the lights were out. Now that she was alone, anything might happen to her. I worried again about her death: that she might die having lived only an unhappy life and that I would never have been close to her. I knew when she was gone, I would regret all the times she had tried for intimacy and I had pushed her away.

That evening, in darkness, I sat on the edge of our bed, my address book open to Tom's number at Noah's in Westchester. I reached for the phone but then stopped myself. I wanted to hold out, to see if I could bear it.

I made myself plain spaghetti with Ragu sauce, and I drank the expensive white wine I'd been saving for a year. It was delicious, light and dry and soft, and I savored every sip. I overlooked Tom's stuff, which filled many of the shelves, and thought about how I might reorganize the living room, how I might make a nice home for myself, even though I was alone and needed to please no one.

"We're always alone," my father liked to say in that doomed voice of his, and I thought how that was true, but it wasn't tragic. I could count on myself, I thought, and I felt strangely giddy.

"Tom and I just broke up but I'm okay," I told Daphne over the phone. "I marched up the stairs, feeling strong, and then I did it. I asked him to leave."

"Do you want me to come over?"

I assured her I was fine, but then I couldn't sleep. The apartment was so silent that every sound—the faucet dripping, Betty Blue shifting in her cage, the wind hitting the window—made me shiver awake. I had forgotten how afraid of the dark I was, how I had always been afraid to sleep alone. Someone might climb through the window, or else alone, submerged in darkness, I might simply disappear. I thought of calling my mother, but I knew that if she were having one of her rare good nights of sleep, she'd get angry at me for waking her. Even if she wasn't angry and I told her what I felt, I worried that together we would lose ourselves to sadness and I might never see my way out.

I must have been asleep when the telephone rang at 5:00 A.M. I lurched awake to hear my own voice on the outgoing message on the machine and then Tom's voice, Tom's breathing, I was sure, though he only half-spoke, half-whispered a sound like the beginning of my name. By the time I got to the machine, he had hung up.

The bright overhead light made my head hurt as I squinted down at Noah's number in my address book. When I dialed it, Noah's father answered, groggy and annoyed. I hung up quickly and waited with my hand on the receiver. Tom must have heard the phone ring and must have known to call me back. My head felt heavy trying to picture Tom in the spare bedroom in Noah's plush house in Scarsdale, a place I'd only seen once.

I waited as the sky became white through my window. Dawns were horrible, I thought, so white, so silent. I sat with my back against the wall, thighs curled to my chest, head down on my knees.

I remembered all the nights Tom kept his back to me. I would wrap my arms around him, my breasts and stomach pressing into his back, and I could feel him tense.

"You're so needy," he said, but still I would try, always I would try too hard to get him to want me.

"You don't want to cuddle?" I would ask in a baby's voice, a voice I hated to remember, a voice I vowed never to use again. "Please?" I'd kiss his neck, the sore from his violin.

He still ignored me, his back to me. His breaths were shallow and irregular. Whatever he was thinking or feeling, he kept it from me.

The morning light washed over the living room where I sat alone. I never again wanted to beg Tom, or anyone, for feelings he did not want to give.

That day, I forced myself to finish my Oakland tape. I moved Betty Blue into the bedroom so the microphone wouldn't record her cawing in the background, and that was the only care I put into the tape. Tom had excellent recording equipment, but still it couldn't compare to the studio I'd used for the rest of the tape I'd sent to the New York City Ballet Orchestra. I only had to add two pieces to it— Iberia and Brahms. I drank two cups of coffee, kept a cigarette burning beside me, and I made the tape in a wired, caffeinated blur, smoking between pieces to keep myself going and barely editing at all. I played recklessly, only half-hearing myself. I remembered the audition and how beautiful I'd thought my Brahms was and how much I'd loved the sound of my own voice singing. I heard the soft violin chords in the background and I made my tone sweet and longing but restrained until that F, my favorite note, so full and rich and solid like a D, but more shimmering and expressive. I poured my heart into the F, sang, feeling my oboe vibrate with voice, my music.

When the phone rang, I felt dizzy, setting down my oboe and rushing to the bedroom. I clamped the receiver under my chin, sat curled with my back to the wall just as I had last night.

"You're there," Tom breathed into the phone. In the background, there were loud voices, footsteps, and a constant tunneling hum like a vacuum. "I kept trying to reach you yesterday, but I kept getting the machine and I didn't want to leave a message. Where were you?"

"Nowhere. Just a lesson. Robin," I explained, but it felt like a lie, as if I had really been with Stephen.

Tom was silent, suspicious, waiting for me to confess. From behind him came a muddy amplified announcement.

"Are you in the subway, Tom?"

"Grand Central. I have to take the train back and forth from the city to Westchester."

I imagined him, exhausted as I was, feeling lost in the crowd of commuters and the ticket booths. He hated being dislocated; he'd wanted our life together so badly. I held the phone close to my ear and waited.

"What are we doing, Gala? Why are we doing this?"

"I don't know," I said too quickly.

"Do you love someone else?"

"No," I answered. It was the truth.

"Don't you love me anymore?"

The rumble of a train faded behind him. I spoke as gently as I could. "It's not a matter of love. We just keep fighting. I can't do it anymore."

He jammed the receiver onto the hook, and the tumult of the train station was suddenly replaced by silence.

I put my tape and application in a manila envelope and went out to mail it. The wind was blustering, stormlike. Papers washed up on the sidewalk, blew around my ankles. The post office was fifteen blocks away and no bus was coming. The bus-stop sign had been slammed by something. The pole was knocked down to an angle close to the sidewalk.

I went to the mailbox on the next block. If they accepted my tape, my audition would be in a few weeks, and I would go through it all again: the sleepless nights, the overwhelming self-doubt. I could not seem to change myself. No matter how hard I tried.

The tape had to get to Oakland in two days. I had been planning on sending it Express Mail from the post office. I leaned out into the street and still saw no bus. I wanted to be daring, to leave it all to fate. I opened the mailbox. Go, I thought, and I dropped the tape into the slot, listened to it swoosh down, and then I walked away.

Alone, I jogged over the ice that covered most of Riverside Park. Daphne was too worried about slipping and not being able to dance. At first, I thought I would let myself go easy, quit my jogging for the winter months, but it made me happy to hear my steady footsteps alone on the packed snow and to feel the fresh, clean cold against my cheeks. I never missed a day anymore and I got faster and stronger. I sprinted the last half mile, pushing myself until my lungs hurt and my body was spent and satisfied.

I kept track of my miles as meticulously as I'd once monitored the speed of my scales. I expected, always, to bump into Stephen. It stunned me with what finality he had vanished from my life. Jogging by 122nd Street, past Manhattan School, any dreamy, tall man in a black overcoat or carrying a black umbrella made my stomach slip slightly, though I erased any thoughts of him as soon as they occurred to me.

Two weeks later, after picking up groceries at the end of my running route, I turned the corner home and saw Pam, also heading to Broadway. A scarf was pulled up to her nose, and her hands were shoved deep in the pockets of her wool-lined leather jacket. I thought I would pretend that I'd never seen her. She had not called me after the rehearsal, and I was too ashamed to try to reach her. She stopped across the street to light a cigarette. She struck four matches and then huddled against a building for shelter. Her cigarette still wouldn't light and she stood there for a moment, hanging her head. Something was wrong, I knew. She turned in my direction and I thought of walking quickly away, but instead I insisted to myself that I no longer wanted to be someone who hid.

She recognized me slowly, squinting first and then waving. I thought maybe she didn't want to see me. I crossed the street to her.

"What's up? Running in this weather?" she said stiffly over the top of her scarf.

"Always. It's the best." I hugged my groceries, trying to sound upbeat and together. I told her nothing, did not mention anything about Tom. I had an impulse to apologize for the rehearsal, for myself and for my playing, but I didn't let myself. Up the hill on Broadway, the aboveground subway tracks made unrelenting angles in the white sky. Hands still deep in her pockets, Pam walked, looking down at the glittery sidewalk.

"I didn't make it to the finals."

"You didn't?" I hated the part of myself that was glad. "Did you speak to Elaine Douvas?"

She shook her head. "The thing is, I know the people who made it—Joe Maritini, Matsudo Fujiwara, Helen Song—and you just know all those people had connections up their ass. Kurt said I should have fucked Tim Camo and then I would have gotten it."

This audition was the closest she'd ever gotten to winning something big. On the corner of Broadway, she flicked her black lighter and finally her cigarette flamed. I imagined tasting the pleasure of her good tobacco with her, and I missed those days when we smoked and made reeds together all afternoon and were the best of friends.

"I'm going to take a bus downtown to meet Kurt after his rehearsal. He's taking me out to dinner."

"That's nice." I smiled at her.

"What are you doing?"

I checked to see if her bus was coming. It wasn't. I had a little time if I wanted to tell her about Tom.

Pam kicked the slammed-down bus-stop sign and said, "Who the hell did this?" Against her black jacket, her short blond hair glowed in the cold sun.

"I did," I said, and she laughed. The bus lurched up the hill.

"If you need me, give me a call," I told her, though I knew she never would.

"I'm fine. Really. At least, as Kurt says, I played well and the right people heard me." She fumbled through her pockets for her change. "Next time, I'll fuck someone."

I tried a little laugh.

"What about you?"

I held my face high, though I knew she was thinking of the rehearsal. "I'm great."

"Maybe we could play some duets again sometime."

"I'd love that," I said, knowing that would also never happen.

"I'll give you a ring," she said as the bus grumbled to a stop in front of us. She got on and I watched her walk down the aisle and sit down by the window. I smiled and waved farewell when the bus pulled away.

On my way home, I checked the mailbox for a response from Oakland, but there was only an unofficial-looking letter with no return address on it. At first, I hoped it was from Stephen. When I saw my father's sloppy handwriting, I felt a moment of disappointment but then an even greater relief. I had not seen my father since Tom's concert. The note was short, just a few lines:

Whatever happened between your mother and me, whatever truth you someday believe, you should always know you had a father who loved you. I did my best and often failed. I often behaved in ways I will never be proud of. Let us go on. I will always be your father, imperfect.

Maybe it was because I was lonely or maybe it was because I truly wanted to forgive, but I called my father, agreed to see him that weekend. Warm, fuzzy snowflakes that did not stick cascaded down the dark sky as I walked along Central Park South to Marissa's house. The shadowed trees in the park were deep and ominous, but along the clean, well-lit sidewalk, tourists in cashmere coats laughed as their kids ran ahead to catch the falling snow. Winters, my mother and father used to take me sledding in Central Park, and I felt so perfect and safe sliding down the hill and then looking back up to find them waving to me from the top. Their long hair, flattened under hats, would be covered with snow, and their arms would be latching onto each other's side. I believed that they would always be together, happy, and that they would never grow old or sad or truly disappoint me.

My father had been with Marissa for many years. I would never know how long or how often.

Marissa met me in the bottom floor of her duplex, in the foyer with a Persian carpet and glass chandelier.

"Your father, of course, has just woken up from a nap and is still getting dressed." She frowned with one corner of her mouth. Red papier-mâché earrings jangled in her permed hair, and she wore a purple Issey Miyake blouse, exactly like my mother's. Her flat, unmusical voice grated in me. "He was up all night worrying about something. Who knows what. He doesn't know how to take care of himself."

"He's a worrier." I checked for him up the oak staircase to where his new bedroom must have been. I remembered that my parents' biggest fights used to start this way, with my mother criticizing my father. "Your father's a baby," my mother would tell me. "He makes everyone else take care of him."

My father lumbered down the stairs, his big toe sticking out of his sock and his shirt half-untucked. His hair was flying in all directions.

"Look at you." Marissa stroked his hair down over his bald spot. "If I don't do this, he'll go everywhere looking like a crazy person."

"I lost my brush," my father said with a silly, pleased smile as Marissa stuck the last of his messy hair behind his ear.

"You lost your brush." Marissa rolled her eyes. "That's something Jason would say."

"That's my maturity level. Sixteen years old," my father said, and Marissa laughed once, then flicked her wrist dismissively, his gesture. In a year, I both hoped and feared, they would be fighting, not laughing.

"So how's my big love?" My father held me for a long time, and I remembered how he had clung to me that night he told me about the separation, bracing us both for what was to come.

"You two spend some time together while I finish up in the kitchen." Marissa directed us into the living room, which looked like an art gallery. A Jackson Pollock painting, a Mark Rothko, and others I didn't recognize hung from every wall. A red tapestry with black animals and threaded gold was draped above the window. It was a long way from the Bronx where my father had grown up, and he seemed small and out of place, his hands clasped in front of him, as he rocked a little on his feet.

"What do you think?" He gazed around the room and I noticed, once more, how milky and sad his eyes had become and how the creases had grown permanent. It was only three months ago that he had shown me around his sublet on Riverside Drive, and I could not tell how long I wanted it to be before he showed me around another new home.

"Where'd Marissa get that?" I pointed to the tapestry.

"Her mother gave it to her last year. The first real gift her mother had ever given her. Marissa was the ugly-duckling daughter. Her mother told her that."

"That's hard to believe."

"We were both outsiders," my father said heavily, as if it were only yesterday that he had journeyed from his father's immigrant world into this one.

"You should be happy. Look where you are."

"Ugh. Forty more years of analysis. That's all I need." He led me over to the shelves by the Steinway piano, which were stuffed with books I recognized from the apartment on West End where only my mother lived now. I imagined my mother locked in the bedroom, bracing herself against the sound of the books being packed up, and then the words she and my father must have said afterward.

I couldn't stop myself from trying to hurt him.

"So now I'm supposed to just forgive you and forget everything you did?"

Caught, my father's face slackened and he looked down. We were standing so close to each other between the shelves and the piano. I wanted to get away.

"I wasn't always good. I tried—"

"Okay, okay. I've heard that all before. It's nothing new." I moved away from him to the center of the living room, but he still stood by the shelves, flipping through a book by Camus. He looked suddenly soft, biting his lower lip, as he stared at the pages. He was my father. He had done the best he could.

"I'm sorry."

"Don't be sorry." He flipped the pages. "You feel what you feel."

The Jackson Pollock with its blue, red, and yellow splashes mocked our sadness and only spoke of life. I wanted to be someone who had more of that, more of those bright colors, more of that joy in me. My father stopped at a page midway through the book and read to himself.

"Listen to this." He pointed his finger in the air and his voice boomed. " 'One must laugh uproariously but without mirth. A mirthless laugh.' "

"Ay." I shook my head. "It's great to see you. Now I'll go home and stay in bed for three days."

"That's me. Mr. Sunshine."

"Don't you know how short life is?"

"I'm on Prozac, I don't know anything. I'm like this." My father made strange faces, his lips contorting, his hands spastic.

"What a nut. They should take you away."

My father laughed that silent, sorrowful laugh at himself.

"When will you learn to be happy?" I punched him in the arm. "I'm serious. Between you and mom . . ." I shook my head to show my disgust.

He asked me how Tom was and I debated my answer. He knew nothing of the past month of my life, that Tom and I had split up or how much I'd been struggling.

"Tom and I broke up." I focused straight ahead at the gold-threaded tapestry, but my father was watching my face with such love that I could barely hold my tears back.

"I'm so sorry, sweetie," he said, and then his arms were around me. I let him hold me. I had needed his comfort for so many months.

Marissa appeared through the living room door, carrying a silver tray with steaming miniature empanadas. My father and I oohed and aahed, savoring the spicy meat scent, and she smiled with her whole face, her voice almost singing.

"I knew you would like it." She beamed. "Your father told me everything."

"See," my father said to me, and then he bit into the crisp crust. "Delicious."

"Jason!" Marissa shouted twice up the stairs. In his own home, Jason looked less of an awkward boy. He had on worn jeans and a big Champion sweatshirt. When Marissa brushed his hair away from his face, he made a disgusted sound and caught my eye. I smiled at him.

"Your mother is a great cook. Do you get this every night?"

"She only does it when she wants to impress people."

Marissa blushed and hid her face a little in her hair, and I saw something softer, something more fragile than I'd noticed before. She reminded me of my mother, before she'd gotten her deepest hurt and then her bitterness.

We four stood around Marissa's tray of empanadas.

"Did you help with dinner?" I taunted my father.

"He never helps," Jason teased my father easily, which surprised me. He wouldn't have done that two months ago.

"Marissa spent all day cooking," my father told me.

"I did not," Marissa said.

"Thank you," I told her, meeting her eyes.

"Well . . . ." Marissa laughed, offering me the tray in her out-stretched hands. "Why don't you have some more?"

She and Jason went to get a plate of smoked salmon, and my father and I were alone together again, the silver tray surprisingly heavy in my hands between us. From somewhere down the long, lux-urious hall, I could hear Marissa ordering Jason around the kitchen. My mind whirled with tears and sadness and joy at how quickly life changed.

"Are you and I okay together?" My father squeezed my arm once as if he wanted to hug me again, but was holding himself back. "You know that's the most important thing in the world to me."

"Yes." I steadied my voice. "Everything's fine."

20

The Columbia General Studies office seemed filled with hand-some young men, waiting on line for applications. A dozen anthropology and philosophy classes in the course bulletin interested me. After practicing, I'd had to force myself to come here, telling myself it would simply be a distraction to study something new, but now I felt giddy with all there was to learn. I imagined that I would receive all A's in my classes, and I would finally have the confidence that all my life I had lacked. My father would be proud of me, too. I imagined him bragging to another professor about me, but then I stopped myself in my thoughts. I no longer wanted to worry about whether I pleased him or not. It was a strange, lonely, but liberating feeling to be without his judgments even for a moment.

I drank cappuccino in the Hungarian Pastry Shop and studied the course listings. All around me, students smoked and drank coffee over their books, and I imagined that I was one of them, no longer an oboist, no longer who I'd always thought I was. It would upset me to be rejected from the Oakland audition, but if I was chosen, I would have to go through all the worry again. And hope. The hope that I might someday play all the Beethoven symphonies with at least a decent orchestra never completely went away.

A Norwegian man, good-looking but very blond, flirted with me from the next table. He was a *National Geographic* photographer on a break from an assignment and was leaving the city in four days. He wanted me to invite him home, I could tell, and I debated it before remembering how depressed these sorts of flings had always left me.

But still it was nice to be free and to flirt, and on my way home, I felt the sexiness of my newly muscled legs and my long hair. It took me a second to recognize Stephen, pacing small circles on my corner in front of Ralph's deli, waiting for me in the cold.

"There you are." He grabbed my wrist. Under his overcoat, he had on a gray nylon shirt, too tight around the neck. "I've missed you." Around my wrist, his fingers were strangely damp, already insisting to me.

"I'm sorry, I'm just surprised," I apologized without having meant to. "I didn't expect to see you."

"Is your boyfriend home?" He nodded to my building, wanting to go up.

I kept my voice matter-of-fact. "We broke up three weeks ago."

Stephen held his breath for a moment, then turned to look at me. "That's good, isn't it?"

"I'm just figuring it out. I don't know yet. So much of what went wrong was me."

Side by side, neither touching nor looking at each other, we walked to Riverside Park. I tried to feel my care for him again as I listened to his voice, slow and gritty. He was telling me about his struggles with the last movement of the symphony. He could not find the perfect ending, that perfect balance between a sad resolution and hope, between closure and open-endedness, which was more like life. The longer we spoke, the closer I felt to him.

"Are you thinking of taking classes?" Stephen nodded to my Columbia course book, still clamped under my arm.

"I'm trying not to look at it as a big deal. I just want to experiment."

"Anything you study can only help you as a musician. It's a good thing, either way."

"I love music." The words felt simple and true, but painful.

"You wouldn't play the way you do if you didn't. You know, though, you're the same person, no matter what."

I nodded, feeling the relief of talking to him again.

"I'm going back home," he said as we stepped around a dirty pile of slush.

"To Mississippi?"

"Just for a month or two. I haven't been able to make my rent. There's this blues project that my grandfather wants me to help him with. I need the money."

Stephen's life was just as unsettled as mine. I remembered his building, the peeling wallpaper and grimy windows, and then I remembered the kindness in his voice when he'd asked me if I was okay after making love. I'd stroked his head down so he wouldn't see my tears.

"How long I stay in Mississippi depends on a lot of things."

"What?" I wanted to know about the woman.

"The grant. Business. Other things." He looked hard at me, wanting to hold my eyes, to tell me something about his hopes for me, but I averted my gaze. I only wanted to make promises I could keep.

We sat side by side on the cold, bumpy stone wall. Two months ago I had been terrified of touching him in public, but now I worried because even when we could, we did not touch. I would end up alone. Alone. I repeated that to myself again and again, but it didn't seem so terrible anymore.

"You have a lot to think about right now. You probably need time to yourself," Stephen said as if he'd been part of my thoughts.

"I do," I said carefully. "But you know me so well. That's what keeps amazing me. It doesn't go away, how close I can feel to you. It's real."

Stephen nodded, rocking himself a little. "If it's real, why can't we plan on anything? When I get back?"

I forced out the words because I knew they were right. "I have to know that I can be alone. I have to do that first. But then, when you're back again . . ." I let my thought go unfinished. My still leg touched Stephen's and he was silent beside me. Faintly, with the breeze, I could smell his spicy cologne, familiar to me by now.

"I'll probably be back in the city in a month or two," Stephen said finally.

"We can get together then," I said, and he nodded. We sat on the cold stone a few moments longer, and then at the same time, we looked at each other and knew it was time to go.

* * *

Chopin's Nocturne in E-flat filled the hallway outside my mother's apartment. For a moment, I thought it was a recording; the tone was so fragile, the dance so unsure, so courageous and sad. One of the turns came out a little unevenly, as if the player's fingers weren't perfectly in shape, and I knew the player was my mother.

"Before I lose what little confidence I have, let me play you something," she said as soon as she opened the door. "I look funny, don't I?" She laughed when I stared at her. She was only half made-up, wearing lipstick but no eye makeup, and maroon rouge on only one cheek.

"I was getting dressed and then I just got seized with the desire to play!" She hurried ahead of me to the living room, her purple bathrobe swelling out behind her.

"You know, your father didn't even want to move the piano into our first apartment. He said it cost too much money because we had to lift it in through the window. Of course, we were already paying extra for his room so he could write."

I leaned into the inward curve of the piano as my mother flipped through the leatherbound book of Nocturnes she'd gotten from her first teacher before getting on the bus to New York.

"I think I'm actually improving." She raised her reading glasses back up to her nose. I liked those glasses. The frames were black, sturdy, and indelicate, unlike her.

"I've been practicing every day, if you can believe it." When she started the E-flat Nocturne, her playing was soulful and dark, and it reminded me of the best parts of my own playing. Before she reached the cadence, she slowed, hesitating, before the resolution, exactly as I would have done.

"It feels good again now. Carlton said I should slow down here, put weight on the B-flat . . ." She closed her eyes and her voice felt ancient to me, as if I were still a girl beside her on the piano bench, listening to her talk through pieces measure by measure. She understood music. And I remembered lying in bed at night, unable to sleep, and listening to her play after she had fought with my father, after my father had slammed out of the house. I would lie in bed, my head under the covers, eyes open to the dark, and I would listen to her play and I would tell myself that everything would be all right.

"You sound beautiful," I said, leaning my elbows on the piano, closer to her.

"See how much my teacher is helping me?" She raised her eyebrows, coy.

"Oooh." I raised my eyebrows back, trying to be natural and playful.

"He taught me to play my turns like this—to toss them off lightly, into the wind."

"I love it." Her playing was better than it had been in years. Her fingers were almost fluid again. "I'm proud of you, Mom."

"You are?" She looked up at me, though she didn't stop playing, and her eyes filled with tears. I tried not to look away and to stay close to her.

"You sound good. You're doing so well."

"One should never give up on love."

"On love? You like your teacher that much?"

"Do I like him that much?" She laughed at the question. "Let me think. Hmmm." She thought with her finger over her lips. "Yes!" she said suddenly, and played a crashing chord with both hands. The piano rang and I took a step back. "In fact," she said, "he is going to come over at eight tonight for dessert."

"He is?" The rare safeness I'd felt around her threatened to disappear. I debated whether I had a right to feel angry that she'd invited Carlton without warning me in advance. I didn't want to fight with her, though.

She disappeared into the bedroom to change, in case he came early. Alone by the piano, I stuck on her sturdy black glasses and considered the fuzzy image of myself in the mirror. I had my mother's delicate, dark features, but my face was round and my body was broad and sturdy like my father's. I was such a perfect combination of both my mother and father; I didn't truly resemble either of them.

"What do you think?" My mother spun around, her gauze, turquoise skirt opening like a flower around her. Her Indian beads and Chinese coins flew up and jangled around her neck. She smelled of flowers.

"Very exotic."

"Not so bad for an old woman." She faced herself in the dining room mirror, and then we sat in the living room, the slate table with the laughing brass Buddha between us. My mother's turquoise skirt blanketed her lap and her chest bones rippled between the buttons of her shirt, but she had gained back some weight. Her cheeks were no longer so hollowed, and her fine, small features had a softness, a roundness, to them again. Some bitterness was gone.

"The next time I see Tom will be next Friday, on Christmas," my mother said, then she made herself laugh. "I know how you love those holidays."

I smiled, even though Tom wouldn't be there.

"It won't be so terrible," my mother said. "We'll make the best of it. That's what life is, anyway. You salvage and then you grow."

I rolled my eyes, trying to tease her, as I hardly ever did, and she surprised me by laughing.

"I know, I'm a silly old woman sometimes. You know what would make the evening special?" She smiled brightly. "I know exactly. If we could play something together. You and I. We could play Handel. At least, I can still sight-read Handel."

I took a deep breath. "I don't want to play."

"Gala!" My mother clucked her tongue, not taking me seriously.

"I can't do it this year. Let Carlton play."

"It would make me happy for you to play. Did you end up sending your tape to Boston Pops?"

I thought of the chain of lies I would have to tell if I lied once now. I made my voice strong as if I had pride. "I sent it to Oakland."

"Gala." She sounded as if she were about to scold me again, but then she leaned forward, narrowed her eyes at me. "What's going on with you?"

I shrugged, reached for Stella on the table, and tried not to feel my mother's eyes on me.

"There's something wrong. What is it?"

I lifted Stella onto the sofa beside me.

"Why don't you want to talk to me?"

I smiled at her to ward her off.

"You know what I think? I think you're just ruining yourself with your lack of confidence. You don't try your best. You sabotage yourself."

I argued against her. "I always tried my best. I don't know why you keep insisting that I didn't."

My mother was silent, her lips terse, absorbing my anger.

"Maybe my best is simply not good enough." My voice was shaking, and for a moment I could say nothing else.

"You know who I was speaking to the other day?"

"No." I shook my head. I knew she was about to pass on some piece of advice some musician had given her about me. She was always talking about my problems with other people.

"I was speaking with Ed Bloom—"

"Mom, I don't want to hear this."

"Why don't you want to talk to me?" Hurt was creeping into her voice.

"I just don't want to talk about this."

"You don't even want to listen to me? He told me all about Alexander technique."

"I've done Alexander technique."

"You've taken a few classes, not a whole course."

"Okay."

"Okay, you'll do it?"

I shook my head. I had taken a lot of Alexander technique classes; I had learned to stand correctly, breathe correctly, as if I were really relaxed. It hadn't helped. For all these years, nothing had helped. I wasn't going to get better. I had tried my best. She would never believe it, but I had. I didn't have it in me to try anymore. Grief came and washed over me, washing away every sound, every sight. I needed my mother to understand, to forgive me.

My mother gripped the neck of her blouse. "Alexander technique has helped a lot of people who can't perform."

I covered my face with my hand. "It won't help me."

"How do you know it won't help you?" Her voice was loose and broken. She understood what I was telling her. "How do you know it won't help?"

I held my breath, tried to settle myself. "Mom, I'm not going to be helped."

"You're not even going to try?"

I reached for Stella, sleeping beside me.

"You're breaking my heart."

"I'm breaking your heart?" I wanted to tell her that she shouldn't say that to me. I wanted to say something back, but then my grief was too strong.

My mother stood up, smoothed down her skirt. I thought she might come to me and hug me. She looked at me as if something had ended, as if she could never forgive me.

"I've got to go."

"Where are you going?" She grabbed my wrist, but I knocked her away.

"You've made me so unhappy." I snatched my coat off the rack. My voice was choked and lost in my quick movements, and I didn't know if she had heard me or not. Later, I hoped that she hadn't. I was all she had.

Outside, the day had passed and the sky was a royal blue with tufts of purplish smog hanging over the Hudson River. Hands in the pockets of my long coat, I hurried from the quietness of West End to the traffic and neon signs on Broadway. The bus-stop glass had been shattered into a million tiny pieces on the sidewalk.

I leaned out into the street. A bus was about five blocks away. Waiting under the empty, still-standing metal frame, I imagined riding all night until the streets were white with dawn. I remembered when Stephen and I had talked about taking a road trip together through the South, and I imagined myself with my feet up on the dashboard, elbow out the window, free. It seemed now I should have just gone with him, taken off. It would have been so unlike me to trust myself, to trust someone else.

"Finally," a woman holding a Sunday *Times* said as the bus lurched to a stop. Inside, the fluorescent lights glared and I sat in a single seat graffitied with blue Magic Marker. I wanted to be freed. From music, from everything. I wanted no more sadness, no more failure. I never wanted to look at myself with such shame again.

Still I played and I had my moments of love. Moments when I thought there was nothing else in the world I could love more than music, moments when I felt so sweet and breaking inside because I knew I was saying good-bye. I did not admit it to myself. Instead, I thought of everything I could to prevent myself from giving up. I told myself that if I left the oboe, I would always come back to this. I would always be lost and stunted by the muddle and doubts and ambivalence that were myself.

I got the letter a week after seeing my mother. The committee from Oakland wrote that out of two hundred applicants they had chosen me and forty-nine other oboists to come for the audition. All I had to do was to sign a form and send it back. Then they would schedule my audition and I would go through it all again: the anxiety I could not seem to control.

I signed the form, stuck it into a stamped envelope, and left my apartment. I walked down Riverside Park with my head down against the wind. Beyond the highway, the ice cracked over the fast river. I held the envelope in my hand. It was thin and weightless.

There was no turning back. If I did not mail the letter, I would stop playing. I might have thought for months about making a decision, but it never felt real. I had flirted with the decision, testing myself.

I sat on the stone wall, my feet dangling. Against the cold, I pulled the sides of my jacket close together, the letter against my chest. On a nearby bench, a mustached man in an old down coat stared with watery eyes out over the Hudson. It was the middle of the day. Hardly anyone else was in the park.

If you give up now, I told myself, you will always feel failed.

I slid off the stone wall, my feet on the ground. I went over to the wastepaper basket. Beer bottles and newspapers, wet and crumpled, were on the bottom. I looked to make sure no one was around and then I tore up the letter. I tore it into twenty pieces and then dropped it into the garbage can.

I hadn't finished yet. I went back up to my apartment. My music was on the living room table, my stand right beside it. I took my stand and music and hid them on the upper shelf of my closet, behind the scratchy army blanket and the old towels I never used. Next I had to take care of my reed-making tools and all my cane. This was complicated. I had so many tools and so much equipment; it all had to go into separate boxes. I didn't want anything damaged.

I used shoe boxes and jewelry cases. I emptied all my jewelry onto my bureau and filled the cases with tools. Then I put all the boxes on the shelf with my music.

Last was my oboe. I wanted to do it without crying. I started to unhinge my case to take one last look. I couldn't do it. I couldn't look at my oboe again. I reclasped the hinge.

21

*O*n sheer panty hose and pumps and my hair in a bun, I answered phones at a long oak desk in the reception area at a Madison Avenue law firm. Calls came in every five minutes, and I had to look down my list of lawyers, then dial their extensions. Long, endless-seeming days blended into each other and then became weeks. It was January, a year since Merkin Hall. Every morning I woke at 7:00 A.M. when the sky was still deep over the subway tracks, and I drank a quick cup of coffee in silence on the couch. With my pumps in a plastic bag, I walked in sneakers carefully over the ice covering the sidewalk, and I huddled on the platform beneath the shelter. If the train took long enough, I could see the sky turn to its daylight gray above the tracks and buildings.

Nights started too early. My apartment, with its fire-escape windows over the alley, was always dark. I turned on all the lights as soon as I got home from work, and after running, I ate in front of the television. Sometimes I went through my phone book, called people I had not spoken to in years. I never told anyone about the oboe. Daphne assured me that one day I would learn to play for fun and simply for the love of music, but I didn't believe her. I believed I would never play again, that it would always make me too sad to hear myself play so much worse than I once had.

I lived for my runs. They were the pleasure and steady structure of my days as practicing once was. I had to rush home to make it before darkness, but as I jogged over the sheets of ice, I would almost forget that any life had happened between this run and the last. Careful not to slip, I could not go as fast as I wanted to, but I went for long runs, always, twice down to the boat basin, eight miles. Sometimes when I felt especially strong and purposeful, I willed myself to go even farther. I was no longer physically unsure as I'd been all my life. My legs had become taut and muscular, and I thought they could take me through anything.

Toward the end of January, Daphne left for India and so I ran alone. Only a few diehards like me jogged in snowstorms or over ice, and we waved to each other as we passed. Once a man who I'd seen regularly slipped on the ice and I stopped to see if he was all right. The next day we met for coffee at Cafe 112. He was a computer programmer and I had to explain to him what an oboe was. He asked me why I had stopped playing, and I reduced it all into one quick reason to end the conversation.

"I couldn't perform." That was somewhat true.

I received a letter from Stephen, along with a tape of his grandfather's blues playing, and as I listened to the soulful, sliding guitar chords, I tried not to let myself feel too excited about Stephen's return, two months from now. I was taking care of myself: I was cooking good, healthy foods and buying myself books on psychology and anthropology to fill my evenings.

The book of Columbia General Studies courses lay, untouched, on the high shelf beside Betty Blue. I had many excuses for not having signed up this semester, the most practical being the money. I'd gotten the New School catalog, though, and some psychology courses seemed interesting for the summer. I looked forward to studying hard, to delving into something new. I realized one thing about myself: I liked intensity. I wanted to be devoted to something.

I'd taken to reading Freud. I'd lie under a blanket on the couch for hours reading his case studies, trying to find myself on every page. I fantasized about becoming a psychologist even though it would require so much schooling and I had often mocked my parents' life-long therapy. My mother had never thrown herself into anything new. It was always too late. She was always too old. She could never give up music completely. But I could. I had shattered my life, but I was still here, still my same old self, no matter what.

* * *

Nearly a month after he had gone, Tom left a message on my machine, saying he had rented an apartment in the West Village and wanted to come over at noon the next day with Noah and move out everything: his records, stereo, television, and the glass coffee table. The whole living room was his; the only thing left would be my sofa.

"If there are things you don't want me to take, let's discuss it," he said cordially, as if he'd decided beforehand on his tone. "I won't take anything that we bought together."

I called him back and we talked logistically, practically, civilly, about what things he would take. He could have been anyone. My mouth tasted bitter as we spoke. Everything was going better, he said, and he couldn't wait for that tour with the Quartet next summer.

"I'm going to stop off in Sicily and meet some of my father's relatives. A whole roots thing."

"That's wonderful. It's what you wanted."

"How are you?" he asked finally.

"Fine." I remembered what I had forgotten for the first time in three weeks: I had stopped playing.

"And my baby Betty Blue?" he asked tenderly, in his boy's voice, and all of a sudden he no longer seemed like a stranger. I half-expected him to start calling both of us all of his sweet, silly names. At that moment, there didn't seem any good reasons why our love hadn't been enough.

When we hung up, I decided I didn't care; I would give up everything except photographs and Betty Blue. I hid all of our photographs and tapes under my clothes in my drawer, attached a sign to Betty Blue's cage, but still, for some reason, I was afraid that Tom would take her from me. I hid her cage on the floor in the corner by my bed, and she stared up at me with her black eyes as solid and blank as beads. She didn't know how much I loved her. She registered none of my care. Even when I told her I loved her, her eyes still looked the same.

At eleven-thirty the next morning, I made myself leave my apartment without looking back, without even photographing it in my mind. I sat in the Bread Shop—run by white Rastafarians in their twenties who had gone to Columbia—and finished off two cups of coffee, two cheese Danishes, and five cigarettes. It was only twelve forty-five.

In Riverside Park, I leaned over the railing, watching the shifting blocks of ice crack and float down the Hudson River, and I tried to think of what it was I wanted from love. I did not imagine a specific man, but I thought that inside myself I wanted to feel a solidness and safety, a steady warmth around my heart.

When I got back home, Tom's U-Haul was still parked outside my building, and Tom was struggling down the stoop with two speakers in his arms. His hair was short, cut above his ears; the curls that I loved were all gone. His face looked harder, older, the angles deeper. He had on a long black coat with a high collar I'd never seen before. It was cashmere, expensive. He loaded the speakers through the sliding side door of the van and, then, in a tone I couldn't read, shouted, "Done," to Noah, who must have been in the driver's seat. When I called his name, Tom recognized me slowly as if it had not been a month but years since we'd seen each other.

We did not kiss each other hello. We stood a few feet apart, our hands stuffed in our pockets. I couldn't stop smiling, for some reason, and staring at his cropped hair, the suddenly unfamiliar angles of his face.

"So you're going on tour to Italy."

"Yeah." He laughed, glancing down at his feet, his new leather boots.

"What cities are you going to?"

For a few minutes, we talked in false, easy tones about the cities in Italy we'd heard were the best and where the best museums were. Noah honked the van horn.

"How are you, Tom? Really."

"How am I?" he said with a short laugh, that same defensive laugh. "I'm fine. How are you?" He said it like a joke, imitating my tone.

"I've been thinking of taking some classes."

"Classes. Why?"

"Just to learn. To read things I've never read before."

Tom nodded, the smile on his face not changing. His life of tours and concerts was so different from mine. If he were with me now, he would have to struggle to understand anything I told him about the oboe or what I wanted for my life.

"My father's sick again," Tom said. "I went to visit him in the hospital."

"Is he going to be all right?"

"He has these things coming out of his nose." Tom clamped his nose with his two index fingers and laughed. "It's bizarre." He looked down at his feet, kicking at the dirty snow on the curb.

Noah honked the horn once more.

"I'm sorry about your father, Tom."

When he looked at me again, his face had suddenly changed back to the face I had known and loved, strained with longing and feeling as he pulled me toward him. We held each other as if we might save each other's life, as if we might still love each other again.

"I better go," he said finally, and I stood there, dumb, as he walked, head down, pausing every few steps, to the van. A few moments later, he was gone.

As I turned to my building, I was sure I would cry. It seemed excruciating that love ended. I walked up the four flights to my apartment, stuck the key into the door. The living room was cleared out. Only my sofa and bookcases remained.

I slid down to the floor in my bedroom beside Betty Blue. I rested my head on top of the cage and told myself I would be all right.

I took New Jersey Transit, a cheaper train, out to Philadelphia. The train jerked flimsily over the tracks, but I did not have my oboe to protect. It had been a month since I had put it away. I stared out the window at the yellow fields and broken-down factories and tried to force away my thoughts of Mr. de Laney. "Give it another year. We'll work together for another year," he'd insisted at my last lesson, and then he'd spent an extra hour, dictating a practice schedule to me.

In Wynnewood, the sky was so clear that the branches looked vivid, animated against the blue. The tops of Cadillacs shined. I felt too light without my oboe and music. I swung my free arms back and forth. I didn't have to worry about playing today.

Mr. de Laney tapped open the door with his elegant, rosewood cane.

"Hello there," he said, gruff and impersonal as always. The skin was slack around his long jowls, and his eyes were heavier and more veined than I'd remembered. Mr. de Laney was old; I'd never truly registered that before. I took a breath, smiled at him. I felt naked and selfish somehow coming here without my oboe. I didn't know what I wanted from him.

"Where is it? Where's your oboe, Gala?"

I smiled foolishly, as if I'd been caught at something. "I have to tell you something."

"All right." He turned away from me. He already knew. "We'll talk then." He started down the stairs to his studio. For support, he held on to the railing, pausing before each new step. As I followed behind him, I had to fight not to burst into apologies.

He lowered himself down to his chair by his reed-making desk where his old oboe lay. The top joint was stripped, the keys in a tiny pile beside it. All of his tools for repairing old pads were in the corner of the desk. On the music stand was his old copy of *Ferling Etudes* and I wanted to laugh, then cry, imagining his diligence, still practicing his exercises.

He folded his arms, gazed up at me from the chair. "I told you many times how talented I think you are. You lost a lot of time. A lot of good training years. And you have these problems." He seemed flustered for a moment. "Sometimes you play beautiful and sometimes . . ." He couldn't find the right words.

"Sometimes," I finished the sentence for him, using Pam's words, "I sound like a duck."

"Well, I wouldn't have said that. I told you that I thought you should give yourself another year."

I stared hard at a corner in the shelves where dirt had gathered. More than anything I wanted to tell him that I would try again, that I would try for another year.

"I was too unhappy," I blurted out instead. "I was too unhappy to go on."

Mr. de Laney frowned and looked down at the small, loose pile of keys on his desk, and it was a few minutes before he spoke again.

"Look. Let me tell you something. When I was studying with Mr. Tabuteau, working on Brahms, one day he told me that I would never in my life be able to do Brahms any justice. I would never play like him."

"He didn't tell you that."

"He told me that and it was true."

"No." I knew Tabuteau was so wrong. I'd heard old recordings of Tabuteau, and really I knew that no one else in the world could play as beautifully as Mr. de Laney.

"He told me that I would never be much more than second-rate." Mr. de Laney's face was stunned as if he were reliving the moment when his teacher had shamed him.

"That was many years ago," he said, his voice practical and impersonal again. I thought he might try to convince me now that I shouldn't quit, that I should keep going. And if he did try to convince me, I didn't know if I would have the strength to say no. Or if I even wanted to.

"Gala, if you're unhappy playing, you shouldn't play. You shouldn't be unhappy."

He leaned back in his chair, regarding me.

"You know, Gala, you're young. You're intelligent. You're pretty."

I blushed.

"You've got your whole life ahead of you. It's the simple truth."

I smiled because I didn't really feel like that. I felt as if I had given up my life.

"Have you thought of anything you might like to do?"

I shook my head. Besides Stephen, Mr. de Laney was the only person who had asked about my life without music with any kind of hope.

"Well, it will probably take a while to figure it out. You'll be okay."

Mr. de Laney leaned forward, his hands on his knees. He didn't seem to know what to say next.

"You have a lot of friends?"

I nodded, but then, so it wasn't so quiet, I said, "Yes, I do. I have friends."

"Good friends?"

I nodded again.

"Gala, you've got to do what's right for you." He stood up from his chair and I realized that unless I did something, we were about to say good-bye.

"You'll be okay." He squeezed my shoulder, once.

"Mr. de Laney?"

I looked up at him. I wanted the courage to say good-bye.

"Mr. de Laney, thank you. Thank you so much."

On the bus downtown to Lincoln Center, I huddled in the back corner on the warm seat above the engine, and I watched Broadway go by. The cold wind blew garbage and bits of snow across the streets and sidewalks, and people walked, hugging themselves, with their heads down. I braced myself as the bus passed the Thalia and Symphony Space, then the trafficked intersection at Seventy-second Street; I had only six more blocks to go. Six blocks until I would see my mother's face and I would have to tell her I had quit, ending the hope that had once joined us together. I closed my eyes and counted the stops, just as I used to close my eyes and count measures when I felt very brave.

When the bus lurched to a stop, I pushed open the doors. The cold rushed up at me but I kept my arms wide, my legs loose traipsing down those giant bus stairs. My heart open, I stepped out into the day.

Alone in front of the fountain, squinting into the snowy wind, my mother might have been the same girl who had first arrived in New York to attend Juilliard, over thirty-five years ago. She held on tight to her funny floppy purple hat with the flowers on it, her long, black cape blowing back behind her. I smiled to see her: her seriousness, her beautiful, mismatched clothes. As soon as she saw me, she called my name so loudly it almost reached me through the wind.

"A Sunday afternoon concert! I'm so excited! You know I just loved standing out here in the snow." She kissed me on the cheek, smiling at me, and I tried to loosen that shut, scared part of me and smile back at her.

"It's beautiful," I said.

"I know you don't love Heinz Holliger, but he's doing the Mozart and I know you love that!"

"I do."

"And you know what I'm working on, speaking of Mozart? The A Major Concerto! I was terrible at Mozart as a girl. I couldn't be light."

I didn't know how I would tell her I had quit. Across Lincoln Center was the New York State Theater where I'd taken my last audition nearly five months before.

My mother led the way into Avery Fisher, her cape billowing up around her ankles. We faced each other on the escalator, and my mother told me about the weekend trip she and Carlton were taking to Overlook Mountain in Woodstock.

"It's going to be lovely." She clasped her hands. "You remember the lookout tower and the burned-out hotel? We used to take the most beautiful walks there in the summer. We had such wonderful times, didn't we? You and I. Remember?"

"Sort of." I fought my need to resist her, to deny any of her happy memories as I usually did. I wanted to try to let her close to me, even just a little bit.

I asked her how it was going with Carlton.

"You know how it is. It's something for the here and now. Not the future. I'm happy for the moment with him. It's kind of funny, isn't it? An old woman like me?"

She laughed fully for the first time in months and my heart ached, homesick for her, my mother. It was true; we had been close on those walks we used to take up Overlook Mountain. Ahead of me, she would climb the trail in her hiking boots and backpack and I'd felt secure and envious, following behind, watching the sturdy muscles in her legs. I thought we would always be together, that I would always be her child and she would always be ahead of me, protecting me from branches and strange animals.

We edged in front of an old couple to our plush red balcony seats. My mother sat up straight, her cape folded in her lap.

"I'm thinking of moving back," she said.

"Upstate?"

"You always said I should, and now I think, why not?" She waved her program in the air, to the possibilities of the future. "What do I have here that's so irreplaceable? You would visit me. Carlton would, too."

"You've already discussed it with him?"

"It's never too late in life for happiness. You have to keep trying. What else can you do? Woodstock is my home. At night I fantasize about being on Magic Meadow again with the wildflowers and the wind." She made a whistling sound like the wind and then laughed.

The chairs onstage were almost filled with the Philharmonic players, warming up. A flute, then a clarinet, then a sweet high note from a violin pierced through the mess of sound. Mr. Barret was frowning at his reed, his bland, tight face pinched up, exactly as I remembered it. No matter how badly I played, I hadn't deserved to be treated so cruelly.

"Don't they all look like penguins up there! White, black, white, black!" my mother exclaimed, just as Zubin Mehta took the podium. Mr. Barret gave his A, his sound much wider and brighter than Mr. de Laney's. It had been over a month since I'd played, but I knew it exactly, how his lips felt coming to the reed, how the sound felt vibrating under his fingers. It had been a mistake to come to this concert with my mother, to think of telling her here. I imagined myself onstage, preparing to play the big solo from *La Scala di seta* as Mr. Barret was, and I knew I would have dreaded it, that all night I would not have been able to sleep and that all day I would have been sick. There would have been no pleasure.

Mr. Barret's solo was, of course, perfect and characteristic of his playing: big and fat, raucous on the last scale. And then Heinz Holliger, the only oboist superstar, was applauded onto the stage for the Mozart. His technique was brilliant; he played all three movements faster, but half as elegantly, I thought, as Mr. de Laney.

My mother's long fingers were nearly in a fist on the armrest between us, and I felt her studying my face. I remembered how disappointed she had been with me during Tom's concert. I thought there had always been this iciness to her at the bottom of everything, as my father had said. When I glanced at her, her eyebrows were drawn together, eyes small, fixed on me. She knew. She knew what I was going to tell her and she wasn't going to make it any easier, I thought, but then suddenly she took my hand and held it tightly between us on the armrest. I could not remember ever having held my mother's hand. Her fingers were long, but bunched at the knuckles, with made-up nails. I tried to relax and to fully take her in: she was my mother, holding my hand, and she loved me. I'd had two parents who loved me; I could keep them both in my heart.

"Well! That was just extraordinary! Wow!" My mother applauded at the very end. She had to be somewhere with Carlton after the concert, and as I gathered up my coat and program and purse, I attempted to gather my courage, too.

Down the escalators, she faced away from me, looking down, and let a middle-aged couple in fur coats stand between us. I tried to empathize with her, to remember all her years of struggle on the piano, and all her hopes and all she had given to me so that I would become what she could not.

"Shall we get calendars?" She leafed through the stacks of calendars and programs at the ticket counter. I kept thinking, after the next stack, the next bunch, I'll tell her. My voice was sort of flat-sounding, ordinary.

"Mom. I quit playing."

Her face changed into something horrible and disappointed, and then she rearranged her smile.

"I know that. I knew since you were over that day." Her hand slipped as she tried to stick a calendar back into the stack. Picking it up, she smiled quickly at me. I thought, if she never forgives me, it's okay.

Outside the cold wind hurled us back against the door. Blustering snow crossed my mother's thin face as she squinted beyond Lincoln Center to the street, holding on tight to her purple hat. She was either going to look at me with pride or she wasn't, but I told myself I didn't need it anymore.

"You're my daughter. You know I love you. No matter what." Her voice was thin, blowing away with the wind. When she put her arms around me and held me, I could feel the effort in it.

"You'll find what you want," she said over my shoulder. "I believe in you. Music is just one thing. One small thing."

I wondered if I would ever believe that. She asked me if I wanted to take a cab with her, but I told her I wanted to be alone.

"Are you all right?"

"I'm fine." I turned my face into a smile.

"Because I could call Carlton and cancel and just you and I could go have some dessert somewhere. Pecan pie with whipped cream!" She smiled brightly at me, but her voice trembled a little.

"Thank you, Mom. I'm all right alone." I'd said what I wanted.

My mother was unable to leave. "Are you sure you're all right? Are you sure?"

"Positive."

"Good-bye, sweetie." She kissed both my cheeks and then held my shoulders. "I love you. You know that?"

"Yes." I did know. I watched her cross Lincoln Center, holding on tight to her hat and her cape, which threatened to fly up around her legs. She waved for a cab delicately, not as my father and I, city people, would, and I thought with pleasure about how she might return to her home upstate.

Before closing the cab door, she turned to blow me a kiss, and then her cab disappeared with others down Ninth Avenue. I walked away into the sweeping wind, past the fountain, past the New York State Theater, my last audition site, and then up Broadway. This was my city, my home, my life. I had done it. I was free.

ACKNOWLEDGMENTS

I would like to thank all the members past and present of my writing group, particularly Andrea Brunholzl and Jennifer Callahan. Without their insight, emotional support, and enormous generosity, I would not have been able to bring this book to completion. I must also thank Kristin Crawford, Jill Einbender, and Sarah Hendon for their steady friendship and love over many years. In addition, I would like to acknowledge Evelyn Streifer, Claire and Al Moreno, and Sanda Lewis for being such essential parts of my life. For their careful editorial advice, thanks to Colin Dickerman, Lucy Rosenthal, Ann Shipley, and Mona Simpson, and for his patience at the last minute, Arthur Maisel at Dutton. And, of course, much gratitude to Elaine Koster, my publisher, and Gloria Loomis, my agent, for taking a chance and working so energetically on my behalf, and to Julia Serebrinsky, my tremendously talented editor, for her enthusiasm and dedication.

Most important, I thank my parents, Ruth Garbus and Martin Garbus, for giving me everything, and my sister, Elizabeth, for being my friend the longest.

The typeface used in this book is one of many versions of Garamond, a modern homage to—rather than, strictly speaking, a revival of—the celebrated fonts of Claude Garamond (c. 1480–1561), the first founder to produce type on a large scale. Garamond's type was inspired by Francesco Griffo's *De Ætna* type (cut in the 1490s for Venetian printer Aldus Manutius and revived in the 1920s as Bembo), but its letter forms were cleaner and the fit between pieces of type improved. It therefore gave text a more harmonious overall appearance than its predecessors had, becoming the basis of all romans created on the Continent for the next two hundred years; it was itself still in use through the eighteenth century. Besides the many "Garamonds" in use today, other typefaces derived from his fonts are Granjon and Sabon (despite their being named after other printers).